*What people say* Y0-DPC-282

## The Duke's Musician

*The Duke's Musician: A Spy at a Renaissance Court* is fascinating! I was transported to the Renaissance...all the intrigues and planning genius that created that era. An extremely complex subject made accessible and fascinating. Bravissimo!
*Judith S, chef—Italian cuisine*

A brilliant story (that) demystifies late medieval Italy. Very believable characters—humankind hasn't changed much in all these centuries. I loved it.
*Charles Diggs, biology teacher*

What a terrific book! The intrigue—handsome men and beautiful women intertwined with the art and music of late medieval times—kept me turning pages as fast as I could read. This was a great visit to another place—another time—filled with beauty and evil, and food for thought in my own time—far better than most best-sellers. This is Harry Potter for adults.
*Paula Diggs, artist*

Superb novel. I was sucked into the experience right away and never left for a moment. Should be read by every literate person. Ought to be a staple in history and literature classes on every level from high school on up.
*Richard Sarradet, history and drama teacher; former actor ("General Hospital")*

WOW!!! This is a masterpiece! Reading the bios put everything into perspective. I'll be the first in line at your book signing! *Eva Loeffler, writer/ housewife*

I never remember finishing a book in three nights. In this case, I did! I went to the Renaissance and didn't want to come back. *Lily Ayzoukian, European actress*

*The Duke's Musician*, by Bernard Selling, is an historical novel that you can't put down. *Alan Wills, businessman*

The only way I really sink into a book is feeling I am there. *The Duke's Musician* is a true story brought to life by action, color, romance, adventure, and characters with whom I can identify. Cecilia (Gallerani) is more than just the obligatory beauty. She has the brains to run a business, courage and all kinds of curiosity including, I suspect, for more men than young William. He is not too perfect, a man of flaws, who loves music and is grateful for his gift. No reason why his future adventures shouldn't be just as absorbing.
*Laura Hitchcock, arts journalist.*

Well, I just finished the book and I am sad it's over. I enjoyed it very much. The second half was really compelling. I guess my favorite part was at the end, when William and Il Moro were talking on the balcony. The book really captured the feeling of the most happy times of life, when everything seems like it is in its right place, so much is possible and the world is spinning in greased grooves. *Mona Lewis, dancer, artist, art teacher*

What a piece of work, *The Duke's Musician*! I thoroughly enjoyed the read and was amazed at the effort put into researching and writing this marvelous story. It's a real work of art. *Dirk Tousley, novelist*

Wm Castle, musician/spy, is a terrific character and a wonderful guide to the period. *Bill Rempel, author At The Devil's Table*

*The Duke's Musician* introduces the reader to the noble families of 1475 Milano as only Bernard Selling can do. A writer and a talented filmmaker, Selling is a master at describing, with elegant detail, the intrigue, sights and sounds of the world of Renaissance Italy. *Tony Morris, Freelance Journalist*

*The Duke's Musician* was wonderful to read. It was informative, educational and entertaining. William Castle as a pioneer in the arena of spiritual growth via music is a fascinating and intriguing read. The idea of new musical instruments and their sounds being foreign to most people hadn't occurred to me. It all makes perfect sense. Hearing a trombone for the first time would evoke feelings and sensations that might excite or trouble a person depending on their beliefs and life experiences. *Jacqueline Davis, writer*

*What people say. . . about the William Castle series*

The William Castle series of novels of the Italian Renaissance is a saga of powerful people in tenuous times. Bernard Selling brings scholarly research to document Italy, France and Spain, a trifecta of forces whose iconic personages Ludvico Il Moro, Charles VIII, Pope Sixtus IV and Leonardo da Vinci unravel Medieval closemindedness and engage the world of humanist Renaissance. A metamorphosis whose seven volumes pulse with the fervor with which William Castle—musician, courtier and spy—negotiates, and leaves us breathless with anxiety for a forthcoming novel of resolutions for this turbulence of brutality, betrayal, beauty and lust, all based on historical fact. *Henrietta Knapp, writer*

A William Castle novel

# The Secret Garden

### The Rise of Ludovico 'Il Moro' Sforza

By

**BERNARD SELLING**

## OTHER BOOKS BY BERNARD SELLING

*NONFICTION*
Writing From Within
Writing from Within: The Next Generation
Writing from Deeper Within
Writing from Within Workbook
Character Consciousness
The Hidden Treasures of Renaissance Milano
The Art of Seeing

*William Castle Series*
The Duke's Musician
Predators
The da Vinci Intrusion
Fortunes's Crooked Smile
Eye on the Prize
The Fall
Coffins

**ISBN: 978-0-9892181-5-3**

Library of Congress Cataloging Pending in Publication Date
Selling, Bernard
The Secret Garden: The Rise of Ludovico Il Moro Sforza
1. Fiction --Authorship. I. Title
Registration No.

Printed in the United States of America
Front cover photography - Sforza Castle, Milano, by Bernard Selling
Book Design: Joe Menkin

Graphics - front/back cover, title page by Joe Menkin

**To Gail, Jeff and Will**

# FOREWORD

This book and the volumes that follow are the product of some fifty years of research and writing on my part. My father loved history and, in that sense, I am my father's son. As an English literature and art history major at the University of Michigan in the 1950s, my fascination with the Italian Renaissance began in classes taught by one of that university's most outstanding professors, Marvin Eisenberg.

Later, during my years teaching at the USAF Academy in Colorado Springs, Colorado, I had the good fortune to introduce young cadets to something about the history of art, including the Renaissance. During that time, a summer in Europe offered me the opportunity to photograph significant buildings, cathedrals, and palaces as well as add to the academy's art history slide collection. On one such outing, I discovered the remains of the castle at Loches, France, where a notable Italian ruler, Ludovico Il Moro Sforza, had been imprisoned for the last years of his life.

Descending into the dungeon, I had a strange and awe-inspiring experience—I had been there before—a bizarre, compelling, even somewhat terrifying sensation. The scratching on the walls, the light from the single window, the dank smell—all were too familiar. This *déjà vu* moment remains one of the most riveting memories of my life.

Ludovico Il Moro Sforza? Why do I know that name? I asked myself, as this weird, moment passed. Slowly it came to me—Il Moro had employed Leonardo da Vinci for all the years the artist/musician/engineer had been active in Milano. It was for Il Moro that da Vinci had created his all-too-famous Last Supper, embracing the haunting words, "One of you shall betray me." This

Sforza character is one fascinating and important person, I said to myself, quickly forgetting about him as I left the castle.

A few days later, I got off the Paris-to-Milano express train and soon found myself gazing at, into and around the enormous Castello di Porta Giovia (the Sforza castle). Its vast emptiness seemed a mute testament to the power once exercised by the Sforza dukes of Milano--Francesco, Galeazzo Maria and Ludovico Maria Sforza. How does such a man go from ruling the duchy of Milano at one moment to dwelling in the bowels of a French prison the next? I wondered.

And so I began to study the life of Ludovico Il Moro Sforza in earnest—after building a career teaching film history, directing short fiction films, marrying and rais-ing two sons, and beginning a second career as a writer and creative writing teacher.

As it turns out, history has little good to say about Ludovico Il Moro. Machiavelli holds him responsible for the fall of Italy to the French in 1499. Lorenzo di Medici's followers and apologists find the Florentine oligarchy of 14th century Florence a far more preferable form of government to the autocratic rule of the Sforza/Visconti family in Milano. Even Shakespeare had a hand in shaping Ludovico Sforza's destiny, naming his gullible hero in Othello 'The Moor'. Later, a 17th century play vilified Sforza in every way possible.

Was this picture of Il Moro accurate? I wondered.

Researching his life through the books and articles available in English, having more books and articles in Italian translated for me, and spending many summers in Italy photographing the Sforza castles, villas, and residences still in existence, I found a dif-ferent picture emerging. Moro appeared to be a calm, reasonable, careful ruler—a forward-looking, highly-educated visionary who ruled wisely, without resorting to the usual violence of the period.

He increased the productivity of his duchy by the careful use of its natural resources while gathering around him men of equal vision such as architect Donato Bramante, mathematician Luca Pacioli, composer and theorist Francinus Gafuri, and, most of all, Leonardo da Vinci whose skills as an engineer were as important to the Duchy of Milan as were his talents as an artist.

Ludovico Il Moro devised the first effective spy system in Europe, one that kept him informed of the thoughts and actions of Europe and Italy's decision makers. Sadly, he ran afoul of a disgruntled former military commander, Gian Giacomo Trivulzio, whose skills worked in Il Moro's favor for a number of years and then against him for an equal period of time.

Of greater significance to Il Moro's survival, the loyalties among the states of Italy were badly divided during the years of his rule (1479-1499). Acquiring reliable allies in the face of the looming armies of France (and later Spain) presented an enormous challenge to Il Moro and the rulers of the other Italian territorial states, Venezia, Napoli, Firenze, and the Papal States.

So here is the product of all those years of research—a fictional story of the life of a talented English musician, William Castle. Related to a powerful Italian family (that of Bishop Branda Castiglione of Castiglione Olona, near Varese and uncle to Baldassare Castiglione, author of *The Courtier*), his 'arc' rests atop the actual events of the times and true-to-life personages at the court of Ludovico Il Moro Sforza, regent and later duke of Milano, as well as patron of Leonardo da Vinci.

Sources for the biographies of the many historical characters which people this series may be found at the end of each volume.

# Table of Contents

# INTRODUCTION

The year 1477 finds the Milanese court of Duke Galeazzo Maria Sforza in turmoil. The duke's assassination at Christmas Mass in 1476 creates an unclear line of succession. In one will, Galeazzo Maria makes his First Secretary Cicco Simonetta regent for his young son, along with his wife, Bona, and close friend, Gian Giacomo Trivulzio. In a second will, known to exist but not anywhere visible, Galeazzo names his brother, Ludovico Il Moro, as Regent. Simonetta and Ludovico Il Moro each fully intend to rule Milano.

Nor are these the only people willing to lay down their lives to rule the duchy, perhaps the wealthiest of the city states in Italy. Ambitious men and women people the court from top to bottom, especially those of the Visconti family, whose connection to power ended with the death of Duke Filippo Maria Visconti in 1447. Having no male heir to carry on the family name, Filippo gave legitimacy to the Sforza family by betrothing his daughter, Bianca Maria, to Francesco Sforza, thus ending the Visconti line of dukes. Nevertheless, Visconti relatives lie in the weeds, ready to assert their rights.

Impressive and tightly wound military figures also fill the court with their ambitions and schemes. Francesco Sforza's longtime friend and ally, the condottiere Roberto Sanseverino, whose family hails from Napoli, Francesco's ally in years gone by, is one such man.

Another family with a strong voice in Milanese affairs, the Castiglioni family, can boast that its head of family, Branda Castiglione, is a much-valued confidant and counselor to both Il Gran Francesco and Galeazzo.

These survivors of Galeazzo's schemes and lusts all intend to leave their mark on the court of Milano. But only one will rule. Who will it be? Simonetta and Trivulzio? Ludovico and his brothers? The Visconti family? Sanseverino and his heirs?

The hero of the first novel, William Castle, is now caught among these conflicting ambitions, unsure where to turn, perplexed by the claims of one side then another, puzzled by orders that, at another time, might seem a betrayal. Yet he has many friends at court and fully intends to survive and flourish within the currents and cross-currents of loyalty and betrayal, truthfulness and deceit, certainty and flux.

*Please note: Actual events and people are portrayed in this book, with some liberties taken. The one completely imagined character, William Castle, is a composite of several musicians at the Sforza court. For more about these characters and the history of Italy during the Renaissance, please see "Living History" and the bibliography section in Appendix II and III of the book.*

# BIOGRAPHIES

*(all are actual historical personages unless otherwise noted (\*);*
*additional biographies may be found in Appendix II)*

## WILLIAM CASTLE (1450— )\*/fictional

 Handsome, adventurous, independent, spirited young musician at the court of Charles, Duke of Burgundy. Skilled as trumpeter and singer; highly proficient on the newly invented brass instrument, the trombone. He seeks an appointment to one of the Italian courts as have many of Burgundy's finest musicians. Family connections feed these ambitions: his uncle, Branda Castiglione, is the chief adviser to Duke Galeazzo Maria Sforza of Milano, possessor of the most glorious collection of musicians to be found anywhere in Europe. To achieve the wealth, power and fame he seeks, William pursues a dangerous and circuitous course of action, one that will force him to become a self-promoting musician, as well as resourceful courtier, emissary—and spy.

## LUDOVICO *"Il MORO"* SFORZA, (1452-1508)

 Third son of Duke Francesco Sforza. Hated by his older brother, Duke Galeazzo, for his cleverness, intellect, vision and unflappability. Regent, later Duke. His nickname, *Il Moro,* was apparently a play on words regarding his middle name, Maurus. His dark complexion may also have inspired his nickname Il Moro (the Moor). (In later years, Ludovico became one of the central characters in Machiavelli's *The Prince.* In Shakespeare's time, Ludovico became the template for the bard's character of Othello, inspiring Shakespeare to address his character as the Moor.) A handsome, energetic, clever, sensual man with great taste and a vision for the future, he was known for his calm in crisis situations (*sprezzatura*). He never allowed his enemies to see him perturbed. Later became the patron of Leonardo da Vinci.

## First Secretary CICCO **SIMONETTA (1402—1480)**

Loyal First Secretary to Duke Francesco Sforza, and later to Galeazzo Maria Sforza. Clever, knowing and very effective administrator and negotiator. Of Calabrian descent, his antagonism toward Ferrante, king of Napoli, knew no bounds. This antagonism alienated him from Ludovico Il Moro when Moro allied himself with the king of Napoli.

## CAPTAIN GIAN GIACOMO **TRIVULZIO (1444-1523)**
(pronounced *John Jacomo*)

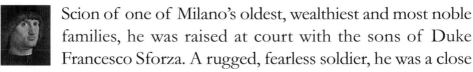 Scion of one of Milano's oldest, wealthiest and most noble families, he was raised at court with the sons of Duke Francesco Sforza. A rugged, fearless soldier, he was a close friend of and conscience to Galeazzo Maria Sforza. Much favored by and closely aligned with Cicco Simonetta, First Secretary of the Duchy of Milano. Initially served as the ranking officer (captain) and one of the governors of the ducal guard, the *Lanze Spezzate*. Competed with Roberto Sanseverino for position as head of the armies of Milano.

## **BISHOP BRANDA** CASTIGLIONE (1412-1483)

One of the most powerful, pro-Sforza figures in Milano, he was Bishop of Como, Count of Castiglione Olona and a respected diplomat under Duke Galeazzo Maria, Simonetta and Il Moro. Friend to the Sforza family and also to Trivulzio and Simonetta.

## CECILIA GALLERANI (1460 (?)—1510(?))

 Wise and beautiful. Considered one of the most cultivated women of the entire period. Lover and consort to Ludovico Sforza. Her portrait was painted by Leonardo da Vinci.

## GENERAL **ROBERTO SANSEVERINO** (1440—1496)

One of the better *condottieri* of his era. Rugged, ambitious, and self-assured. Was a trusted captain in the army of Duke Francesco. Rose to the command of all the Milanese armies under Duke Galeazzo Sforza. Is a first cousin to Duke Francesco. Mistrusts both Trivulzio and Simonetta. Sanseverino's hatred of Simonetta lay in his family's ties to the ancient nobility of Naples. Simonetta and his clan, on the other hand, are upstarts from Calabria in the kingdom of Naples. After the death of Duke Galeazzo, he maintains close ties to the Sforza brothers.


\*Fictional

*ADDITIONAL BIOGRAPHIES MAY BE FOUND IN APPENDIX I — pages. 267-271*

Italy, 1480

Duchy of Milano, 1480

R. Ticino

Mesocco

Bellinzona

Varese

Bellagio

Como

Sesto Calende

Novara

Milano

R. Ticino

Vigevano

Pavia

Tortona

Genoa

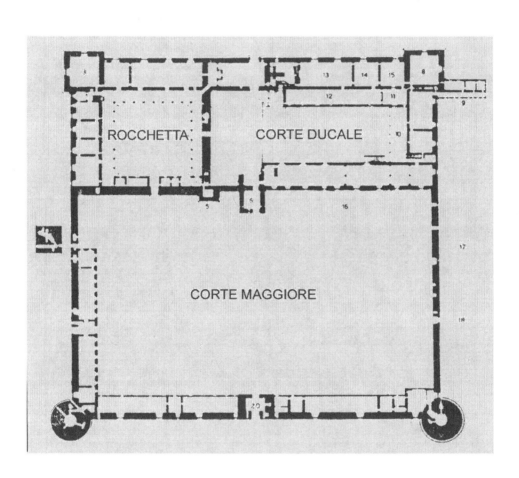

ROCCHETTA

CORTE DUCALE

CORTE MAGGIORE

# PART I

# 1

## *Return*

*The Rhone River*
**LYON, FRANCE**
January, 1477

**T**he small merchant vessel battled the freezing winds of the Ligurian Sea and turned inland at Marseilles where the Rhone River met the sea. The vessel sailed northward, up the Rhone, tacking this way and that, struggling to make progress against wind and snow. At times, it had to be towed by horses and ropes when the wind, snow, and flow of Alpine water made the trip almost impossible.

William found himself impossibly cold. His hands and feet had become numb and the wind soon snuffed out any small fire that the crew attempted to maintain on deck. Never in his life had he been so cold or so alone.

Finally, after three days fighting the winds on the Rhone River, the ship made port at Lyon.

William stomped his feet on the deck and worked his fingers back and forth, seeking warmth in those parts of his body. Ever so slowly, they came alive. He limped down the icy gangplank, careful of his footing, his knees stiff and unresponsive.

At the end of the wharf, he displayed his credentials to a guard who took him to the officer in charge. The Frenchman examined the papers then led William to a stable where he saddled the only horse available, a dirty gray mare. Once on horseback, he found a measure of strength and rode in all haste toward the residence of the king.

Arriving at the castle late in the day, he addressed the guard at the gate who pointed down a road leading into the hills around the city. "They are hunting," the guard muttered through chattering teeth.

William clicked the reins of his horse and rode off as fast as the beast could take him. Snow fell in large flakes, mixed with thick, heavy clots of sleet that stung the skin like pointed arrow tips. The sight, sound, and feel of snow blanketed the road ahead of William. Despite the heavy coat, warm cap, and gloves he wore, he felt the chill of winter deep in his bones as he trotted through the French countryside.

So it was that he found himself on this lonely, desolate road seeking out the young princes. For the many weeks of his journey, his mind had been full of unanswered questions. *Why is my uncle so frantic to find the brothers? Are the assassins of Galeazzo only three of many who intend to eliminate all the heirs to Francesco Sforza?* He got to thinking about Simonetta and Trivulzio. *How much power do they intend to hold for themselves?*

Then he remembered a few phrases he overheard Simonetta and Trivulzio mutter as they climbed the stairs to Bona's apartment. *"...everything is going as planned. Soon there will be nothing in our way..."* He had not thought much about it at the time, but now, yes, Simonetta had the look of a man who would stop at nothing to get what he wanted—the power to rule Milano. Captain Gian Giacomo Trivulzio, too. The soldier certainly had the compelling personal qualities that caused people to follow in his footsteps. *But what did he want?*

In the distance Willliam spotted three figures on horseback, heading in his direction. He spurred his horse to a gallop. As the three approached, he suspected they must be Ludovico and Sforza Maria Sforza, with their attendant, Pier Pontremoli, all bundled up in winter clothing. He waved as he neared the trio, reining in his horse as he approached.

Ludovico recognized his young friend and stopped his horse. "William? What a surprise. What are you doing here? No, wait...," he laughed. "Let me guess. You played a few wrong notes and now you are in exile with us." He chuckled even as the ice froze on his lips.

William shook his head. "My uncle instructed me to come." He passed the packet of letters to Ludovico. "It is about your brother."

Il Moro opened the top letter, a message from Bishop Branda.

---

## DUKE GALEAZZO SFORZA ASSASSINATED BY GIROLAMO OLGIATI, ANDREA LAMPUGNANI AND CARLO VISCONTI

---

Ludovico absorbed the message at a glance. "Galeazzo dead?" His mouth fell open in amazement. "I cannot believe this." He crossed himself, stared at the ground for a moment then looked up. "Ah, Galeazzo, Galeazzo. Those unnatural urges of yours brought you to a sad end." He shrugged. "Still, it is hard to believe that anyone would make such an attempt."

"I was a witness, Signore," William spoke in a hushed voice. "He was stabbed by three men, each with a serious grievance.

The duke's will gives Simonetta the position of co-regent to the young duke so Trivulzio and Simonetta now rule Milano...."

Ludovico's eyes narrowed, his eyes becoming small, hot slits in his face. "A new will?" Anger and rage vied for expression. "Well, well, well."

An hour later, Ludovico, Sforza Maria, Pontremoli, and William sat in the comfort of a small roadside inn. In the main room where meals and wine were served, a warm fire burned in the fireplace. The brothers stared into the fire. Ludovico glanced over at William. "Explain again, what 'abide by a decree of consent' means."

William held his hands up to the warmth of the fireplace. Though the four men had been sitting in front of the fire for almost half an hour, they remained bitterly cold. "Simonetta and Trivulzio control the regency," he began. "They desire that you overlook the objections you may have to what they have done. In return, you and each of your brothers will be provided a palazzo in Milano, a fixed income for life, and titles of some significance if you do not create obstacles to their rule."

Sforza Maria shook his head in wonder. "They believe we would allow ourselves to be duped and humiliated all over again, simply to play a role in the chorus while they step to the center stage of history? Bah!!" He spat into the fire. "They are fools!"

Ludovico stared into the fire. "Our father intended for us to rule," he murmured, "First Galeazzo. After him, Sforza Maria, on down the line. Ascanio entered the clergy so that on the day he becomes cardinal he will assist us in ruling Milano."

"Well, we shall have none of it!" Sforza Maria's face became red with the heat of burning logs and the hearty burgundy wine. "We will take what is ours!!"

"From this moment on, we will paint history's portrait of Milano in different colors," Ludovico declared. "The adventure upon which we embark will bring one thing—the duchy of Milano shall rise above all the states of Italy—perhaps above all the states of Europe." He put out his hand toward Sforza and Pontremoli, who laced hands with him. "Do you join us, Master William?"

William smiled. "I know so little about these matters, my lord. I serve my uncle, who is devoted to your well-being. At the moment, I am charged with seeing you safely back to Milano."

Ludovico chuckled. "*Comprendo.* You sit on the fence, leaning slightly in our direction. *Correcto? Si?*"

William laughed in agreement.

"It is better that way," Ludovico continued. "We know you to be discreet in all things. Sometimes it is better to have a sympathetic ear in high places."

With muscles taut and ambitions soaring, the young men continued to eat, drink, and enjoy each other's company. Before they retired, Ludovico took William aside. "You observed our brother's final moments?"

The young musician sighed. "I did indeed, Signore. Very troubling. In a church of all places. I was deeply shaken. The trombone was at my lips when the shouting began. We never played a note. Perhaps someday the world will hear Weerbecke's Masses and admire them for what they are. A new kind of music never heard before."

Ludovico reflected on the Englishman's words. "Yes, I can imagine the truth of that." He ran a finger under his chin. "Galeazzo was good to his musicians. Very good. Under Trivulzio and Simonetta, the court will look quite different."

William's shoulders slumped a little.

The four men returned to the castle of King Louis XI. Ludovico informed his majesty of the events that demanded their departure. The king provided a squad of French soldiers which escorted the brothers and William to the dock where they boarded a small caravel which would take them down the Rhone River to Marseilles and then Genoa.

Not far from the dock where the caravel floated, a young man with a glove on his left hand fingered a dagger. He appeared annoyed, perhaps even dismayed.

As Il Moro, his brother and Pontremoli boarded the ship, William scanned the crowd for any sign of danger. His eyes came to rest on the figure of the young man moving through the crowd.

The vessel cast off and drifted slowly down river. The figure stopped, drew out his dagger and raised his arm as if to throw it. William glimpsed Ludovico at the railing of the ship lost in thought. William reached out and grabbed the prince, hurrying him away from the railing. The dagger whistled by Moro's head and buried itself in the mainmast.

Although Il Moro apparently failed to notice what had happened, William glanced up, eyes alert, searching the crowd that lined the shore for the face of a would-be assassin. The man had disappeared. William turned to the mainmast and pulled the dagger out of the sturdy oak. He stuffed it in the pocket of his greatcoat.

Ludovico gave William a long, searching look. In fact, he had been very much aware of the attempt on his life but kept his demeanor calm and undisturbed.

"Simonetta and Trivulzio do not intend to share their power with us," he whispered to William. "Not even this much." He held his thumb and forefinger close together. "Bishop Branda was quite right." The two men exchanged glances, tight-lipped. "I have much to thank you for." Moro touched the musician on his arm.

William thought about the would-be assassin. As he watched the cold breath from his mouth freeze in the mid-winter air, he also thought of Solice. His dearly beloved Solice—his complicated and perhaps not entirely transparent Solice. The picture of her changed—becoming that of a corpse with a knife stuck in its bosom. He reached in his pocket, took out the knife he had taken from the mainmaar and examined it. Hmm—.

As the captain showed Ludovico Il Moro and Sforza Maria below decks where it was warmer, William thought long and hard about the situation the brothers faced. *If Simonetta had sent an assassin to end the lives of the two brothers, what kind of reception would they get when they arrived in Genoa?* Moreover, he wondered, *what will happen to me if I am found in the company of the brothers upon their return?* A plan began to take shape in his head.

The vessel sailed down the Rhone River, past the city of Marseilles, tacking this way and that with the wind behind them, then into the open waters of the Mediterranean Ocean. The seas were rough and gale winds forced the ship to shorten sail for hours at a time.

Ludovico stood atop the forecastle of the vessel, during the entire voyage, staring into the huge, cresting waves before him. Often Sforza Maria stood beside him. Together they seemed to be defying Neptune's slashing, thunderous blows breaking over the bow with such force that the small craft was driven under-water for long moments before emerging. William and Pontremoli took cover from the huge swells that swept across the deck of the galley.

Unable to sleep at night, each of the crew of twenty oarsmen was so tossed about, so frostbitten that no one was able to perform his duties. Deep worry lines appeared on the face of the young captain, a gentle soul unused to command in such raging storms. With his crew unable to maintain the coxswain's pace, slowing the craft to a virtual standstill, the captain slipped and stumbled over to Ludovico.

"Signori, I am sorry. The crew is near frozen. We must make port. The crew is exhausted and almost frozen to death."

Ludovico stared into a huge wave that rose before them. The great wave crashed over the bow, driving him backward until he clasped the rigging of the foremast. He paid little attention to the danger, simply staring out into the mists and the jagged clots of foam surrounding the little vessel.

Pale with seasickness, Sforza Maria turned and stared into the eyes of the captain, sneering, "Not on your life, Capitano," and fingering his dagger. "We will remain on course." His eyes had a wild, feral look to them.

The captain shuddered. "Perhaps the storm will abate. If it does not, well, then—" he shrugged as if port were inevitable.

Sforza Maria glared at him through squinted eyes. "We shall press on no matter what the storm does, won't we, Captain?" Their eyes met for one intense moment, and the captain turned back to his tasks. Within the hour the storm quieted.

The following morning, they sailed close to land. Genoa lay only a few kilometers to the south "We must find you a place to stay that is safe," muttered William to his two friends. "A place where no one would expect to find you."

"The castello of Donato del Conte," Sforza Maria offered. "He is a loyal friend of the family."

"Very well, I will go ashore, find him and speak to him on your behalf," William replied.

A few kilometers north of Genoa, Sforza Maria directed the captain to put the caravel into a small cove and allow himself, Ludovico Il Moro, and William to go ashore, near the small town of Trento. The captain complied.

William watched as the brothers and Pontremoli headed into town. The brothers were certain they would not be recognized if they stayed at an inn often frequented by members of the family. Sforza Maria galloped off at a fast clip. Ludovico waved to his friend and trotted off at a more leisurely pace. Pontremoli rode off more slowly, still suffering from seasickness.

The Englishman turned and walked toward a nearby stable, rented a horse and rode into the mountains where he intended to reach Donato del Conte's domain before nightfall.

As he rode, William's mind floated back to the conversation he had had with Ludovico Il Moro Sforza the previous year-the moment when Il Moro's vision of what Milano needed in order to achieve greatness became visible. From that point onward, William had to consider the enormous risks he would be forced to take *if he were to help Il Moro become the ruler of Milano*, for that was the route that William had chosen.

Ludovico stared out at the endless rows of vines heavy with ripe grapes. He threw a leg over his horse and slid to the ground. Walking over to the nearest vine, he plucked a white grape and tossed it into his mouth.

"Che bella, eh?" William patted his horse and dismounted.

"Such a gift. Such a gift. Unlike any offered to God's other children." He walked over to a vine, plucked several more grapes and tossed one after another to William.

Grabbing them out of the air one at a time, William dropped them on his tongue. "Uh, uh, uh...deliziosa beyond belief."

"Si, si, deliziosa. None better." Ludovico dropped to his haunches and dug his fingers into the soft, black dirt. He looked out toward the mountains barely visible in the distance then got to his feet. He ambled over to the canal and gazed up its length. "The waters of the Alps flow from those mountaintops down into the valleys of the Ticino, the Adda, the Serio, and the Oglio rivers, nourishing our soil. Everything those waters touch turns into something fresh and ripe and sweet-tasting for us and the people of Lombardy."

William smiled. "Nothing in England looks even remotely like what these vineyards produce."

"But it is a gift that need be nourished." Ludovico got to his feet and ambled over to the canal bank, knelt down and scooped up a handful of water. Foul green liquid spilled out of his hand. "From a distance it looks pure, like the mountain waters that flow down to us in spring. But we need canals—better ones than this—from the foot of the Alps south to the Po. The canals we have are rotten and inadequate." He got to his feet and walked back to his horse. "They need tending..."

William listened in silence.

"...while our beloved brother spends his time attacking the virginal daughters of the great families of Lombardy," Ludovico sneered. "At this rate our family will lose everything... and the illustrious name of our father, Francesco Sforza, will be forgotten."

"Surely that will not happen, Signore." William's voice expressed surprised concern. "Is it possible?"

Ludovico gazed at the mountains in the distance. "My father came to power through force of arms. Duke Filippo Visconti hired him to raise an army to protect the duchy, giving his daughter to my father in marriage, but the duke did not name my father heir to the throne when he died. Following a period of Republican government, my father engaged the city, surrounded it and forced it to surrender to him."

"Yes, my father told me as much," William agreed. "'No man is the equal of Il Gran Francesco' my father used to say."

The young prince gestured toward Milano, the unseen city to the east.

"Force of arms will go just so far. It will protect us from invaders who attack from outside the duchy. But what of the discontent within it?" He paused to let his words sink in. "Citizens, as well as their rulers, must have a voice in how they are governed. And that voice must be educated by the best minds in history—the best philosophers, the best thinkers and observers of human nature—"

"A state ruled by artists and philosophers, as Plato advised?" William offered.

"Ruled, no. Governed, yes."

"You have given this much thought."

The prince laughed. "I have had a great deal of time to think. Too much."

William remained silent, wondering where this discussion would lead.

Il Moro turned toward him. "Now, tell me this—. You are an artist of great talent and reputation."

"Grazie, Signore."

"Do you not feel that, when you have played your best, a great truth about the nature of things, about the presence of God, makes itself known to you?"

"I do, yes. Especially the 'musica nuova.' It is of this world and pleases the ear; nevertheless, it still evokes a feeling of God's presence."

"What if the new music and the new art of Signorelli and Verrocchio, of Ghirlandaio and Ghiberti were to govern the way man sees the world rather than those grim sculptures that surround the entrances to the cathedrals of the north with their terrifying pictures of hell and damnation. Would this not have a great and positive impact on the energies of the people of our duchy?"

"It would, my lord."

Ludovico once again looked to the north then glanced at William out of the corner of his eye. "You understand what talk of this kind means, my young friend."

William bit his lip. "The church would brand us heretics—betrayers of its teachings."

Ludovico stared up into the blue sky. "Visons of hell may be appropriate for the lands of the north, lands which see the sun for only a few weeks or months a year. But for those of us born south of the Alps, we have paradise on earth right here—and our garden must be tended, not alone by force of arms but also by the richness of intellect and the purity of the soul."

"So the nature of man is good; he does not suffer from original sin. His inclination is to benefit his fellow man?"

"That is what I am suggesting?"

"And evil? What about evil? Is man's heart not at bottom the possession of the devil? Are men not possessed in large measure by evil?"

Il Moro laughed from deep within his chest. "Ah, a thoughtful man. How excellent." He brushed his hands together, got to his feet and strolled over to his horse where he wiped his hands on the saddle's blanket. "Evil surrounds man's heart, but it is not his heart. Thus man must be able to perceive and defeat the evil intentions of those around him, without having his own heart corrupted."

"How do we accomplish that, my lord?"

"Every man must be educated to the limit of his capacity." Ludovico strolled over to the canal, hands on hips. "Those who govern need to employ men of vision who grasp the power of nature and can turn that power to man's purposes—the power of water flowing from the mountains, bringing fresh water to the cities, and removing waste, just as fresh water cleanses the body inside and out. We need men of vision to inspire one another to be productive and seek a better life, as orators and artists. We need men who know the past to resurrect the best of the past and remind us of our mistakes so we will not repeat them again."

"Just as Pontano in Napoli writes of the just ruler in order to rein in the intentions of King Ferrante?"

"And this fellow in Firenze who lived in the time of Cosimo di Medici, what was his name...? Bruni. Leonardo Bruni."

"A very ambitious dream, my lord Ludovico."

The young prince clapped William on the shoulder. "Not a dream, my young friend. A plan. A map of the future." He chuckled. "Not even the Florentines with their Platonic Academy have so clearly seen the future." His chuckles grew and grew until the trees around him rang with his laughter.

"Well, then, a worthy goal, my lord," William whispered almost to himself. "A very worthy goal."

"Indeed." Ludovico's voice turned cool and calculating. "A far cry from the self-serving ambitions of Galeazzo Maria, my brother." Ludovico spat out these last words as if they were soaked in vinegar.

As William finished his reverie, he could see that he had traveled many kilometers. The castello of Donato del Conte lay nearby, just across the valley. He smiled to himself. *So far the brothers' return has gone well. I wonder if it will continue to do so.*

"The brothers Sforza here in Genoa?" boomed the voice of Donato del Conte as William stood before him. A huge smile crossed the large, open face of the good-natured del Conte. "Of course they will be welcome here." He clapped William on the back. "Bring them here."

William returned to Trento, told the brothers that they would be welcome at del Conte's castello then returned to the vessel. Boarding the ship once more, he wondered what kind of reception he would receive in Genoa. It didn't take long for his suspicions to be confirmed.

When the tiny carrack landed, several of the *Guardia Republica di Genova* met the vessel as it docked and boarded it. The men searched the vessel, but found nothing unusual. However, they were not about to let William go free. The four members of the Guardia Republica pointed William to a horse. The musician mounted up, and the five men galloped up the road that led over the mountains and to Milano.

At the top of the pass over the Appenine Mountains, the Guardia Republica troops were met by members of the Milanese ducal guard, the *Lanze Spezzate*, who accompanied William to Milano. *Simonetta wants to know what I have been up to,* William thought to himself as they approached the walled city.

"Before I meet with the First Secretary, please allow me to make myself presentable," he said to the captain of the guards as they passed beneath the Genova portal to the castello.

"My orders are to escort you to the First Secretary as soon as we arrive," the young officer replied.

"The First Secretary would be deeply offended if I presented myself in an unkempt manner. Moreover, my uncle, Bishop Branda Castiglione, is one of the First Secretary's closest friends. His quarters are just down the hall from those of the First Secretary…"

The young man thought for a moment. "Very well," the officer replied at last as they came to a stop at the courtyard of the Corte Ducale. "You will have half an hour to yourself."

In the great hall of Donato dal Conte's castello, del Conte, a large man with a huge appetite for life, provided a fine luncheon for his guests. Donato finished off a pheasant breast, downed his glass of French claret and leaned forward in his chair. The topic of Galeazzo Maria's death soon followed.

"I suppose we knew it was coming," Donato frowned.

"Indeed," muttered Sforza Maria. "Had we been nearer, we could have preven—"

"*Au contraire*, my friend!" laughed Donato, an urbane man who spoke five languages and owned a fleet of ships that plied the Mediterranean. "Had you been in Lombardy, the rumors of your involvement—would they have fallen on deaf ears as they do now? I think not. Simonetta has created a climate of distrust of you and your brothers, but no one here takes the rumors seriously."

Ludovico and Pontremoli sat and listened as Donato and Sforza Maria discussed recent events.

During a lull in the conversation, Ludovico offered his views on the new regency of Simonetta and Trivulzio. "We believe that the regency for little Gian Galeazzo ought to fall to ourselves, his uncles, not Simonetta. The Sforza family ought to rule the duchy."

Del Conte pursed his lips. "Galeazzo's will published by the chancery named Trivulzio as regent to young Gian Galeazzo. Many of us were quite surprised. We thought that would be named, Ludovico. In fact, I heard Duke Galeazzo say that you were the best person to occupy that position."

He paused, squinting his eyes as if trying to see into the future. "I suppose he had in mind for all of you to fight it out among yourselves—a last gesture of contempt toward those around him." He shook his head with apparent sadness. "A most cynical man." He shrugged his shoulders. "And the duchy continues to pay for his ill temper."

"Such is the flaw of monarchy," Ludovico replied with a sigh. "Intrigue never ends." He drew a mulberry tree in the dust on the table.

"Indeed!" answered del Conte, laughing. "Genoa is a republic like Venezia, yet the intrigues are no less than those of Milano. Incredible!"

Ludovico Il Moro glanced over at his brother and then at del Conte. "Do we have the support we need to take over Milano?"

Donato shrugged with uncertainty. "The city wants peace at this moment, more than anything else…" he admitted.

Ludovico leaned closer, waiting for more.

Del Conte continued. "In your absence, Simonetta has waived several of the taxes, freed many political prisoners, and has distributed free wheat in areas ravaged by last summer's famine. He has made himself popular."

Sforza Maria got to his feet and paced the hard stone floor. "Our peers must be persuaded that government in our hands will be much superior to rule by Cicco Simonetta,"

Ludovico nodded in agreement.

"We must become more visible," Sforza Maria continued.

Del Conte pursed his lips.

"Having our young brother, Ascanio, named head of the *Consiglio Segreto* would be a good first step, would it not?" asked Il Moro.

Sforza Maria gasped. "You wish to place our heads directly in the noose?"

"No longer will we idle away our time as we have done for the past ten years," Ludovico spat, his eyes alive with a fire seldom if ever seen before.

The brothers got to their feet, exchanged warm hugs with Donato, bade him good-night and retreated to their bedrooms. Pontremoli remained by the fire.

Donato stared into the fire in the fireplace. "Word that they are here will surely reach Simonetta's ears, and he will insist that the Fregoso family attack us." He sighed.

Pontremoli nodded in agreement. "We will have to trust that young William has the means by which our lives will mean something and that safe harbor can be found for us all."

The lord of the castello looked up, a hint of a smile crossing his lips. "Indeed," he replied, the nervousness in his voice quite obvious.

Approaching his uncle's apartment in the castello, William knocked on the door. He heard some shuffling of feet inside, and the door opened a crack.

"Yes?" a weak voice asked. "Ah, William." The voice brightened and the door opened. "My beloved nephew. Come in, come in." Still dressed in his nightshirt, Bishop Branda stood in the early evening darkness, unshaven and tired-looking. "Pardon my appearance." His voice was weak and hoarse. "A bit of the ill humors, the ague, I guess the English call it." He tried to laugh.

"I am sorry to see you like this, Uncle."

The elderly statesman took note of the four guards who accompanied his nephew, ushered the young man into his apartment, and shut the door. He put on a robe, motioned for William to place another log in the fireplace, then he sat down close to the fire.

"Help yourself." He pointed to a decanter of *Grappa Lombardia*. "Now then, what have you to tell me—before we go to see the First Secretary?" His eyes sparkled as his spirit returned.

"Sforza and Ludovico are with Donato del Conte in Genoa. They are safe there, for the time being. They seek an audience with Simonetta and Trivulzio." William poured himself a glass of grappa and took a sip.

"No doubt they do." Branda seemed as alert as an owl. "I imagine they want to establish their right to rule, eh?" William raised his glass and nodded. For several moments, the bishop sat back in his chair and let the fire warm him. Finally he turned to his nephew. "How do you assess the brothers now, as opponents of Simonetta and Trivulzio?"

William took another sip of wine and leaned back in his chair. "Simonetta is the old dog—righteous and suspicious. His greatest weakness is that he both respects and fears the Sforza name. Trivulzio is another matter."

Bishop Branda gazed up at the ceiling.

"Like his mentor, Duke Francesco, Gian Giacomo knows no fear. But he has no reputation as a ruler. Sforza Maria possesses a clumsiness in his person and in his thinking that would be a significant obstacle to ruling Milano." William paused.

The elderly statesman trained his eyes on his nephew. "And Ludovico?"

William nodded his head, up and down, and stroked his chin. "God in heaven, if ever a person was born to rule, he is the one. He thinks several steps beyond everyone else, has the interests of the state in his heart, and is conversant with the best aspects of his father's rule." William shrugged his shoulders. "He has the same charisma as Trivulzio...I suppose it will be between those two."

Bishop Branda's eyes flickered in agreement. He leaned toward his nephew. "We must find a way for the brothers to meet with Duchess Bona. If they are to achieve anything at all, she must be persuaded to help."

William nodded in agreement.

The elder statesman got to his feet, clapping his nephew on the shoulder. "Now I think we are ready to seek out a moment of Simonetta's time." He went into the other room to dress. All thoughts of ague and depression had disappeared.

An hour later, William and his uncle faced Simonetta and Trivulzio as they sat across a desk from the First Secretary and the captain in the dark recesses of the chancery office.

Simonetta stared at the bishop, his forehead creased by a dramatic frown. "You contacted them without my permission?"

"The situation was turbulent." The bishop squinted at Simonetta. He was not used to being quizzed about his decisions. "No one knew who was in charge, who needed protection, who was part of the plot—who wasn't."

Trivulzio got up from the desk, ambled over to the window, turned and stared at the bishop and his young nephew. His expression was impossible to read.

"Perhaps so," the First Secretary continued. "But why your nephew? Perhaps he has fallen under Ludovico's spell, as have so many others." Simonetta glanced at William, looking for a hint that his words had unnerved the young musician, or struck a revealing truth. But William remained impassive. Simonetta turned back to the bishop. "Or are you both traitors?"

The bishop chuckled at the thought, throwing up his hands. "Our loyalties are to the duke of Milan, as they have always been, and to those who care for him." Bishop Branda straightened up and folded his arms across his chest.

Simonetta winced. He was getting nowhere with the two and was growing restless. "Since we have been charged with the care of the young duke, your loyalties are to ourselves—Capitano Trivulzio and myself—."

"Of course," the bishop replied softly, without malice.

William looked Simonetta in the eye. "Yes—"

The First Secretary appeared satisfied and continued. "Did either one indicate he planned to oppose us?"

"They want more say in the government of Milano than they had under their brother," William answered.

"That is their intention?" Simonetta leaned toward William who shrugged. The First Secretary squinted at him.

"As to the brothers…" Bishop Branda inquired once again. "…we ought to tell them something."

"Very well. Let them know, I will be happy to receive them. Why would I not? They are not our enemies." Simonetta got to his feet, pleased in some remote way.

Leaning against a wall, Trivulzio watched from one corner in the room, the expression on his face hidden in the early morning shadows of the cold February sunlight streaming in through the windows. His arms crossed, he hardly breathed.

In the opposite corner, William listened, quiet as a mouse.

"They will have safe passage." Branda stated, as if ticking

off the conditions of a truce between warring parties.

"Of course, of course." Simonetta grimaced then turned to the boy at his elbow who was writing down every word being spoken. "That is enough for today, Giovanni." The boy got to his feet, bowed, and disappeared into the gloom of chancery's back offices. "That boy is a marvel," he smiled. "Fascinated by history. Remembers everything. Writes as well in Latin as he does in Calabrian and Lombard."

William returned to his chair next to his uncle, folded his hands over one knee, open and relaxed in the manner his uncle had taught him.

"They have nothing to fear." Simonetta stopped in front of the bishop. "But my offer is as it was before—a palazzo for each, income of 75,000 ducati per annum in perpetuity, and a written guarantee that they will not interfere in the regency." He glanced at William. "Your thoughts, Messere Castle."

"My thoughts?" William reacted with surprise.

"Si...si." Simonetta smiled at him. "Considering the time you have spent with them, no one knows their intentions better than you." More than a hint of sarcasm surfaced at the edges of the First Secretary's voice. "Will they take the offer?"

William got to his feet, walked around the long table and leaned against a chair. "Put yourself in their shoes for a moment, my lord. You would see their frustration. The indignities they have suffered. Galeazzo treated them badly, with little respect, humiliating them at every turn, his own brothers. They seek to be worthy in the eyes of their father."

"What are you saying, *Signore*?" Trivulzio's deep voice rumbled from the corner.

Bishop Branda held up his hand.

William went silent.

"My nephew's point is well-taken. Give them something to look forward to, something more than indolence and retirement. Make them ambassadors to the states of Europe, or Firenze, Venezia, the Papacy or Napoli, as Duke Francesco did to his wife's Visconti cousins. Otherwise—"

Trivulzio stepped out of the corner. "No 'otherwise'! They will do as we tell them to do!" He slammed his fist on the table. "I know these brothers. I was raised among them. Not one of them has the backbone to stand up to us. Tell them that they will—"

Simonetta raised a hand to Trivulzio's shoulder, gently pushing him away from the table. "Bring them in. We will talk." He stood up. The meeting had ended.

As Branda and William got to their feet and walked toward the door, Simonetta intercepted them. "An excellent report, William. I can see you are following in your uncle's footsteps—helping to keep a dangerous situation under control."

"Thank you, First Secretary." William bowed. "I appreciate your understanding of our efforts. Governing the duchy of Milano can be no easy task." Simonetta nodded and squeezed his shoulder, much as Bishop Branda had done earlier in the morning. William realized the two older men were demonstrating the kind of affection toward him that they would give to their own sons; yet they were, at the same time, deeply suspicious of him.

"We have not forgotten your ambitions, William. One day you will be able to return to your calling," Simonetta assured him, and closed the door.

In the hall outside the chancery, William and his uncle ambled down its length.

Branda walked on in silence for some time. Finally he spoke.

"I see a long, painful time ahead of us, my boy. Simonetta appreciates the strength of the Sforza name, and has some compassion for the situation the brothers are in. Trivulzio—?" He shivered as he walked. "Trivulzio is a changed man. He has come to love power. He sees it as his birthright. And he has no respect at all for the sons of Duke Francesco."

Coming to the end of the hall, the two men stopped. Branda spoke in a whisper, knowing that at court here in Milano, the walls had ears. "Go find Sforza Maria and Ludovico and tell them to come to Milano. We will arrange a place where they cannot be attacked. But advise them to watch their tongues." William bowed and headed out the door.

*The Chancery*

# 2

## *Confrontation*

*The Chancery*
**CASTELLO DI PORTA GIOVIA**
MILANO, ITALIA
February, 1477

**C**icco Simonetta sat at his desk, staring out the window. He was a careful man, cold by nature, often inhospitable even to friends, seldom if ever given to emotional outbursts or ill-thought-out decisions. Since coming to power after the assassination of Duke Galeazzo Maria Sforza barely a month before, he found that he enjoyed the power to make things happen, to force men to do his bidding and to direct the affairs of a major European state.

A commoner born in Napoli with no connections to the nobility of Milano, he had found a place in the government of Francesco Sforza, rising quickly in the esteem of the calm, forceful *Il Grande* Francesco. Never for a moment had he thought that he would be in a position to rule Milano. Fate, however, had brought him to this place. As he stared out the window, he knew one thing for certain—he would never give up the power that he possessed for anything in the world. Few men had or would ever have the command of others' lives that he could wield. He savored that feeling.

He understood quite well why Duke Galeazzo had acted as he had—without scruples or concerns for others' feelings or wishes. Simonetta, however, was scrupulously moral and intended to rule in a manner quite different from Duke Galeazzo—no luxuries, no artists with their egos on display, no display of wealth and luxury—garments laden with gold and silver, choirs of musicians for chapels and cathedrals, parades and festivals, courtly entertainments of all kinds. No, he intended to rule Milano in the simplest way possible—through the rule of law.

His mind came to rest on the brothers Sforza, with whom he would meet in a few hours. What to do about them? The people of Milano loved the brothers, so dispatching them by means of the dagger, the sword, or poison was out of the question. He suspected that sooner or later they would make a mistake—allowing their egos to become visible—and he, Simonetta, would pounce on them like a cat—ever watchful, always alert.

At the very least, he was certain the Sforza Maria would make such a mistake. The younger brothers, Ottaviano and Ascanio, could be led easily enough. The problem was Ludovico Il Moro. That young man seemed to live a charmed life. Highly educated, a favorite of his father, he spoke seldom, always with care, maintained an easy, pleasant disposition no matter the circumstances, yet no one knew what he wanted, or what he planned. Yes, Ludovico Il Moro would bear watching.

Simonetta was pleased that he had employed young William Castle to do the watching. The young man was an opportunist, through and through. If the court of Milano no longer had use for him as a musician, he would find another way to be useful to Simonetta. His understanding of Ferrante I of Napoli had been quite astute and had enabled Ferrante and Lorenzo di Medici to end their feud. As a way of thanking the young Englishman, Simonetta had given young William a wonderful present—the Castello di Vezio on Lago di Como. William had been pleased and grateful—and now owed Simonetta a debt of gratitude.

Yes, Simonetta loved power. Most of all, he enjoyed watching others grasp for little tiny rewards that he bestowed. Likewise, he could take way as easily as he bestowed and high on his list of those he wished to diminish were the Sforza brothers. Very shortly, they would grovel and cringe in much the same way that they had done when Duke Galeazzo was alive. Ah, yes, the march of *Fortuna*. Simonetta smiled to himself. It was a beautiful thing to behold.

Early that afternoon, the brothers and Pier Francesco Pontremoli set out for Milano, full of high spirits, brave sentiments and deep misgivings. Willam had assured them that in meeting Simonetta at the former palace of the Visconti dukes of Milano, they would be safe from harm. No soldiers would be within striking distance.

William rode at the rear of a column of the brothers' own soldiers from the castello at Vigevano. William saw that Sforza Maria remained suspicious of his loyalties. Ludovico saw the wisdom of keeping him at a safe distance from their actions.

The day was cold and clear, the sky a deep blue and the sun a warming disk as they cantered toward Milano. The Duomo—the magnificent cathedral of Milano—shimmered in the distance. Not far away they could see the great castello. Church and castello dominated the horizon.

Before long Porta Genova, the nearest entrance to the city and the castello, became visible. Sforza Maria held up his hand, and they reined in their horses. "Let us think about our place of arrival." He glanced from one brother to the next. "Perhaps, a more fruitful, a loftier, more august entrance is available to us."

"Porta Romana—?" Ludovico offered.

"Exactly." Sforza Maria's beefy face exploded into a smile.

Ottaviano fidgeted in his saddle, anxious for the action to begin.

Circling the city to the southeast until they reached the road leading to the Porta Romana entrance, they followed it northward until at last the walls of the city were visible. In a few more minutes, the imposing Roman arch loomed before them. The brothers slowed their horses to a walk. The Milanese soldiers guarding the entrance recognized them instantly, saluted, and waved them through.

William observed the young men as they rode beneath Caesar's arch. He sensed that their mission was now, in its own way, as important to them and as noble and as ambitious, as was Caesar's journey north to confront the Gauls fifteen hundred years before.

With as much dignity and martial carriage as they could muster, they directed their horses up the Corso di Porta Romana, toward the center of Milano. Word spread quickly that they had returned. The streets filled with well-wishers who clapped and waved as their horses advanced over the brick-paved streets. First Ottaviano, then Ludovico and finally Sforza Maria dropped any pretense of impassivity and grinned, nodding and waving to the crowd that followed them to the Duomo. Their private militia of ten soldiers preceded them and followed them.

William continued along behind the soldiers, ever watchful, intent on picking up the scent of danger.

The brothers dismounted, entered the cathedral, and marched toward the great altar which sat at the junction of the nave and the transept. William remembered the last time he had been here—Galeazzo's murder. His throat went dry. His stomach turned over. Soon there would be more conflict and violence.

The three princes stopped at the altar. They found Galeazzo lying in state—hands folded across his chest in a peaceful repose, one he had never embraced in life. It suited him well. Each man knelt for a moment, crossed himself, entered a pew, and prayed for several moments. They arose together and walked down the nave to the entrance of the great cathedral, still incomplete after four centuries of work.

In the bright sunlight of the piazza, the shimmering spires of the church created a halo behind them. Thousands of happy, cheering Milanese surrounded them. They waved and mounted their horses, cantered, then galloped toward the nearby Palazzo Arengo.

The brothers dismounted and entered the ancient palazzo, a place that reeked of their Visconti ancestors—tapestries, coats of arms, paintings all testified to the lengthy Visconti rule that stretched many centuries into the past.

A *Ragazzo del Camera* (youthful servant) showed them into the Sala des Anciens where meetings with dignitaries throughout Europe had taken place for centuries.

"I remember this place quite well," Ludovico observed as the four men were ushered into the room, empty save for a half dozen chairs arranged in a circle. Ludovico gazed at the whitewashed ceiling. "One day this ceiling will echo the power of the Sforza name," he whispered, extending his arms in all directions. The young men sat down. William took a chair in the corner of the room near the door.

Half an hour later, Simonetta entered the room.

The brothers and William got to their feet.

"I am most happy to see you all looking well," Simonetta smiled.

"We thank you, Signore, and wish you equally good health," Sforza Maria replied. "We are delighted that you have continued to guide the state with the same mastery you exhibited during the reigns of Galeazzo and our father, Francesco." The two brothers touched their hearts twice, saluting their father. Simonetta answered with two taps of his heart. Everyone took a seat.

The First Secretary appeared older and wearier than when William had seen him last. He had acquired a slight tick to his mouth, as well. *Power debilitates this man,* William realized. He noticed Ludovico also gauging Simonetta's capacities. *Were it not for Trivulzio, would Simonetta consider handing over the reins of government to Ludovico and Sforza Maria?* William wondered about that.

The old man held out a hand to Sforza Maria, who took it without hesitation. Simonetta then extended his hand to Ludovico. But as Moro raised his own, Simonetta removed his hand, barely grazing Ludovico's. The elderly man got to his feet, came around his desk and hugged Ottaviano.

*Hmm, he is more afraid of Ludovico than his brothers,* William observed as Simonetta returned to his seat.

"You had a safe journey back from Francia," murmured the First Secretary, "…and a quick one." He tried to smile, the weariness apparent in his voice. "You must have ridden with the wind."

William observed the awkwardness of the introductions, the grandiloquence, and the flourishes with which each side engaged the other, seeking out impertinences and missed protocol.

Simonetta folded his hands over one knee. "So tell me, how can I help you?" He stared at Sforza Maria.

The eldest of the three brothers got to his feet. "Our father rebuilt the Castello of Porta Giovia after the ravages of the Ambrosian Republic. Every room there has his stamp, his sign, his emblem. The duchy is prosperous because he brought peace to the realm, stability to the government, and wise and thoughtful management to all its resources."

"Indeed."

"Our father saw to it that every member of his family—sons, cousins, friends such as yourself—contributed to the well-being of the state."

Simonetta smiled in agreement.

Sforza Maria continued on. "But our brother, Galeazzo, did all he could to keep us from our destiny—our family's destiny. We wasted our lives in idle pastimes. Our father would never have approved."

"And you wish to—" Simonetta drew him out.

Sforza Maria leaned toward the elderly ruler of Milano. "We believe—we know—that we are entitled to a place in the government of Milano – first, as head of the Consiglio Segreto, and, second, to share in the regency of our nephew. It is what Galeazzo himself wanted."

Simonetta lifted himself to his feet and paced about. "I have known you since you were born. I served your father and brother for more than thirty years. I believe I know and knew their thoughts and feelings on every matter. About the first issue, you are quite correct. Galeazzo kept you at arm's length. You were unfairly denied a position in government, but when rumors surfaced that you planned his assassination, is it any wonder that he feared you?"

Sforza Maria opened his mouth to object, but the First Secretary held up a hand. "Not for a moment do I believe you were involved. Such a thing is beneath the sons of our beloved Duke Francesco. Nor would I dream of keeping you from your rightful place in government."

Ottaviano smiled at these words and started to speak.

Ludovico glanced over, gaving him a fierce, squinty-eyed look that wiped the smile off the young man's face.

The First Secretary continued on. "We extend to Ascanio, the presidency of the Consiglio de Guistizia." The old man opened his arms. "That should satisfy your first need. As to the second, well, the intentions of Galeazzo are spelled out in his will. We will be happy to provide you with a copy. The young duke is to remain in my care, assisted by Gian Giacomo Trivulzio."

"That is not satisfactory!" Sforza Maria jumped to his feet. "This is just more of the same treatment we received at the hands of our brother. Perhaps you are the one who poisoned his mind against us!"

In a moment of unconcealed glee, Simonetta leaped to his feet and stuck his jaw in Sforza Maria's face. "Perhaps yes, perhaps no, but you are in no position to protest, are you?" He snapped his fingers, and three guards appeared at the door. "You dare to walk in here and talk to me as if I were a schoolboy! I, who have run the duchy of Milano for a quarter of a century while your foolish brother paupered the treasury with gaudy display, spectacle and— of all things—this absurd assemblage of musical talent? Your father would turn over in his grave to see the way his spoiled children behave with the wealth of the state." Simonetta wiped the spittle from the corners of his lips.

Sforza Maria and Ottaviano leapt to their feet. Ottaviano's right hand seized the dagger he wore at his belt. Simonetta took a step backwards, fearful of the outburst.

With a languid ease about him, Ludovico rose from his chair. "My dear brothers, this is nonsense." He looked from one man to the other. "We all desire the same thing— the well-being of Milano. Dear Simonetta, we are but young men who seek to drown ourselves in such activities that will better the state. If we are spoiled, then it is because we have been idle too long. Send us on a mission as ambassadors or as heads of an army." His voice was soft and pliant, almost pleading. "We are young men, and we need to spend our time doing good work."

Simonetta stumbled. Expecting attack, he heard only a heartfelt desire to be of worth—through the netting of Ludovico's seductive words. His head bobbed up and down, trying out a number of scenarios. He mumbled to himself, "If I...well, perhaps... Genoa...hmm...." He looked up with a smile. "Yes, perhaps there is something that will put you to the test. Succeed in this and, who knows—" He clapped Ludovico on the back and left the room.

In the streets of Milano, the brothers were mobbed by citizens who cheered them with greater enthusiasm than ever before. Ottaviano, the youngest and handsomest, threw kisses to all the children, to the winsome young ladies and their mothers, and grandmothers as well. Teenage girls tossed garlands of flowers in their path. Soon Ottaviano was festooned from head to toe with red and yellow roses and carnations. As he rode past, girls were seen to faint from excitement.

Ludovico and Sforza Maria cantered along behind Ottaviano, quieter and more dignified, each hiding a smile. "It was a good idea," Ludovico whispered to Sforza Maria, "letting him go first."

William continued to watch and listen, almost invisible behind the young princes and the soldier who protected them.

"The more popular we become, the less likely we will be to end our days at the point of a sword!" Sforza Maria waved as he saw the nobility of the city saluting them from the porticos and balconies of their *palazzi* bordering the *strada*. "I thank you, brother," he said under his breath. "But for your quick thinking, I would have landed us in the dungeon." He put out his left arm. Ludovico, cantering along beside him, reached over and clasped hands with Sforza Maria.

*Caesar might have done something like that all those centuries ago,*

William reflected, observing that each of the brothers now sat in his saddle a little straighter than before their trip to the castello.

Most of those in the crowd saw the gesture and sensed something important—a spirit of some kind—kindled in the young princes. Something in their carriage or the determination in their eyes awakened the crowd to the triumphs of their father, Duke Francesco.

A few moments later, they passed through the entrance of Porta Genova, leaving the crowds behind as they cantered back toward their home in Vigevano.

After a long day of hunting a week later, with the winds warm, the sky a deep, rich blue, and birds singing and crickets chirping, Ludovico and Ottaviano rode into the courtyard of the castello at Vigevano. A train of servants followed behind. Sforza Maria and William ambled out to meet them. "Hail, brothers," he waved, "how was the hunting?"

"Many quail and two deer," replied the usually quiet Ottaviano, "all with the crossbow." He showed his older brother the lethal weapon he used to bring down the birds and the deer in the private park that spread out below the castle.

Ludovico and Ottaviano dismounted, leaving the horses to the servants. Sforza Maria handed Ludovico the document that William had brought from Milano.

"At last we hear from Simonetta."

As he read Ludovico read the document, a look of simmering fury passed from Sforza Maria to his younger brother. "He offers us each a palazzo of our own and a share of our mother's income," Sforza Maria muttered.

"Excellent!" replied Ottaviano.

Ludovico glanced over at Sforza Maria. "With a condition, no doubt, that we cease to cause them any trouble, henceforth leaving the governing of Milano to them."

Sforza Maria threw back his head and laughed as they crossed the vast courtyard and headed for the great hall. "That is exactly his condition."

Entering the great hall of the castello, they sat down at the dining table. A servant hurried out of the kitchen with some fruit, a breast of quail, wine, and cheese.

"Damn, I am getting fat with idleness!" Sforza Maria gazed at his great bulk in a mirror.

"Those muscles of yours were made to crack men's heads." Ludovico wiped the sweat from his brow. "You should join us more often. We actually have to run after these birds and animals, you know. Keeps us in fighting trim."

"How do we answer Simonetta?" asked Ottaviano, running a hand through his thick, wavy hair.

"We accept the palaces and the monies," Ludovico replied. "But we insist on an active role for ourselves. A diplomatic mission, an army command—"

"Simonetta will never trust us to do what is best for the state, or himself," answered Sforza Maria. "If we succeed, we gain power."

"Ah," smiled Ludovico, "but do not forget our friends. Every day, Countess Beatrice, Tristano's widow, speaks to Bona on our behalf. She is well received by Marguerita, wife to Capitano Trivulzio, as well. Many of our friends, the Borromei and the Castiglioni families in particular, speak to Simonetta often, reminding him that we are quite popular with the citizens of Milano, and they do not want to see their princes idle."

"You really believe things will turn our way?" asked Sforza

Maria.

Ludovico got to his feet, gave his brothers a knowing wink and sauntered off, tossing an orange in the air and catching it behind his back.

William watched as they enjoyed their evening of idle play. He sensed that Simonetta and Trivulzio had something to worry about. Not from Ottaviano, or even Sforza Maria who were used to idleness; anything else seemed like too much effort. But Ludovico Il Moro was a different matter.

The following morning he bid the princes goodbye and returned to Milano, wondering what the future held.

Beneath the warming sun of a bright spring morning, Duchess Bona and several of her attendants sat on the grass of the courtyard of the Corte Ducale listening to Cecilia play the lute and sing. "And the lady of the castle, she lay for a hundred years, just waiting for the day when her knight, he would return...." To each verse she sang a refrain in French, *"Voulez vous le retour du roi, madame, voulez-vous lui revenir?"* (Do you wish for the king to return, madam, do you wish for him to return?)

Inside the ducal chapel, William put away his instrument. Only three people had shown up for his morning concert, not one of them members of Simonetta's or Trivulzio's entourage. Likewise, the concerts, performances and religious celebrations featuring other musicians of the *Corte* had seen attendance falling off during the past few weeks. Trivulzio's aversion to pomp, display, and performance had made itself known. He loathed musicians and artists, giving them wide berth when he happened upon them. He had, however, always been more than cordial to young William.

The strains of a *frottola* came to William's ears. He stepped out into the courtyard and saw Cecilia singing. A twinge of surprise clutched at his heart. He had seen her several times since her return, but always at a distance, as if she were taking pains to remain remote. A yearning welled up inside him——to touch her, to feel her breath on his cheek....

Just as he moved to turn away, she looked over at him and smiled. Those beautiful white teeth of hers glistened in the sunlight. *Oh, for another of those kisses.* He had thought about her, her mouth, the swoon, ever since the day they had met. They seemed destined to be together, that much he had known.

But now? So much had happened. And he didn't even know if he would be in Milano for more than a few weeks or even days. The duke of Ferrara had written inquiring of his availability. The king of Napoli had also sent him a note praising his work.

That smile of hers! It had lit him up—and shone on his dark, melancholy side— the humble, even unworthy side. He felt himself a better person—a bit more noble, less self-serving, more aware of what she must be feeling. *Perhaps the song was directed at me. Certainly she seemed to be singing from the depth of her soul.* His mind was a jumble of thoughts, hopes, strange and feverish inclinations. "Remember," his father had told him before his departure for the continent, "no woman is worth more than a moment's reflection. Enjoy them. Suffer them. But do not waste time on them."

At last Bona's damsels rose and headed for Bona's tower, Cecilia with them. *Not even a nod, a wink, nothing*, he observed. His heart sank. At the last moment before disappearing around the corner of the building, she turned and gazed at him—sadly, it seemed to him—then slid out of sight.

William's head sank. He realized he had been holding his breath. He sighed, letting out the air in his body. She had forgotten him, he had to admit. Or she had given away her heart to another man. That awful possibility filled his being. *Another man tasting that beautiful body of hers, breathing in her intoxicating scent, filling her thoughts. Ahhh!*

Never in his life had he felt so alone. The *corte* of Duke Galeazzo was dissolving before his eyes. No one paid him any mind. He had no country. No loyalties. No following. No friends. And this magnificent young woman, this light, thoughtful creature! She had descended, as if from some celestial place, gifting him with fantasies of the two of them becoming one, like a raindrop falling on a leaf, then to the ground, as if it never were.

# 3

## The Composer's Lament

*Parade Ground*
**CASTELLO di PORTA GIOVIA**
June 1477

**M**artino Lactarella tossed the remainder of his few worldly possessions into the back of a two-wheeled cart and closed the gate. He turned to his friend, William Castle, who watched, a sad look on his face. Martino embraced William. "Well, Englishman, take care of yourself. I am sorry it wasn't a happier experience. We came so close, eh?" He ambled to the horse hitched to the wagon, patted its head, then climbed up to the driver's seat.

"No doubt I will be following you in short order," William replied.

"The court of Ferrara is quite hospitable to musicians." Martino squinted in the bright sunlight. "Though no court will ever rival the one that Duke Galeazzo created. Try not to think about what would have happened to our fortunes had the duke been killed as he was *leaving* the cathedral—after we performed the mass."

"It is hard not to think about such things," William muttered.

Martino glanced around the empty courtyard. "This place has the look of death. Weerbecke, Compere, Guinati—all have left. You will be lonely, my friend." Martino's face turned sad. "Let us hope that Milano does not go the way of Burgundy." With that he took the reins in his hands. "A word of advice. The first time they offer you a gold florin—take it. The second time—say no.

Tell them you would prefer a sinecure—a small vineyard, taxes from one thing or another."

"Oh?" William shot back.

Martino, the *trombeter* laughed. "They only trust people who have property, or want property." He shook the horse's reins and clicked the horse and wagon forward.

As William headed toward the servants' quarters where he had been housed since the death of Duke Galeazzo, a *ragazzo* hurried up to him and handed him a message. "The First Secretary wants to see you right away." William nodded and followed the youth.

The boy knocked on the door of the First Secretary's chambers. "Enter," a voice growled from inside the room. The door opened.

Sitting in the dim light of his quarters, Simonetta poured over a book, using a magnifying glass. Some distance away, Trivulzio stood looking at one of the many books lining the walls of Simonetta's chambers.

"Come in, come in." The First Secretary waved William inside. The place was dark, illuminated only by a half dozen candles. The room was a burnished red mahogany color, warm, and comfortable—inviting, yet secretive, with an aura of reflection to it. The young man took a seat across from the First Secretary. Trivulzio appeared from the darkness and took a seat in another chair at the table.

"So, my young friend, I would like to ask you how you have enjoyed your stay in Milano." Simonetta's voice was pleasant, almost musical. "But I know that few of us can say we have enjoyed these last few weeks and months." William slumped in his chair and picked at his nails. "I know that your friends have all deserted us for Venezia, Ferrara, Napoli. Too bad. Soon, perhaps you will be leaving as well?"

The musician shrugged then dropped his head in agreement. "I suppose so."

Trivulzio leaned a little closer. "Perhaps there is a way for you to stay—at a profit."

Glancing up at the soldier, William gave him a look filled with suspicion.

"Oh, no, no. Nothing untoward," Simonetta chuckled, shaking his head. "No, no." He got to his feet and began to pace around the room. "You see our beloved duchessa is unhappy. The death of her husband, the absence of music and dance, it is a trying time for her. She needs to be entertained." Simonetta sat down. "She has asked for you by name. Her husband so loved your playing."

"Oh?" William sat up a little straighter. "I didn't know she knew of me."

"On the contrary," Trivulzio gave his friend Simonetta a little grin. "She is well aware of your talents."

"The news from Burgundy has reached her ears." Simonetta hid a smile.

William grimaced. "I had nothing to do with that young woman's death."

"No, of course you didn't," replied the First Secretary. "And so long as you stay here with us, you will be safe."

"Safe?"

"There are rumors that *Le Batard* has sent someone to take revenge, for her death and his honor." The First Secretary rubbed his hands together. "So long as you remain with us, we shall endeavor to identify anyone who would do you harm."

With the cuff of his sleeve, William wiped the perspiration off his forehead. "I will be happy to play for the *duchessa*."

The two older men glanced at each other, each with a pleased smile. "Very well. Tomorrow, the *duchessa* will see you, after she has dined." Trivulzio's eyes remained impassive, but an unmistakable gleam shown through them." He handed William a small pouch which jiggled with the sounds of coins.

As he left the chancery, William noticed two ragazzi glancing in his direction. *Why do they look at me?* He wondered. Then he realized that the guard outside the chancery office had given him a similar look. *What is it? All I did was...* Then it hit him: they saw him putting money in his clothing. He cursed himself for being careless, just as he had been in France when he left his belongings in the cart while he went swimming.

William reminded himself that one of the dirty little secrets of life at court—the many instances of small-time thievery. With so many young boys and girls of good families doing the bidding of the adults at court, considerable amounts of money were stolen by the ragazzi who had free rein of the court.

Of course no one dared steal anything from the duke. His violent temper and wayward habits protected him from that. Most of the ragazzi had the good sense to keep their hands off truly valuable items such as jewelry, ducati, and the like. But a few soldi on a desk or a nightstand?

Among the ragazzi di camera themselves, quite a bit of money changed hands. William had heard rumors of some young ragazzi taking money for sexual favors. He had heard of such things at the court in Burgundy, too. Not in England. But perhaps he was just young and naive at the time.

As he reflected on the glances that the ragazzi had given him, he realized that in the years he had been at court, he had taken great pains to make himself indispensible to the wealthy and powerful at court. But he had not a single trustworthy ally among the younger people at court. Perhaps of greater importance, he had no network of acquaintances who would relay information to him. *Hmmm. That will have to change, or I may wake up one day with a dagger in my back.*

He had to admit that such a scenario was a real possibility. Murders had occurred at court, most of them the result of jealousies. Arguments over possessions and lovers were not uncommon. The court was a small *citta* composed of every class of person from very rich to very poor, and within such a citta very good and very bad people could be found. The threat of banishment from court—the disgrace, the shame, and humiliation—served to keep most of the young people in line.

But some of the young people came to court ready to defy the order of things. Who could say whether they had been fawned upon by nannies, teachers, and others responsible for their care, or if rebellion simply lay in their natures. They defied even naked, brutal authority. *Young Zimarro 'Bieko' da Corte seems to be one of those sorts*, mused William.

Handsome, easy-going, and confident, da Corte seemed quick with a reply or a joke, qualities that had ingratiated him to Duke Galeazzo. The youth seemed to be one of the rising stars of his court. Nor had he suffered since Galeazzo's death. He was everywhere in evidence—delivering messages, ready to serve a glass of wine, poised at a lady's elbow to take a wrap. Never more than a cough or a sneeze away from wealth and power.

As he pondered these concerns, William asked himself who among the youth of the court would be a good ally? He suspected that for all her apparent coldness and indifference, Cecilia remained a friend. But who else? Then he recollected a tall, thin young man at the chancery who seemed especially diligent—forever working—even late at night. What was his name? He poured through his thoughts. He remembered it rhymed with something:

*fortress, rocca, courage, chorus, castello* — ah, ah, that's it, Tolentino. Yes, *next time I am in the chancery, I will make a point of talking to him.* William smiled to himself. He felt proud at never leaving any stone unturned in his search for success. His uncle would be proud.

In the duchessa's chambers, William and a viol player finished a cheerful frottola to the applause of Bona and her ladies-in-waiting. He bowed in appreciation. As he put away his instrument, he caught the glance of a young, dark-haired beauty out of the corner of his eye. She averted her eyes but her hands fluttered in the Italian manner. William laughed to himself. *These Italian women are such a delight.*

Soon the duchessa dismissed all the young ladies as well as the viol player and took her place at the head of a small table. William joined her as he had for several weeks, sitting next to her.

She pulled a small sack from a pocket and shook it so the three coins within clinked together. "Your playing is miraculous, Englishman. It has brought us much pleasure in our time of grief." She placed the sack next to the cuff of his sleeve.

"I thank you, Duchessa." He stuffed the pouch inside his breast pocket then fell upon the wine, cheese, and *langosta* that her servants placed before him.

She cast a sly smile in his direction. "Tell me, boy, do you find me attractive?"

William almost choked on his food. He glanced into her eyes then returned to his meal. "You know the answer to that, *la mia duchessa.* Your beauty is the envy of every woman in Milano." He wiped his mouth on his sleeve.

"Oh? Is that so?" Bona gave him an inquiring look. She took a napkin and wiped the corners of his mouth. "You men! You're just like my husband." The widow got up and went to a window seat filled with pillows. She motioned for him to follow as she stretched out on the long, wide seat. "But why have I had such difficulty getting your attention?"

William followed her to the seat and stretched out, reclining on one elbow. He gazed at her ample bosom, the plunging neckline of the loose-fitting garment, and wet his lips. "While the nectar and ambrosia you have been feeding me these last few weeks is tasty, it appears that there are other, spicier things to sample here."

Duchessa Bona laughed. "At last, this tune moves in a proper direction."

He pushed back his blond and brown hair and ran a finger along her neck, around her shoulder, across the top of her bodice. "Is this really a good idea, Duchessa?"

She stopped his finger, put it between her teeth and bit softly. "It would please me…" she purred. "You would not find it distasteful."

He took her hand in his. "My dear, let me be truthful. No man is going to say no to a beauty like you." She blushed. "But let me speak to you honestly." He gazed into her eyes. "I understand what you have lost." He kissed her hand with tenderness. She listened. "You loved the duke very much. No man can replace him." Her body began to droop. He moved closer to her. "I know what you have lost." Tears began to fall from her eyes. He put an arm around her. She buried her face in his neck and cried softly. "Go ahead," he cooed. "I know how it feels."

The tears flowed from her eyes as she held him closer and closer.

"The girl, Solice, up north, must have been utterly mad for you."

He buried his mouth in her sweet smelling hair.

"And before her?" she asked.

"An Irish girl at the court of the English king. I wanted to stay, but my parents had ambitions for me."

"Poor boy," murmured the duchessa, taking his chin in her hands and kissing his lips, sinking her teeth into them.

He untied the loose string holding her bodice in place, revealing her dark-nippled breasts. He was surprised to find one of them pierced by a ring. "Wha—"

Again she buried her face in his neck, this time stifling a laugh. "It was the duke's desire. I have three such rings on my body. You can guess where." Again she stifled a laugh. "He had this long golden cord—and would run it through the rings. Then he would sit at the other end of the room and draw me closer as he sat studying his papers."

William stared at her, fascinated and aghast. "Is that not cruel, not a painful thing to do?"

She chuckled. "I would try to resist. The pain would be too great, and I would give in. Sometimes it took hours." She unbuttoned his shirt. "Do you like pain?" She reached inside his shirt and squeezed the nipple of his breast.

He winced. "Not especially," then lowered his head to her breast and bit the large dark nipple of her other breast.

She began to swoon. "Take me," she whispered. "I need a man." He put his hand between her legs, finding it deliciously wet. "I thought you English were cold people," she murmured. "I was wrong."

"It takes a few logs and a hot burning fire to warm up these bones," he admitted. She laughed.

She moved his hand away then nestled her head to his chest.

"It is so good to feel a man's body next to mine. A real man."

He kissed her lips softly. "There is a matter which we must discuss. If we do not, I may get myself killed, and that would not satisfy either of us." She looked at him in surprise. "We both know that I was brought to you by the First Secretary. I report to him every evening."

Bona gazed into his eyes, running her hands through his hair. "Yes, I know. Everyone thinks me a stupid woman, because I am so emotional. But I do know what goes on."

"Had I not mentioned this to you, you would never have trusted me."

She kissed his lips. "You want me to trust you?" He nodded. "Then we will make love, the most passionate love you have ever had from a woman," she grinned. "Afterwards, you will tell Simonetta what I want…when I have done with you." She touched the bulge between his legs. "Although perhaps I won't let go of you so soon…"

He laughed, leaning down and licking her breast once again, pulling on the nipple ring with his teeth.

"Ahh!" She winced then chuckled. "I think I can trust you, Englishman. I want to." She turned serious. "Now I want you with me. I will have you killed if you deny me."

"Umm," he murmured in her ear. "That is even more compelling than the nipple ring." She laughed. "However, before we begin…" he caressed her cheek.

"Yes…?" Her eyes grew wide with desire.

"Your husband's brothers wish to see you. Will you receive them?"

The duchess stared into the young man's eyes. She brought his head down to her lips. They were full, dark, soft, and inviting. "Of course," she whispered.

Simonetta and Trivulzio sat in semi-darkness in Simonetta's apartment as William settled himself. They shared a bottle of wine and exchanged pleasantries.

"Now then, my friend," urged the old man, "what do you have to tell us today?"

"I am afraid I have some unhappy news for you, First Secretary."

Simonetta leaned closer, rubbing his hands together. "Oh? And what is that?"

"The duchessa is aware that we meet every week, and that I tell you everything that goes on."

"Oh? How does she know that?" Trivulzio's smoldering voice echoed from the darkness of the room.

The young Englishman leaned back in his chair. "I told her so."

Simonetta jumped to his feet. "You what? Why did you do that?"

"Because I do not wish to continue spying on her." William found himself pouring out his frustrations in a torrent. "I wish simply to be the musician that I am. I came to Italy to perform as a musician, not to play frottolas in some chamber and then tell all the gossip that went on."

The First Secretary got up, came around and sat on the corner of his desk. He glanced at Trivulzio, whose nose and forehead were visible in the bare stream of light coming through the window. "Then perhaps you want something more." He paused for effect. "We have been known to provide those who serve us well with property that has income attached to it."

"That would please me greatly, First Secretary. But I do not wish to continue to be the confidante to the duchessa." He fell silent. The other two men remained silent as well. Finally he spoke again, this time with a little laugh. "There may be another who would serve your interests better than I."

"Oh? And who would that be?" The sarcasm in Trivulzio's voice was thinly veiled.

"Tassino, the assistant carver in the duchessa's kitchen. He has caught her eye, I suspect her heart as well," William answered.

"Ah, well, that is good information." The First Secretary walked back behind his desk, took a small sack from a drawer and handed it to the Englishman.

William handed it back. "What I tell you is simply information she herself could have told you, or that you would have found out in a few days."

Trivulzio laughed. "We already knew this, my friend. But it is good that you have told us. We would not want you...holding anything too close to your chest."

"I just want the opportunity to join my friends in Napoli or Ferrara. I am no spy. I am a musician."

"You are an excellent spy, and, yes, one day you shall join your friends. You have what few spies have—a sense of honor and the ability to gain the trust of those around you," the soldier answered.

"I understand your impatience with the parlor games we are playing," added the First Secretary. "But the stakes are very high. We will have another assignment for you before long. Be patient." He handed the sack of coins back to William. "Your next assignment or two will gain you more property. Perhaps with a small villa attached. A sinecure against the vagaries of chance."

William's lips twisted into a sharp blade of a smile. "From the roasting spit into the fire."

"*Que?*" Trivulzio's deep-set eyes narrowed.

"I was reflecting on my days at the court of the Duke of Burgundy," William answered.

"*Casar alla padella nella brace* (from the frying pan into the fire)." Simonetta hid his smile. Trivulzio nodded. The elderly First Secretary searched William's face for a sign of enthusiasm. "Perhaps," he added, "we can find other inducements."

A look of uncertainty crossed William's face. "I do not follow you, First Secretary."

"A proper introduction. An opportunity for something to flower. An assurance to a certain young lady's parents of a compari relationship that will flow from ourselves…." He glanced at Trivulzio who nodded in agreement. "To them and their children and their children's children, if you are successful."

A tiny flicker of understanding crossed William's face—Simonetta observed Cecilia's swoon those many months ago. *He knows my passion for her and offers an introduction, an opportunity, an assurance of a compari relationship that is more valuable than gold.* Simonetta's words flooded his brain, making him light-headed. He gripped the back of the chair he had been leaning against and steadied himself. *They entrust me with a mission no one else can accomplish.* Pride welled up inside him. Then another voice laid claim to the truth of the matter. *More likely, no one else is fool enough to take it on.*

William put out his hand. Simonetta took the young man's hand in his own.

Trivulzio laid his large hand upon those of the other two men. "We do not expect you to be in any danger, my young friend. The task will be more a challenge to your powers of persuasion than to your courage—"

"The first of the labors of Hercules," Simonetta chuckled. The two men laughed in concert.

William found himself intrigued. His eyes came to rest on a beautifully crafted chess set sitting on a small table behind the First Secretary. Each piece was in its proper place, except for one black pawn standing alone in the middle of the board. It begged to be taken off the board with a simple move. *Hmmm. What got the pawn so far out in front? The thrill of the unknown? Its strength? Or a foolish risk?*

Some days later, Bishop Branda's coach pulled up at a roadhouse near Vigevano. The bishop got out of the coach. Moments later, Ludovico, Sforza Maria, and William rode up and dismounted. The two brothers climbed into the coach, slipped into the empty spaces beneath the two seats and disappeared from sight. Bishop Branda and William climbed in behind them and sat down on the seats hiding the brothers. Once the brothers were hidden, the bishop signaled the driver to move. The coach sprang forward.

At the entry portal to the Castello of Porta Giovia, the coach stopped. A guard peered in and saw only William and his uncle. He waved them through.

Circling the vast parade ground, the coach lumbered through the portal that led to the *rochetta* in the south corner and the Corte Ducale in the northwestern section of the castle. The coach came to a halt at the entrance to the tower of Duchess Bona.

As he and William climbed out of the coach, Bishop Branda requested that the guards bring the duchess and her visitors some food.

"And get a little something for yourselves," the old man grinned.

The three guards were happy to comply. After all, Bishop Branda was a truly important person and well liked by all who knew him. When the guards left their posts, the brothers slipped out the other side of the coach, unseen.

Inside Bona's apartment, Ludovico with sat the young duke on his lap, mussed his hair and laughed with ten-year-old Gian Galeazzo. Sforza Maria and Duchess Bona looked on.

"So you have no idea what happened to Galeazzo's instructions, investing me with the regency of the boy?" Ludovico questioned as he played with Gian Galeazzo.

The duchess frowned. "None. I am sorry. I didn't know what to do. Your father always trusted Simonetta. So did my husband. I had no reason not to."

Moro looked into the eyes of his nephew, smiling. "We intend to run the government, whether Cicco Simonetta likes it or not. We have a plan."

"No matter what your plan, dear Moro," the duchess sighed, "I have no wish to make trouble for old Simonetta." She embraced him. "You are in my prayers."

A knock at the door jerked Ludovico to his senses. The surprised look on his face gave way to suspicion.

The duchess put a reassuring hand on Ludovico's arm. "It is now 10:00 pm. I am only permitted to see my son from seven to ten in the evening." The duchess waved the two men toward an adjoining room.

"Must I go, Mama?" muttered the petulant ten-year old duke. "I want to stay and play with Uncle Moro."

The duchess bent down on one knee and embraced him, tears in her eyes. "Don't worry, this won't be forever." She touched his lips with a finger. "And say nothing of your uncle's visit. Understand?"

Ludovico moved over and kissed the boy on the top of the head. He and Sforza Maria disappeared into the other room. The knock came a second time.

Bona opened the door and led her son into the grasp of the unseen figure in the hallway. The door closed.

Ludovico emerged from the other room and enfolded his brother's widow in a long, loving embrace. "You loved Galeazzo with all your heart, my dear. Despite your sorrow, a sorrow that would age a lesser woman, you are more beautiful now than you have ever been.

The duchess flushed and took Moro's hand as she led the brothers to the door.

William and Bishop Branda watched as they stood against a wall, close by.

Darkness had fallen by the time the Sforza brothers slipped down the stairs, staying in the shadows. At the bottom of the stairs, they waited until the guards had their back to them, then entered the bishop's coach. In a few moments Bishop Branda and William followed. Each sat on one of the seats, the brothers again secreted in the hollowed-out seats of the coach. Branda knocked on the wall of the coach and the vehicle moved forward.

Fifteen minutes later, the coach stopped in front of the church of Santa Maria della Grazie, a few blocks from the castle. Ludovico and Sforza Maria climbed out of their hiding place.

"You will be safe here," murmured the bishop. "Tomorrow night, the monks will see you out of the city."

Sforza Maria shook hands with William and his uncle. "We are grateful for all you have done. We will be in touch."

The two men climbed out of the coach and melted into the darkness. Bishop Branda stared after them. "What do you think? Have they the strength of character to stand up to Simonetta and Trivulzio?"

William shrugged. "Trivulzio is very resolute. Moro has vision and patience—that is true. And the good will of the king of Napoli. However, I doubt that they will ever defeat Trivulzio in battle."

"Trivulzio treats those who come into conflict with him very harshly," observed Bishop Branda. "A bad sign. He is losing the good-will of the people of Milano. From here on, we must give help to neither side more than the other. At least until we see who will succeed and who will fail."

William agreed. "I will do as you say."

Obtaining horses from the monks of Santa Maria della Grazie, Ludovico and Sforza Maria rode out to Pavia where they found their younger brothers, Ascanio and Ottaviano, waiting for them. The brothers embraced.

Sforza Maria explained the plan to his younger brothers, then took Ascanio aside. "You will remain here in Pavia with Pier Francesco," he counseled. "Should we fail, we must have someone on whom we can rely, someone who is above suspicion."

Returning to the others, Ascanio, a quiet, modest, astute young man of twenty chuckled, "Ah, I am to stay behind and assume a Christ-like repose while my brothers take on all the danger...and have all the fun."

Ludovico stifled a laugh at Ascanio's succinct, playful summary of their plan.

The following morning the brothers gathered together, each

pondering his feelings toward Galeazzo's death. Some of the recollections were of a friendly nature, but more often than not each recalled a tense, competitive, usually painful encounter.

Then each spoke of Tristano, their bastard brother, some twenty years older than any of the duke's legitimate sons. Not one of them recalled any encounter that was less than affectionate. For a few moments, they all fell silent in memory of Tristano.

"Now we must endeavor to put Milano back in the hands of those who deserve to rule," muttered Sforza Maria to his younger brothers. The others agreed. "We must sound out all those we can trust."

For an hour they went down a list of those whom they believe to be fully in accord with their desire to rule. Finally they came to Bishop Branda and his nephew. "Young William has been a great help to us, so far. Yet he receives many favors from Simonetta. Property. Income. I have heard that Simonetta has offered him a compare relationship to a certain young woman's family, in return for a marriage contract. Are you certain you can trust William?" Sforza Maria muttered in Ludovico's ear.

"He was born of the best, the most noble and reliable stock to be found anywhere. Build your marble edifices as you will, beneath them lies the stone of an unbreakable foundation. The members of the Castiglione family are such stones. Not one of them has ever played us false, or been less than transparent."

He paused for a moment and chuckled. "Put simply, the court of Milano under Simonetta and Trivulzio will be much too austere for a young man with his ambition. If he does not know this yet, he soon will, which we will turn to our advantage."

Sforza Maria shrugged. "He may admit to working for his uncle, but who is to say the *ducati* from Trivulzio and Simonetta do not also influence him?"

The two younger Sforza brothers gazed at Sforza Maria, then at Ludovico.

Ludovico folded his arms across his chest. "Patience, brother. Patience."

Cicco Simonetta and Gian Giacomo Trivulzio walked around the small garden within the walls of the ducal court.

"The brothers are restless, First Secretary," observed Gian Giacomo. "They will cause us no end of trouble in months to come."

"Very true," replied Simonetta, his hands locked behind his back. "If anything happened to them, we would suffer the consequences."

Trivulzio nodded his head in agreement. "Perhaps we need to pay more attention to those who support them."

The aged First Secretary stopped and gazed at Trivulzio. "Umm, yes," he responded. "A very good idea. Whom do you propose to watch?"

Gian Giacomo threw an arm around his friend's shoulder. "Donato del Conte," he answered. "I have it on good authority that the brothers spent many weeks with del Conte in Genoa after their return in June. Let us watch del Conte."

The First Secretary smiled. "And now would be a good time for us to look in on our young charge, Duke Gian Galeazzo, to see if he is well and happy."

"Indeed…" muttered Trivulzio, bored with the details of ruling the duchy of Milano.

As Simonetta opened the door to the nearest building, Trivulzio called after him. "And Count Castiglione, what about him?"

The aged First Secretary turned and thought for a moment. "Do not worry about him. Men of a certain age are of no concern."

Trivulzio took several steps toward his mentor, Simonetta. "And his nephew?" He folded his arms across his chest. "Something tells me he begins to think for himself."

Simonetta paused at door, lost in thought for a moment. Then a sinister grin crept across his craggy features. "Another mission, perhaps to France, for that young man. All kinds of things can happen on a mission." His eye brows rose as if he were asking a question. He closed the door behind him.

Trivulzio smiled to himself. "Yes, a mission to France. Perfect."

# 4

## *France*

*A Courtyard*
**CORDIER'S VILLA**
MILANO, ITALIA
July, 1477

**W**illiam sat in the courtyard of Cordier's villa practicing his trombone. The French tenor had provided his place where William could live and practice, at Bishop Branda's suggestion, knowing that Cordier usually stayed with his wife and family closer to the castello. The courtyard offered a wonderful place to play with the sunshine warm on William's back and head, the breeze very slight and the sounds of his horn amplified by the stucco walls and porticos lining the four sides of the courtyard.

At first he had thought that the Frenchman offered him the villa as a courtesy. He felt much honored and appreciated. Then a bill had arrived at the end of the month for fifty-seven *scudi* (57s). The Frenchman had not loaned it to him at all—the villa was a rental. Not an unfair price, he paid it within the hour. He laughed to himself, observing that those whose wealth was newly gained often behaved this way. Nothing ever came to pass unless a contract and a healthy income were attached. Even his uncle, whose power, position, and prestige flowed out of the family's four hundred years of devotion to the well-being of Lombardy, operated this way.

The sound of horses clopping up to the doorstep came to his ears. Putting the horn down, he got to his feet. Before he could take two steps, he found himself welcoming his uncle—Bishop Branda—almost out of breath, but in good spirits.

William had been expecting his uncle to arrive about this time and had the villa's cook prepare a modest luncheon. The two men sat down to a mid-day meal of fish and salads capped with a good Lombard wine from the area of Minaggio. "Delicious, so delicious, *nepote*." The bishop appeared to be savoring good news. "You choose your wines quite well."

"Well, Uncle, you have something on your mind. Are you going to tell me or must I make guessing a habit?"

Bishop Branda leaned back in his chair. The expression on his face turned from one of satisfaction to one of deep concern. He leaned closer. "Galeazzo's reign created much confusion among the states of Italy...and Europe." William nodded, recalling Cordier's outrageous treatment of the Neapolitan ambassador. He reminded his uncle of the incident. "King Ferrante was certain that Galeazzo had ordered Cordier to drop that piss pot on his ambassador's head."

The bishop began to chuckle then laugh—louder and louder.

William joined him, recollecting the moment. "I wish you could have seen those two men. Can you imagine how that piss stank? Cordier had just had lunch. It reeked of asparagus, garlic, and onions." The two men continued to laugh and laugh.

When the bishop had calmed down, he said, "Ferrante then sent some very nasty letters to the First Secretary, threatening to make life miserable for us and our allies, principally the Florentines. But you solved that problem." Branda's face screwed up in discomfort. "Now it is the king of France who is unhappy. You may recall that Galeazzo took great pains to ally himself with Burgundy a few years ago. The king has not entirely forgiven Milano for that."

"So, you have in mind for me to…" William motioned for his uncle to get to the point.

"The First Secretary is sending an emissary to Lyon to meet King Louis XI. Since Bona has close ties to the king, she has it in her head that her tenor, Cordier, ought to perform for her brother-in-law, the king. Simonetta and Trivulzio are loathe to agree to this but do not want to offend the duchess." Branda's expression became earnest. "They want you to keep an eye on Cordier. They don't trust him and think he may have put Bona up to all this. Follow his every step. Thankfully, you are acceptable to King Louis. He knows of you and is anxious to hear you perform."

The young Englishman smiled at the thought of playing for the king.

"If your mission comes to a successful conclusion, you will be given a pass that will ensure a safe journey to Bruges."

William recollected Simonetta's last words to him: '*Your next assignment or two will gain you more property. Perhaps with a small villa attached. A sinecure against the vagaries of chance.' Apparently, word moves quickly that I am trustworthy.* He smiled to himself. "I will do my best." In his mind he imagined a dinner at Simonetta's apartment with Cecilia and her parents, the offer of a dowry, a sinecure, and her hand in marriage. *Yes, things are going well.*

The two men got to their feet. "Very well, nephew. I wish you all the best…"

"Uncle, there is one thing more," William interrupted.

Branda's eyes crinkled up in amusement. William was beginning to think several steps ahead, like himself and Duke Francesco, so many years ago. "Certo."

"I would not dare take this magnificent instrument out of the city of Milano." He held up the beautiful horn that Jacopo Trombone had made for him. "I would like for Jacopo to make me another one, brass, yes, but perhaps not so carefully ornamented as this."

The bishop nodded in agreement. "A wise move. No need for us to trumpet our wealth." He chuckled at his own joke. William laughed with him. "Consider it done."

Slowly William turned serious. He stared at his uncle then leaned toward the older man. "And what of Ludovico Il Moro?" He inquired. "What will happen while I am gone?"

Bishop Branda said nothing for several moments. Finally he answered in a soft, almost inaudible voice. "A great deal will happen quite soon. It is just as well if you are out of the country."

William picked up his wine glass. Bishop Branda did the same. The two men clinked glasses. "To the future," William mused.

Standing on the bowsprit of the tiny ketch, William hung onto one of the staysail halyards that looped downward from the top of the foremast to the bowsprit. He gazed intently at the shore, looking for the first sign of the city of Lyon. Pushed by a strong southerly breeze, *Euridyce* had sailed up the Rhone River at a good clip. The late summer air hummed and buzzed with life. Sailing craft of every kind plied the river. Beautiful country, he had to admit, although he could not help remembering his most recent unhappy experience within the borders of France, a few years before.

The voyage from Genoa to Marseilles had been uneventful. A summer squall had pushed them well out to sea, making them fair game for marauding pirates from the Algerian coast. Passengers and crew of the little vessel understood the risks. They became irritable and nervous. In the end no pirates had been sighted. Perhaps it was no more than a rumor after all. The passage up the Rhone pleased everyone, except the musicians. Despite wonderful scenery and temperate weather, the musicians never emerged from below deck. All remained too sick to leave their hammocks.

Half an hour later, *Eurydice* sailed around a bend in the river, revealing Lyon just ahead on the western bank of the river. Dominating the countryside around it, the castle of the king of France stood like a sentinel overlooking the glassy surface of the river.

As the ketch docked, William turned toward the gangway amidships, expecting Cordier and the other musicians to appear. One by one, they came on deck, pale from two weeks of seasickness and card playing below decks. In all, ten singers and five instrumentalists staggered into the light of day. Cordier wore a strange smile. William wondered about that. He considered for a moment the possibility that the singer might have been given different instructions from the ones he had been given. *In fact, Cordier might be taking orders from more than one patron.*

As the musicians debarked at a loading dock, a steward welcomed them and the king's ambassadorial staff, then escorted them up a winding path. William noted that throughout the journey, Ambassador Marco Trotti had kept to himself, never talking to the musicians who laughed, sang and told jokes below decks, when they weren't vomiting. Trotti's staff was also quiet and dignified, even somber. William wondered why. The musicians had no such concerns.

On either side of the path leading up the hill, young girls in tight bodices festooned with ribbons hurled flower petals in the direction of the newcomers. The musicians relished the courtesies the king had devised for his guests. Arriving at the end of the path, numerous carriages awaited them, along with four of the king's trombeters who raised their herald trombetti and sounded a salute.

A handsome, gray-haired man stepped out of the lead carriage and shook hands with Trotti and the famous tenor, Cordier. Once the passengers had boarded the carriages, they were whisked along a broad expanse of road that led up to the castle. The air warm, the sun bright, the musicians laughed and sang as the young girls hung on to the doors of the carriage, waving to the onlookers.

As the carriages approached the fortress of Lyon, William spotted great numbers of armed men gathered around the castle. Squadron after squadron of the king's army stood at attention and saluted as the ambassadorial party rumbled past. Each mounted soldier wore a suit of chain mail with a white cloth over-garment on which were sewn the insignias of the king's lancers and the fleur-de-lis of the French kings.

William frowned, recognizing the difference between this army and that of the Milanese. As his eyes followed the ranks of lancers, archers, and artillery, the old discomfiting chill raced down his back. Somehow the spectacle that lay before him did not bode well for the rulers of Milano. The army of Louis XI was fit and ready to attack. *Attack whom? Attack what? Attack where?* William questioned. He shivered as he watched.

At the castle, stewards showed the men to their rooms—dark and gloomy despite the freshness of the air and warmth of the sun. The entire place reminded William of the court of Burgundy at Bruges, before the death of Charles the Rash.

That night the musicians gathered in the great hall of the castle. Dressed in crimson and black, they cut dashing figures. A sumptuous dinner appeared as well as sufficient wine to send their spirits soaring. The king, a tall, thin man in his early fifties with long features, entered to the playing of many trombetti and much applause.

"Welcome to France, Monsieur Trotti," he smiled.

Trotti stood and bowed.

"We are most happy to have you with us. For too long, the Duke of Burgundy came between us." The king looked around at his courtiers who nodded their approval of his words. "Fortunately Charles the Rash now rests in the company of men who no longer have such earthly ambitions." The members of his court received his little joke with laughter and more applause. He held out his hand to the ambassador and motioned for everyone to sit down.

Trotti motioned for his aides to stand up. "Great and illustrious, most powerful and serene majesty, Louis of the house of Anjou, King of all France, conqueror of Burgundy—our beloved duke, young Gian Galeazzo Sforza and Reggente Cicco Simonetta, First Secretary to the Duke of Milano, wish you the best of everything. You have earned the respect and envy of every man, woman and child in the entire duchy. We treasure your friendship. We are guided by your wisdom. We know the strength of character, the perspicacity and sagacity that guide your every move."

The king glowed at this wonderful display of rhetoric. No one could flatter like the Italians. Not the English or the Spanish, certainly. No, the Italians were expansive in their praise but not beyond the boundaries of possibility. He hid his smile as best he could, but from ear to ear his mouth widened with pleasure.

"With this in mind we offer you a number of gifts." Trotti ticked off half a dozen priceless gifts—a sword belonging to Julius Caesar, a dozen casks of fine Lombard wine, three lots of silk from Tuscany. Half an hour after he began his encomium to the king, Trotti concluded. "Moreover, Majesty, we have a very special treat for you, in addition to the sweet offerings of our wonderful tenor, Monsieur Cordier." Once again, he bowed to the king and backed away.

"Ah, no one could have delivered a finer speech, Minister, than what we have just heard." The king smiled with pleasure as he motioned for Trotti to sit. "Now we must live up to the reputation you have created for us in which you have extolled our person as the finest example of kingship to be found anywhere." Louis turned to Cordier, the tenor. "And what gifts have you brought us, Monsieur Johannes?"

The tenor got to his feet, bowed to the king and then sang an unaccompanied motet in which the king's many virtues were extolled once again.

Louis got to his feet, came over to Cordier, kissed him on both cheeks, took the singer's hands in his own and pumped them up and down. At length, he turned to Trotti. "You mentioned a special treat, Minister?"

Trotti waved a hand in the direction of William Castle. "We are most fortunate to have at our court the premier brass player of our generation, your Majesty." Trotti motioned William to his feet. The Englishman bowed to the king. "This afternoon he will play for you an instrument called the trombone, invented by our own Jacopo Trombono. We hope you will delight in the sound of this most unusual instrument." William took his trombone from its leather case and signaled the other instrumentalists to do the same. In short order, William, a second trombonist and two trombeters began a short piece for the king.

The music cascaded in every directions—the sounds of the horns echoed throughout the room, bouncing off stone walls and high ceilings. The king turned in one direction, then another. William had written the short piece with great care, paying attention to the spaces needed for the sounds to penetrate vast spaces then return moments later. He had created the parts so that they would answer one another, using the echoes as additional instruments.

When the piece ended, Louis sat down in his chair, speechless. At first William thought that his little motet had displeased the king. His heart sank. Then Louis began to applaud. His servants and musicians also clapped their hands with great enthusiasm.

Trotti smiled and continued. "It may be of some interest to your Majesty that the English king, Edward IV, so disliked this instrument that he banned the instrument and its player, young William here, from his court…for evermore."

The king laughed at this gesture of understanding and clapped his hands with delight, as did the others in his retinue.

The queen leaned over and whispered in her husband's ear. Louis nodded and then beckoned William over to the royal couple.

"My wife tells me that you, Englishman, were the one who actually freed her sister from the grasp of that wretched Charles of Burgundy. Is that true?"

William bowed before the king and the queen. "I was deeply honored that our Lord above chose me to bring her to safety. Duchessa Iolanda rewarded me handsomely. I am deeply in her debt."

The king whispered to the queen who nodded in agreement. He turned back to William. "Come see us in the morning, Maestro. And bring Cordier with you." With that he rose to his feet. Everyone in attendance did the same. As the royal couple marched from the room, Trotti, Cordier, and the other members of the Milanese court crowded around William, congratulating him on the beauty of the instrumental motet and wondering what the king had said to him. William smiled at everyone, but said nothing.

In his room that night, William lay on his bed thinking about the morning to come. A fool or a person with excessive ambition might speak of his yearnings and his accomplishments the next morning, in order to further his career. Making the king of France an ally would be no small accomplishment. *No,* he decided, *I am here for another purpose. What did his uncle expect of him?* He concluded that first and foremost this was a diplomatic mission. Trotti was an experienced diplomat, and Cordier for all his affectations and ambitions had plenty of experience. What would a man like Trotti be looking for? He put himself in Trotti's shoes, imagining the mission unfolding as it had—the king well-disposed toward the Italians. Why would that matter?

Little by little, he found himself looking at the Italian mission as if he were the king of France. The Italians appeared to be children—playful, colorful, articulate, artistic, pleasing in every way—but still children. He imagined row after row of French soldiers outside the walls of the castle, thousands of them, all serving under the banner of the king of France.

He thought back to the recent history of the French military, how it had learned the art of warfare after its defeat at Agincourt in 1306, nearly two hundred years before, culminating in the defeat of the Burgundians at Nancy, in 1476, a little more than a year ago. *If I were king,* Castle told himself, *I would be wondering what to do with my army. This vast standing army needs to be fed, clothed, and paid. Above all, it must pay for itself.*

It dawned on William that this must be what occupied the minds of Simonetta and his uncle, Branda. What would the king of France want next? William could see that the Milanese wanted France as an ally and would go to great lengths to achieve this. He wondered what all of this could mean?

Then the answer appeared to him from out of nowhere. A sinking feeling hit him in the pit of his stomach. For the sake of Milano's well-being, either he or Cordier might be offered to the king as a kind of ransom or bribe. William sighed and tried to fall asleep, but a feeling of dread had taken hold of him and would not leave. He turned and watched Cordier asleep in the other bed, and wondered how the Frenchman would feel about returning to the French court.

The next morning the two men were escorted into the king's chambers where Louis and his wife dined. The two men bowed, keeping their eyes on the floor. The king chuckled, waving formality away. "I honor you as my equals, gentlemen. Two of the finest musicians anywhere." He invited them to be seated and the four shared a sumptuous breakfast.

The meal finished, the king whispered to one of the stewards. The old man hurried away and returned accompanied by a young man with smiling eyes and an easy manner. "*Mes amis*, I wish to introduce you to the prize of our court, Monsieur Josquin des Prez." The men bowed to one another as a group of singers entered behind Josquin.

For the next twenty minutes, Josquin and the choir sang a short section of a mass the young Frenchman had composed. Owing much to Gregorian chant but with lines that were more openly contrapuntal and less tied to the text, Josquin's music bespoke genius. William heard it; Cordier heard it. Their eyes met in recognition: *The man is one of us.* The king smiled as he studied the two men exchanging glances. A nod from the king and Josquin, the young Frenchman, departed.

"Talented, eh?" The king leaned forward. The two men agreed. "Anyone residing at this court would be honored to compose alongside this young man."

*Good God, I was right. He intends to keep us here.*

"I have concluded a very important agreement with Trotti," the king went on. "One that is especially advantageous to the Milanese. To show his appreciation, Reggente Simonetta is willing to part with one of his most talented musicians, to see this agreement to its most favorable conclusion." The king glanced from one musician to the other.

*God in heaven, look down upon me now,* William thought to himself.

Cordier went to the king and knelt down. "If it pleases your highness, I love Milano almost more than life itself…"

*Oh, oh.*

"The duke was good to me, as were his First Secretary and Bishop Branda Castiglione, but I am, at heart, a Frenchman." The king reached toward the tenor, his hand outstretched. Cordier kissed the ring on the king's finger as if it were a cardinal's. "You honor me with this invitation, since it is in the best interest of the courts of Milano and France and I accept."

Louis of Anjou rose. He lifted Cordier from his knees and embraced the man. Then he turned to William and bowed. "Although I desire to have you at my court, I cannot steal both of you away at one time."

William bowed. "The opportunity to serve your majesty and to create music alongside a talent the size of Josquin's…why anyone with any sense would die for the opportunity."

The king chuckled to himself, pleased by this expression of warmth and good fellowship from an Englishman. He rose and escorted the two men to the door. As William started to exit, the king held his arm for a moment, drawing him back into the room. He led the Englishman to a corner of the room where they could not be overheard. "You will pardon me if I am a little indiscreet, *Monsieur*, a little bit too direct. You were the Englishman accused in the death of Solice d'Anselm, *n'est pas?*"

William pursed his lips and frowned.

The king read his expression. "We know you were the one. You wish to go to Bruges and pursue the matter…to find the person who murdered her, *ce n'est pas correct?*"

"That is true." William glanced up at the king. "Sadly I have no idea who might have been responsible." He shrugged. "If you have any i…."

"*Regrettablement,* no. I do not." Louis shook his head. "If I knew that, some of my problems would disappear. Tell me," the king almost whispered, "...do you know anything about a diary she kept?"

Shock permeated William's body. *Another man who knew something about Solice's life!* He almost wished he were staying in Lyon. "A diary...she did say something about a diary, but I believe it to have been more of a journal of advice to young women at court."

Now it was the king's turn to express shock and surprise, and a little dismay.

William caught the look and wondered what else the king knew. "Was anything else in the diary, besides advice to the young?" William shook his head. "No, not that I am aware of."

Perturbed, Louis let William's arm slip from his grasp as he shrugged. "Thank you, Monsieur Castle. If you remember anything, or learn anything, I am your friend, and the information might well tell us the identity of the man or woman who killed her."

The two men walked to the door and shook hands. William bowed.

"Your pass to Bruges will be ready this afternoon. For your protection, ten of my men will accompany you. The territory of Burgundy which we now control is quite unruly. We will ensure your safety." Louis gave the young Englishman a half-smile. "You are a credit to your people. Who knew the English had a soul leavened with music and wit?" He clapped the young man on the arm, leading him to the doorway. "I know your uncle, Bishop Branda. An impressive person. Very trustworthy. Goodbye." The king closed the door.

William walked away. *In a week I will be in Bruges. At last, I will be able to bury some ghosts.*

The following morning William said goodbye to Cordier and

the Milanese musicians, mounted his horse, rode toward the commander of the French soldiers and saluted him in the Italian manner with a closed fist to his heart. *"Bonjour, capitain."*

*"Oui, oui,"* muttered the Frenchman. "However, Monsieur, do not salute me as a man of military rank. You must understand, in *L'armee Francais*, civilians do not salute men of military rank."

*"Oui, je comprend, capitain."* William replied. Disliking the man's insufferable attitude, he thought to reveal that he, too, possessed military as well as diplomatic rank. "I hold the ran…" spilled out of his mouth.

The captain gave him a cool, searching look. *"Oui, Monsieur?"*

William stopped himself. *Don't be a fool.* He shrugged off the question. It would be better if the officer knew less rather than more.

The Frenchman signaled for his troops to move out.

For the next three hours, the men rode northward at breakneck speed. William wondered why they did not board a sailing craft and sail up the Rhone River. It would have been a shorter and more comfortable trip. The winds appeared to be favorable, which was unusual on the Rhone which often required that ships going north be hauled by rope and oxen along the bank. But no, the winds seemed favorable.

William didn't like what he saw. Something gnawed at his insides. Something was not right here.

At midday, the officer brought the ten-man troop to a halt, and they dismounted. Each man broke out a sack of food and a bottle of wine from his saddlebag. The captain provided William with food and wine without so much as a 'hello' or a welcoming smile.

As William rested his aching back against a tree, he heard a voice—a very familiar voice.

*"Mon Dieu,* the English, they are worms, *ami."*

The musician instantly recognized that voice. His senses were suddenly alert. Where had he heard that voice before? Where?! Ah! It struck him. That man was one of those who had robbed and almost killed him! *Christ! What have I gotten myself into?* He resisted the urge to turn and confront his attacker. He realized that he must be extremely careful.

Finishing his plate of food, he pretended to doze off and then awoke in need of a stretch. He wandered away to piss behind a tree. There he caught a glimpse of the attacker. Sure enough! There stood the thick-bodied man with the arms of a blacksmith. With him was another of his attackers. The feeling of dread raced up and down William's spine. All of this could have been orchestrated by the king, in which case he would be at the mercy of his captors. He would have to play the innocent.

For several hours more they rode north. Once the sun began to sink in the west, the troop pulled up at an inn. He was given a room to himself, but the captain took charge of his belongings, including the horn. *He supposes I cannot move without my baggage.*

That night he heard footsteps outside his room. He got out of bed and waited behind the door, his dagger at the ready. The sound disappeared down the hall.

As the bell in the village bell tower struck midnight, he eased out of his bed, fully-clothed, ready to move. He tied the laces of his boots together and hung them around his neck. Pushing open the wooden shutters, he stared up at the moonlit sky. *A gorgeous night. I wonder if I will live to see another one.* The window from which he observed moon and stars looked out over the roof which slanted downward at a steep angle. Some three stories below lay a garden. *Nasty. Very nasty.* A risk he must take.

He climbed up onto the window sill then eased himself onto the roof. He started to slide and dug his fingers into the wood shingles. A nail stuck out and ripped the skin of his middle finger, but it gave him something to hold on to. Little by little he lowered himself toward the edge of the roof. He glanced down.

Not far below him, a small balcony jutted out into the darkness. *If the French soldiers occupy that room, then I am dead.* No matter. He would have to risk it. He lowered himself until his feet touched the railing of the second floor balcony. The room appeared unoccupied. Then he lowered himself down one more time until his feet touched the balcony of a first floor room. It was as dark as the one above.

Dropping to the ground, he spotted the stable. A quick dash in the moonlight brought him inside where several horses lay in the predawn gloom. *My God, it has taken me five hours to get here?* He couldn't believe so much time had elapsed. He roused a horse in the first stall, saddled it, and led the sleepy animal out into the open air. In the early morning light, he recognized it as the captain's horse and smiled to himself. *So be it.* He paused and reflected on this trip to France. *Too eventful. Much too eventful.* Perhaps in a few weeks he would be able to figure out all the currents of ambition and intention that he had encountered. *Let the other horses go,* a voice inside him advised, but he decided not to do so. He would have a good head start. That would be enough. He leapt up onto the handsome mare and galloped away from the inn.

Once again he had won his freedom by being careful and low-keyed in his assessment of the danger around him. As always, it was not the danger in front of him that needed his attention—it was how he reacted to the danger that would keep the blood flowing in his veins. *A good lesson, William. A very good lesson.*

Riding hard, he made it back to Lyon by sundown the same day. He cantered along the river until he found the docking area.

*Eurydice* still lay at anchor. He found a clump of trees in which he could hide, and he slipped inside, concealing himself in leaves and branches. All that night, he waited and watched.

The following morning turned out to be gray and gloomy. Fog shrouded the river and drifted over the dock where the ketch rocked in the gentle waves. Through the gloom, William noticed the workers on the dock loosening the lines holding her fast to the dock. *She is preparing to sail,* he said to himself. The soldiers who tended the little ship all night were being replaced by the morning watch.

In the fog, he slipped down to the bank of the river where he found a rowboat. In the gloom, no one would notice him and the boat leaving shore. He rowed out into the river for some distance until he was out of sight of anyone on the dock, then headed for the ketch, away from the notice of anyone on the dock or on shore.

"Hey, up there!" he called out, keeping his voice low, but loud enough to reach the deck. A head leaned over the railing. William recognized the face of a second trombeter. The man disappeared from sight. A moment later a deckhand appeared and lowered a rope ladder down to him. He noticed the ship was now underway, and breathed a sigh of relief as he climbed up the ladder.

On deck he looked around. Safe at last. The musicians as well as Trotti's staff all gathered around him. He made no explanation. The minister, Trotti, escorted him to his small cabin.

Having no reason to distrust Trotti, a man well-known to his uncle, he confided his tale.

"A nasty turn of events," Trotti frowned after William had completed his story. "Tell no one, except your uncle. I do not know the meaning of this. Perhaps Reggente Simonetta will know, or Bishop Branda." He gave William's shoulder a quick pat and left the cabin. "I will try to find out what I can." He smiled. "We do have friends at the court of Louis XI."

Through a porthole, William stared at the city of Lyon, growing smaller and smaller in the distance. He wondered what to think of the recent events that had befallen him. It occurred to him that Simonetta may have orchestrated everything that happened—if he disappeared, who among those at court would care. He began to dread his return to Milano, fearful that Simonetta had at last divined his strong sympathies with the Sforza brothers and their cause. *Well,* he thought to himself, *the future will be most interesting.* He rubbed his neck.

Two weeks later, William and his uncle sat in the library of the bishop's villa in Castiglione Olona. The cool October weather had set in, and the fire in the fireplace cast a warm glow on the faces of the two men.

Bishop Branda eased himself closer to the fireplace, a blanket over his knees. He looked perplexed. "The First Secretary did not authorize Trotti to release either you or Cordier to the king. I suspect the king invented that story, and Trotti was loath to go against the king's wishes. But someone was acting without your best interests in mind." The bishop's face was a mask of conflicting emotions—deep concern, fear of betrayal, a sense of the futility of keeping one's thoughts and actions private.

"Am I to go on missions for the First Secretary not knowing whether I will return or not, Uncle? I came to Milano as a musician, an artist—not as a pawn in some political mystery play." The heat of his words filled the room.

The older man leaned back in his chair and stared at the ceiling, remaining silent for some time. Finally, he lowered his chair to the floor. "A pawn, you say? Well, my boy, the rules of this game are ever changing. You are in a position to play it with success so long as you remain flexible and loyal to the Milanese cause."

A cynical laugh escaped the musician's lips. "What is the Milanese cause, Uncle? It isn't the Simonetta cause or the Sforza cause or even the Castiglione cause. I see little loyalty in that."

The tone of the young man's voice caused the bishop to sit up straight and study his young relative. "Really, you see little loyalty? Perhaps you need to look harder."

"Do I? You seem to have figured out how to stay alive without offending the various parties intending to further their own causes. Simonetta trusts you, Ludovico trusts you, Trivulzio trusts you. Everyone. How am I to do that?"

"How indeed?" Bishop Branda chewed on his lip for several moments. "You begin to see the flaw in having Cicco Simonetta in a position of such power. Rule by a Calabrian who hates the king of Napoli…"

William gave his uncle a questioning look. Then he pulled a document from his pocket, one that accused Simonetta of keeping money from the church benefices that once went to the musicians for himself, much to the displeasure of the writer. "Many seem to see it as well, Uncle."

The older man read it. "The accusations are true. Moreover, the First Secretary has made old allies uneasy." A rueful expression crossed his face. "Where will it all end?" he asked, almost to himself. "Before long, we may at last have to choose sides, William. We may have to decide once and for all in whose hands the well being of Milano will best be served."

"What does this have to do with my trip to Francia?" William got up and paced the floor. "Unless of course the First Secretary now distrusts me and is inclined to put me in a position where you cannot protect me."

The bishop squinted his eyes. "It is possible." He fell silent for several moments. "From now on, we will keep you a little closer to home." He nodded his head up and down.

William's eyes came to rest on portraits of Castiglione family members reaching far back in time. "Is this what the family has been doing for centuries? Deciding the fate of kings, dukes, and pretenders? My mother's family was filled with artists and musicians. I am more like them, I think." He faced his uncle. "All I ever wanted to do was play music and be the best I could be at it."

Branda reached into a small container at his elbow and pulled out several raisins. He flipped one after another into his mouth. "The best, yes. And you wanted wealth and recognition, both of which you are well on your way to achieving. Be patient. Be careful."

"Patient...careful?" William's lips turned down at the corners. "I watched Cordier sniveling at the feet of Louis of Anjou. Disgusting. This mission to France..." A sigh escaped from deep inside him.

"William, listen to me. You are an artist and a fine one. A very exceptional one. But art and music have always served the hand of those who rule. The sculptures at Chartres and Vezelay, or Giotto's magnificent paintings in the Arena chapel, all were done for purposes of promoting the stories of the Catholic faith. The sculptured head of Augustus back in Roman times or Gattamelata's mounted figure—both were done to promote their leadership. Gregorian chant, as well as Ambrosian chant, was created to instill a deeper level of feeling in those needing a greater sense of transcendence. Your music has not yet defined itself or its purpose—it may yet be for the greater glory of God, or it may be for the glory of a singular man." He paused to let his words sink in. "Who or what, we don't know yet."

William gazed out the window at the faint sliver of moon that glowed in the sky. "You're right, Uncle. We don't. I understand what you are saying."

"Do you? Do you really understand? Cicco Simonetta will never be celebrated in the way that Duke Francesco and King Alfonso I of Aragon were celebrated. His deeds become more self-serving every day, I am afraid." His voice dropped to a whisper. "But I believe that one of the remaining Sforza brothers will one day be celebrated in the same breath, and with the same words as those used to describe Duke Francesco."

"The same breath—really? Are you sure?" William eyed his uncle with suspicion. Bishop Branda's words carried more than a hint of treason in every syllable.

"No. Not at all." Branda's voice returned to normal. He smiled. "Perhaps Simonetta will right himself. I will do all I can to help him do so. But the *ducato* (duchy of Milano) deserves good government. I intend to see that she gets what she deserves."

William turned and stared out the window. He now saw his uncle as more than an aging ascetic faithful to his church and family. He saw a firebrand. The Ambrosian Republic had been formed when Branda was a young man. Many noble families like the Castiglioni participated in it. No doubt he had as well, probably in the background. That was his way. So here was his uncle, naked before him, his republican sympathies out in the open for William to see.

He wondered if his uncle had been a part of the plot to assassinate Duke Galeazzo. No, he would never believe such a thing could be true. Branda was too wise, too dispassionate to align himself with so violent an action. But here in Italy assassination was an approved method of ridding a city of an unbridled and unwanted despot. He knew he could never ask his uncle such a question. But he also understood that his uncle had a very deep passion for good government. No doubt other noble families in and out of Milano felt the same way.

It occurred to him that Gian Giacomo Trivulzio's family had as much of a claim to leading the ducato as did the Castiglione family, although the Trivulzio name was linked to military valor and the Castiglione family to less visible service. William wondered what role 'Fate' and 'Fortuna' would play in the events of the next year or so. Something would happen. That was a certainty. And he did not want to be caught in the middle. Or perhaps the middle was the place to be, favoring neither one side nor the other. He rubbed his neck, as if he could not breathe. The feeling came from the discomfort of an imagined rope drawn tightly around it.

The bishop snored softly in his chair, his blanket fallen on the floor. William picked it up and placed it over the old man's legs. A good human being, his uncle. He aimed to see that this good man lived a long time. At the door, he heard the older man stir.

"Good night, William." The voice was soft, even tender, like a mother's. "You are better than a son to me."

William gazed at this wondrous, generous, thoughtful, perhaps murderous man. "Tell me, Uncle, do Simonetta or Trivulzio suspect that your sympathies lie elsewhere?"

"I think not. They have no reason to be suspicious."

"Of course not. But suppose I turned down another mission, might they not be a little suspicious? Or if I went on a mission and disappeared altogether, might that also be a sign to them? Perhaps I should return to England...." William sighed, with resignation.

The bishop stirred. He picked up a bottle of wine at his elbow and poured himself a glass, then drank. Then he gazed at his nephew and shook his head back and forth. "Ah, my boy. My dearly beloved nephew." He took another gulp of wine. "With the death of Charles the Rash a few months ago, Burgundy ceased to exist. The duchy's nobility, like Le Batard, spread out across Europe like rats leaping off a sinking ship." The bishop waved his wine glass at his nephew. "While he searched for a safe haven, Le Batard posed no threat to you." The bishop's face sank into the shadows. "But he has found that safe haven and his brother-in-law, Edward IV, listens to Batard's ravings, 'I must have revenge on him who brought about the death of my fiancee.'

William blanched. *Tracked down, murdered in some alleyway, alone, forgotten.*

"I will do all I can to protect you," Branda assured him. "But England? No."

William leaned his long frame against the door. *No more England.* He sighed. *Damn Batard.* He nodded toward his uncle. "Very well. I will continue to play this game, the way you instruct."

He stepped away from the door and sat down. The candle on the table next to the bishop flickered and went out. They sat in darkness, each man alone with his thoughts.

# 5

## Conspiracy

*A Footpath*
**CASTELLO DI BORROMEO**
ANGERA, ITALIA
March, 1478

In the late night darkness, several figures on horseback worked their way up the steep incline leading to Castello Borromeo, three hour's ride northwest of Milano. Ludovico and Sforza Maria were among those making their way up the slope.

As Ludovico dismounted at the entryway to the castle, the moon floated out from behind the rainclouds. The young prince glanced down at Lago Maggiore shimmering in the early spring moonlight. "If Donato del Conte is as good as his word, then the most powerful of Milanese nobility will be at this meeting," he muttered to Sforza Maria. The noblemen had gathered, one by one, over several evenings so that suspicions would not be aroused.

In the library of the castello, Ludovico and Sforza Maria greeted Pietro Pusterla, Giovanni Borromeo, Antonio Marliani, and Donato del Conte. Each man's face was a mask of serious purpose and deep concern—brows furrowed, lips drawn, jaws clamped shut.

"Welcome, Sforza Maria and Ludovico." Giovanni Borromeo was the first to speak. A handsome, energetic man with an ancient pedigree, Giovanni's merchant class banking interests extended well past the Alps. "Ludovico, the great success you and young Ottaviano enjoyed in putting down the rebellion in Genoa has made the Sforza brothers the toast of Milano, and therefore much beloved in our fair citta."

"And much hated in the castello," added Pietro Pusterla, a long-faced man with white hair and an air of tiredness about him.

"Yes, that is the case, isn't it," muttered Antonio Marliani, a man of medium height with a large, pugnacious jaw and a rather small head, made more prominent by baldness and unseemly red blotches covering it. But he was a very rich man, having benefited from family estates in the Val Mesolcina at the head of Lago Maggiore, as well as astute investments in the salt trade. Little went on that Marliani did not know about.

Sforza Maria got to his feet. "Our thanks to each of you for coming here this evening. The risk is great, that we know." The jaws of each man tightened visibly. Sforza Maria was quite right, the risk was considerable. "I believe we all know why we are here."

"We are of one mind, I think," del Conte frowned. "Simonetta is Calabrian, a member of the Guelph party, the pope's party. None of us trusts him to work on our behalf. His Calabrian friends will soon occupy all the key positions of power in Milano, and we will be left out, as you have been."

"I concur," added Pusterla.

"Agreed," Borromeo murmured.

"Yes to that." Marliani gave a frustrated shrug of his shoulders.

Ludovico stood and surveyed the room. "My friends, we are not gathered here to air our personal grievances toward the regents but to give ourselves an opportunity to assess the well being of the duchy. Is the duchy of Milano better or worse off than under my brother, Galeazzo Maria? Would it be better off if my family were again in control of the regency?"

The men sighed.

"We allowed ourselves an unseemly pettiness," Pusterla agreed. He looked around the room. "Let us put aside our own personal slights and irritations, amici."

Borromeo stood up. "Simonetta lowered taxes on goods produced in Milano which made many people happy; however, he raised taxes on goods coming into Milano. In addition, the banking industry is suffering. The Medici have closed up their office in Milano. Genoa is taking much of the trade that would come by land. The banks are moving their branches to Genoa. Many of the French, German, and English merchants are going by sea rather than risk the uncertainties of trade in our citta."

"Indeed," Marliani concurred. "The economy of Milano, the best in all Europe save for Venice for twenty years now, suffers under Simonetta. But a greater problem is the *Consilio de Guistizia*. We have a most even-handed system for dispensing justice, one of the best in all Europe. When Galeazzo was alive, he was the final arbiter and, by and large, made decisions based on what was good for the duchy of Milano."

Marliani paused and looked around him. The others wore sympathetic expressions on their faces. He continued. "Simonetta does not do that. His decisions always favor the Guelph party and his own Calabrian friends and family. Often the decisions he makes are laughed at or ignored. Trivulzio, to his credit, refuses to attack individuals in disputes before the consilio. His army is poised to defend Milano from attack by its neighbors, not to attack its citizens."

"I know just the opposite to be true," Pusterla snarled. "The Lanze Spezzate police the streets of Milano. Many of my family have felt the horses' hooves of his ducal guard."

Sforza Maria raised his hands. "So we agree, do we? Milano is suffering and will not right itself under the rule of Simonetta and Trivulzio?"

"The question of course is what do we do about them? How do we rid ourselves of these people?" Pusterla posed the question no one wanted to answer. "I, for one, do not wish to risk position or property unless we have a clear and workable plan and an excellent chance of success."

At that moment, another man entered the room—Roberto Sanseverino, the powerful-looking condottiere and former *Capitano Generale* of Duke Galeazzo's armies. He towered over the others gathered around him. "Sorry to be late, compari," he apologized. "I suspected I was being followed, so I left a track more difficult to follow than that of a piece of wet pasta." He gave each man a baleful look. "I hope each of you was as careful."

The men glanced from one to the other, several with guilty looks on their faces. Each man embraced Sanseverino, who gave special attention to Sforza Maria and Ludovico. "You see, cousins, I told you they would come." After he lifted Sforza Maria off his feet, and then Ludovico, the warrior turned serious. "What I heard was—how do we deal with Simonetta?" All nodded. "Perhaps a frontal blow, in church."

Instead of the laugh he expected, the room fell into silence. Sanseverino said no more.

Sforza Maria took the floor. "Since the attempt on Lorenzo de' Medici's life by the Pazzi, who as we all know were prodded into doing that venal deed by the relatives of the pope, Firenze has grown closer to Venezia while the pope allies himself with Napoli."

The others nodded their understanding.

"As to Milano, Lorenzo de Medici has drawn Simonetta to his

side," Ludovico continued the narrative. "King Ferrante has contacted us. He will provide the money for us to raise an army to bring down Simonetta."

The others looked around the room. Some faces expressed agreement; many were uncertain.

"We risk a great deal," Marliani frowned. The candles in the room flickered with a burst of thunder and lightning. The furrows in his brow appeared to be impenetrable crevices in the bluish cracks of lightning.

"It can be done," Donato del Conte affirmed.

"Agreed. It can," chided Sanseverino, squinting at Marliani.

The others looked to each other, especially Borromeo, on whose shoulders much of the financial burden would fall if the Neapolitans proved unreliable.

Pusterla, Borromeo, and Marliani huddled together. Finally they turned back to the others and stated their decision. They intended to go forward—to success or death. After a few minutes, their business was concluded, and Borromeo ushered them to the door.

Once the men dispersed, William Castle appeared from a small alcove off the library.

Borromeo gave William a hard look. "Your uncle will be satisfied by this, will he not?"

William clapped the older man on the shoulder. "He will. Only Ludovico knows I was there. I could not identify anyone if I were asked. I saw nothing. But I can tell my uncle what he needs to know."

Borromeo frowned. "We cannot go forward without him."

"I assure you, after this meeting, he will be where you need him to be."

The Count of Angera sighed. "I was tossed aside by Duke

Galeazzo, and then by Simonetta. I am desperate to join the ranks of the living."

"I understand," William smiled in the gloom of the library. "My uncle will support you, but will not actively work for Simonetta's downfall. He made that clear to me."

"That is enough." A hint of a smile crossed Borromeo's heavy features for the first time.

Rain poured down the battlements of the castle of Angera as the men gathered at the gate, looking down the steep, slippery slope. Hour after hour they waited, hoping the rain would abate.

The first to leave the castle in the early hours of the morning, del Conte made a last minute decision to head back to his fortress in Genoa rather than his palazzo in Milano. He had been one of those whom Sanseverino had awakened to the danger of their meeting.

Unknown to him, he had been watched. Where others decided to wait out the rain and go unnoticed in the early hours of the following mornings, Donato was clearly recognizable from the large peacock feather he wore in his hat, even in the rain.

Galloping at a fast pace toward the mountains separating Genoa from Milano, he had the misfortune of encountering a unit of Trivulzio's Lanze Spezzate at the border. Spirited and jovial as always, he made no attempt to run. Simonetta had had members of the guard shadowing him for days.

William and his uncle stood on the parapets of the Castello di Porta Giovia in Milano, gazing out over the city. "Two days ago, Donato was arrested and confined to Monza," Bishop Branda observed.

"A bad omen, yes?" William liked Donato's energy and spirit.

"You are sure that he did not see you at the gathering?" the bishop quizzed.

"Quite sure, Uncle." William shifted from one foot to the other, at the time certain that Donato had not seen him, but now a little less sure.

Branda gave his nephew's shoulder a reassuring pat. "You have done well." Yet even the self-possessed bishop could not entirely conceal his anxiety, pressing the thumb and forefinger of his left hand into the corners of his tired eyes.

Hands and feet manacled and chained to a wall of the dungeon, Donato hung in his cell for days on end without food or water. *God help me,* he thought. *I have been forgotten.* With nowhere to relieve himself, he was left to fester in his own body waste.

Before long, delirium took embraced Donato's mind. Words of the great poet, Dante, came to him. "Abandon all hope, ye who enter." *Already,* he realized in a panic, *I have sunk to the first level of hell, and I have not even met death....*

On the fourth day of Donato's captivity, Simonetta came to visit him. "Well, *il mio caro,*" the old bureaucrat gloated, "this is a sour pickle you have stuffed in your mouth. And I see no way out for you."

"I have wronged no one," whispered Donato in one of his few lucid moments.

"Oh, now, let's not be *ingenuo,* my Lord del Conte," simpered the elderly First Secretary. He motioned for the guard to enter with a barrel of water and place it out of Donato's reach. Simonetta picked up a cup, cracked open the lid at the top of the barrel and dipped the cup into the fresh water. He sipped it, letting the water slide down the corners of his mouth. Donato turned away, unable to watch. Simonetta threw the remainder of the water in Donato's face.

*Aaaahhhh,* the poor man screamed as if he had been burned by fire.

"Soon you shall feel the full range of our vengeance," Simonetta's eyes bulged with enjoyment. "Unless you confess to plotting against the state and name your co-conspirators, the Sforza brothers and Roberto Sanseverino. Otherwise, who knows what will happen to you, Donato del Conte?"

"I have wronged no one," repeated Donato between sobs.

"We shall see." Simonetta brimmed with energy for the task at hand as he strode out of the dungeon, slamming the heavy oaken door behind him. "Five lashes," he told the guard as he stepped into the hall. "Then stretch him on the rack and starve him another three days. By that time he will tell all."

Shortly after Simonetta had left, Donato received two visitors—Bishop Branda and his nephew. Dressed in his priestly garments, the bishop attended to Donato in an official capacity.

Bishop Branda examined del Conte and found him to be near death. "Donato, can you hear me?"

The Genoan opened his eyes for a moment. He seemed to recognize nothing, his mouth so parched that he could not speak.

"Ah, my son, this is a very bad thing they have done to you. Such unspeakable cruelty."

William observed a warmth and compassion in his uncle that he had never seen before.

The bishop grasped Donato's hand. *"Buon giorno,* Donato. I guess we have seen better times, haven't we?"

Donato looked up and seemed to recognize the two men. "Good boy. Good boy. Sforza boy, good boy."

Bishop Branda walked to the door of the cell. "Bring the castellan down here," he ordered the guard. "I have something to say to him."

In a few minutes the castellan appeared and bowed to the bishop.

"You are to bring food and water to the prisoner, young man. He is near death, and you have obtained nothing from him for he knows nothing."

"I cannot do that, Bishop Branda. I have my orders," the young castellan explained.

The bishop's eyes turned cold with fury. "Did you hear what I said?"

The man hesitated then ducked out of the cell and returned soon after with water and a few pieces of bread.

After Donato drank the water and ate some bread, the bishop spoke softly into his ear.

Later William took his uncle aside. "I have never seen a man suffer so much at the hands of another," he murmured, appalled. "What did you say to him?"

Branda smiled. "I instructed him to do whatever he could to save his life. If it meant accusing Ludovico of plotting to kill Simonetta, so be it." The grin widened on Branda's face. "'But,' I said, 'make sure the accusations are bizarre in the extreme. Include members of Simonetta's family in the plot.' Donato seemed to understand. I blessed him. He slept. From here on, he is in God's hands."

The two men fell silent. William could see that Donato's suffering had affected his uncle, who believed deeply in legitimate authority. The assassination of Duke Galeazzo had done away with that legitimacy. His uncle was now wrestling with the question of what constituted genuine authority.

Throughout the city, small bands of citizens marched up and

down the streets waving colorful banners that read,

---

## RELEASE DONATO
## DEL CONTE.

---

Among several of the groups were members of the Sforza clan—Ludovico, Sforza Maria, Ottaviano, as well as members of the Sanseverino family, including several of General Roberto's sons.

Trivulzio's mounted Lanze Spezzate circulated among the *popolo*, pushing the crowds with their horses, trying to disrupt and unknot them without injuring anyone. He was mindful of the Sforzas' intention to agitate until the *popolo* were ready to declare Simonetta cruel and unfeeling.

As he passed down the streets of Milano, Trivulzio, a popular figure, waved to the citizens of Milano. No one was willing to stand against the powerful, compelling figure of Trivulzio. On a street not far from the Duomo, Trivulzio came within a few feet of Roberto Sanseverino, who quickly disappeared into the shadows of the late afternoon.

Trivulzio strode into the Sala del Asse in the Corte Ducale and greeted Simonetta. "The Sforza are leaving the city. The crowds have dispersed and no one was injured," he grinned.

"Donato del Conte confessed last night," Simonetta smiled. "His will is broken. When things have cooled off, when Il Moro and his brothers have given up, then we will release him." He frowned. "If only we could go after Borromeo, Pusterla, and the others, but it would be futile."

Trivulzio turned to go, but the old man put a hand on his sleeve. "One more thought *amico*. In Napoli, King Ferrante is a thorn in our side. He continues to hold out the prospect of providing money and arms to the Sforza brothers. We need to find a way to stop that kind of help."

"True," the warrior concurred. "However, a more direct approach would be to summon the brothers to a meeting, take them captive, and imprison them for a while. That would root out their silly ambitions."

Simonetta clapped Trivulzio on the back. "Thoughts worth pursuing."

A few days later, Simonetta sent William to meet with the brothers, offering them another meeting in which he promised to find something useful for them to do. Outwardly at least, he still hoped for a peaceful solution to his problems with them. The brothers read the message William delivered with considerable skepticism. They were almost certain that the First Secretary had plans for them that were not in the least peaceful. However, in the end, they agreed to meet with Simonetta, but only because they had numerous friends and relatives planted throughout the city, looking out for their well-being when they returned to Milano.

As the brothers cantered through the Porta Romana entrance to the city on their way to the agreed-upon meeting place, William was one of those who elected to guard the brothers against the unexpected. He rode through Milano disguised as a friar. Keeping the brothers in sight, he loped along on horseback, his eyes alert for any sign of trouble.

So far he had seen nothing out of the ordinary. Then two blocks from the meeting place at Piazza St. Ambrogio, he noticed unusual movements in a nearby shop. Spurring his horse, he saw that the shop was jammed with soldiers, their pikes ill-concealed on this hot July afternoon.

Glancing down the block toward the piazza, he spied a number of alleyways that could easily be hiding places for an ambush. He rode closer, and saw that, yes, each alleyway was filled with armed men. He crossed to another block. More men in hiding. *God in heaven, it is an ambush!!*

At that moment he spotted the three brothers cantering toward the square.

William put the spurs to his charger and raced down the street. Galloping across the square, he waved his hands at the brothers, a prearranged gesture signaling danger.

Ludovico and Sforza Maria caught the sign, turned their horses around and raced off in the direction from which they had come. Milanese soldiers flooded out of the alleys and buildings in an effort to pursue them. Ottaviano was frozen in place. General Sanseverino, who had ridden into Milano with the brothers, grabbed the reins of the boy's horse. Together they followed hard on the heels of Ludovico and Sforza Maria.

The small group broke through the poorly organized rush of armed men, dashed up the street, and rode hard toward the nearest portal to the city. A group of soldiers at Porta Genoa attempted to stand in the way but yielded to the pounding horses' hooves of the onrushing quartet.

Once out of the city, the brothers and their friends pulled up, breathless.

"We can no longer trust anything these people say to us," growled Sanseverino. "I am off to Venice to raise an army."

"Go with Sanseverino," Sforza Maria ordered Ottaviano. "It is no longer safe for any of us in the city, or even at our castles."

Ottaviano nodded in compliance. The two men galloped off in the direction of Venezia.

Sforza Maria and Ludovico galloped toward Vigevano in silence, defeated. "I worry about our friends," Sforza Maria said at last when they stopped to rest.

"I worry about the duchy," murmured Ludovico.

In the chancery of the castello, Simonetta greeted Trivulzio, his face wreathed in smiles. "We have at last cornered the brothers," he smirked.

"Indeed," muttered Trivulzio.

"They found a reason to avoid meeting with us, so we can now demand that they be sent into exile...and we can confiscate all their property."

Trivulzio shrugged. "Exile, humph," he glowered. "These young men are up to no good. Better that they should meet the assassin's dagger during their exile, otherwise they will continue to plot their family's return to power."

"What you suggest is not impossible," Simonetta replied. "But we must be very careful. You saw what the imprisonment of del Conte meant to the people of Milano. Imagine what would happen if they thought we had murdered their beloved young princes."

Trivulzio looked annoyed. "The people of Milano are sheep. They will allow themselves to be herded by whomever exercises sufficient strength."

Simonetta sat down in his favorite chair, leaned back and put his fingers together, thinking. "What you say may be true, but we are not yet strong enough to exercise such power." He smiled at Trivulzio and raised his finger. "But there will be a time when we will be strong enough." He got to his feet. "Our new taxes are filling the treasury. Within the month, you will be able to begin recruiting a new army to aid our friends in Firenze and defeat the forces of the king of Napoli."

The look of disenchantment on Trivulzio's face gave way to pleasure. The thought of leading an army against the king satisfied his warlike urges. Up to the present, he had been no more than a captain in the Lanze Spezzate. But now he would lead the army of Milano against one of the better commanders in all of Italia— King Ferrante's eldest son, Alfonso, Duke of Calabria. Success against the Neapolitani would ensure the love of the Milanese people…and the opportunity to dispatch the Sforza brothers as he saw fit. Yes, Fate was handing him just the opportunity he sought. He smiled to himself. One day, perhaps not that far off, he—Gian Giacomo Trivulzio—would be Duke of Milano, just like the man he admired most in all the world—*Il Grande* Francesco Sforza, Duke of Milano.

The two men shook hands, and Trivulzio departed the chancery with a light heart. Tonight he would ride north to Mesocco, his familial castle, and spend the weekend with his beloved wife, Margaret, whom he saw far too seldom and whom he treasured above all others.

# 6

## EXILE

*Church of St. Ambrogio*
**PAVIA, ITALIA**
March, 1478

The requiem mass for voices and brass choir by Josquin des Prez turned into a thing of beauty as performed by William and members of the choirs of St. Ambrogio in Pavia, ancient home of the Visconti family.

Inside the vast expanse of the cathedral, the music soared. Ascanio, Sforza Maria and Ludovico knelt in prayer in a pew close to the altar. The magnificent sounds of two trumpets and trombone located in the choir loft echoed throughout the church.

When the mass ended, each of the brothers sighed, eyes red with grief. The young men rose as one body, genuflected as they left the pew and hurried to the entrance of the church.

Outside, well-wishers from many parts of the duchy had gathered to mourn the passing of the much-loved young Ottaviano Sforza. Among those present, Countess Beatrice d'Este, sister of Duke Ercole of Ferrara and the widow of the brothers' older, deceased, natural brother, Tristano, seemed most deeply moved.

An attractive woman of forty-five, Beatrice embraced each of the brothers. "Our dear sister, Duchess Bona, extends her best wishes," she offered. "We all loved Ottaviano very much."

"A terrible accident," Sforza Maria lamented. "Drowned while trying to escape. The soldier he spied, as he tried to cross the river, was not even one of Trivulzio's troops." His head swung back and forth. "A bad omen."

Beatrice gave him a sad smile. "As sweet a disposition as anyone I ever met."

Ludovico, who had remained silent for a long period of time, turned to Countess Beatrice. "Tell me, dear sister, Simonetta holds Bona close, does he not? Therefore, very few people have contact with her or her son?" The countess nodded her head. He remained lost in thought then spoke. "What do we know of our young friend, William Castle. Is he still one of her favorites?"

A wicked look crossed the young widow's face. "As he is much loved by the ladies of the castle, I put a thought in Bona's ear some time ago—that she request of Simonetta that William keep her company with his magnificent playing." She laughed at her duplicity.

The young prince chuckled then motioned her away from the crowd. "*Per favore*, Signora. Let us go meet him."

As members of the choir came out of the church by a side door, Countess Beatrice waved to William.

The young man strolled over.

She kissed him on both cheeks as if he were a member of the family. "William, how are you?" she enthused.

"Amico!" Ludovico embraced William, wearing a big smile. "We knew you to be a fine musician but never expected such excellence."

The musician grinned with embarrassment. "I feel honored to be part of a service for your brother who was so loved by us all."

"Indeed, it is very true," the young prince lamented. Then he brightened. "I regret I have been so out of touch." He put his hand on William's arm and lowered his voice. "We all owe you a great debt."

William nodded his head ever so slightly.

"Had it not been for your sharp eyes and your warning, we might not have escaped the net that Simonetta had drawn around us. We were foolish to agree to meet with him."

"I am happy to have been in time, my friend." William wiped the perspiration off his brow, remembering their narrow escape. "We were very lucky."

"We are also in your uncle's debt for it is he who arranged the exile without our having to trust Simonetta or Trivulzio."

"He has the trust of all sides," William agreed.

As the two men spoke, Countess Beatrice excused herself, leaving them to speak in private.

In an instant, Il Moro changed the subject. "Your magnificent playing has earned you a place at the side of Duchess Bona?"

"The duchess has found my playing to be a great consolation to her in her grief."

"Interesting and valuable news." Ludovico smiled then looked around for his brothers. "We only have a few moments before the Lanze arrive." He extended his hand and gave William another embrace.

"I hate to see you go into exile once more, *amico*," William muttered.

"One day when you are father to the many children around you, we will call each other compare." Ludovico gave him a confident grin. "I am quite sure we will see each other before long." With a quick smile, he walked away, intending to speak to his sister-in-law, Countess Beatrice, before she departed for Ferrara, her home.

Ludovico found the countess climbing aboard her carriage. "One wonders why anyone so talented as William remains while Martino, Weerbecke, Compere and the others have all left—" Ludovico observed.

"Some say he and Bona are lovers," Countess Beatrice murmured in his ear, "…and cannot leave. Others say he is on Simonetta's payroll. Without question he has the ear of Duchess Bona."

Ludovico watched the retreating figure of the young man. "Keep an eye on him, dearest Countess Beatrice. His uncle is one of our strongest supporters, and William would never betray his uncle."

Sforza Maria and Ascanio strode up to the carriage. "Thank the Lord our friends are not here," Sforza Maria said in a whispered voice.

"This is a bad time for them." Ludovico looked around to see several ranks of Milanese guards marching toward them. "They are coming for us, brothers." Each gazed into the eyes of the other. "It has been a trial for us—the deaths of Donato, Ottaviano, Tristano—"

"Where will it end?" Ascanio wondered.

"Their deaths will not be in vain," vowed Sforza Maria, putting an arm around his brothers. He turned to Ludovico. "One of us, you or I, must one day be duke of Milano." He turned to Ascanio. "And you will be pope. On that day, the Sforza shall rule all of Italy."

Ascanio stood almost in shock to hear of such dreams.

"We owe it to the memories of all who came before," Ludovico pledged. "Our grandfather, Muzio Attendolo, our father and brothers, to make Milano the most wonderful place on earth, the most productive, the most tolerant and the most just."

The brothers were moved by Ludovico's simple declaration.

"The Pazzi attacked our friend, Lorenzo de Medici," Sforza Maria said hurriedly, seeing the Milanese guard halt in front of the church. "Simonetta stands with him against the pope and King Ferrante in Napoli. Very soon Reggente Simonetta will send

Trivulzio south to aid Florence."

The guards marched toward them.

"Once he has gone south," Sforza Maria whispered, "look for—"

A *tenente* of the Lanza Spezzate arrived at the small group and stopped next to Sforza Maria, who declared in a loud voice, "Well Moro, dear brother, enjoy your stay in Pisa, and you, Ascanio, perhaps in Perugia you will take up the law, eh?"

"Enjoy Bari, dear brother," Ascanio smiled as he embraced Sforza Maria and then Ludovico.

"Be ready to act," Ludovico whispered to each brother as they embraced. Sforza Maria and Ascanio turned and walked toward the horses that waited for them. They mounted up, each quickly surrounded by a squad of twelve horsemen who would ride with each of them to his place of exile.

Ludovico Il Moro lingered for a moment, watching them ride away. At the last moment, he leaned over to Countess Beatrice. "There is someone you can trust to pass information to me, if necessary." He whispered in her ear. "The damsel to Duchess Bona—Cecilia Gallerani." The duchess nodded.

Months before, Ludovico Il Moro and Sforza Maria had rested for a night at the Gallerani farm on the long journey from Donato del Conte's castle in Genoa to the meeting with Simonetta in Milano. Il Moro had charmed each family member who in turn offered the brothers whatever help they needed. Moro had also been quite taken with young Cecilia. He wasn't sure about her feelings toward him. Now the time had come when she could help him— if she chose to do so.

He mounted his horse and was quickly surrounded by Milanese soldiers. He waved to his many friends and family members and rode away to exile in Pisa.

From her coach, Countess Beatrice watched as the brothers cantered, galloped, and trotted away. She was surprised to see that each sat in the saddle with such fine posture as if defeat were far from his mind. Or perhaps the young men were only hiding injured pride. But no, the brothers had talked in great earnest before they were separated. Pride seemed as far from their minds as fear.

At times like these, she missed Tristano. Strong, thoughtful, steady, courageous. Some twenty-five years older than his brothers, he was deeply valued by every member of the family. Such a man to lose. Duchess Bona, too, must be very lonely these days. She thought about Moro's whispered comment, "There is one person we can trust," and smiled to herself. Later today she would have a nice talk with Duchess Bona about young Cecilia. She signaled the driver to return to Milano.

Cecilia Gallerani trotted her mare up to the family villa and dismounted. The weather was chilly, but the sky clear and blue. She brushed the perspiration off her cheeks and smiled as her mother came out of the house. Angelica frowned as she handed a piece of paper to her daughter.

"You are wanted back in Milano," sighed the older woman. "Just when I thought you had had enough of court life."

"It has its rewards," the girl smirked to herself as she went inside, reading the document as she walked.

"At least the duke is not a worry for you." Angelica sat on a couch in the living room of the small villa.

Cecilia sat down beside her. "This sounds like an order, not a suggestion or a request. 'You are hear by ordered to fulfill the duties and responsibilities agreed upon between you and so and so,' signed, Bona of Savoy, Duchess of Milano.' What do you suppose is going on?"

Facio came into the living room and sat down. His wife poured a glass of wine, cut off some pieces of cheese and broke off a chuck of pane for him.

"How are my *bella signorina* and *signora?*" He massaged the wrist he had been using to write documents for the last few hours, went to the fireplace and threw another log on the fire.

"Our daughter has been ordered back to Milano," Angelica replied. "I have heard it is nothing but chaos. People are attacked on the streets."

"It is true," Facio sighed. "However, I will be returning to Milano in a few days. If she must go, I will find a way for her to remain protected." He turned to Cecilia. "I am sure the Portinari family would be happy to have you stay with them in the city. You can fulfill your obligations to the duchess for a few hours each day and remain safe at night."

Cecilia said nothing. She remained lost in thought.

The older woman studied her daughter's face. "She has a young courtier who is mad about her, Papa."

"Yes, yes. I know," Facio sipped his wine slowly. "Well, that wouldn't be much different than our own meeting, would it, my dear?"

Angelica smiled, remembering the past, savoring it.

Cecilia turned to her mother. "Is that true?"

Her mother gave her a slow nod. "You must consider how different things are now. Your friend today may be your enemy tomorrow. Be careful of your alliances, romantic or otherwise. Great men and women fall with breathtaking speed. The unexpected will happen as a matter of course."

"I can see the wisdom of that," Cecilia acknowledged.

# 7

## PISA

*A Dominican Monastery*
**PISA, ITALIA**
March, 1479

Time passed with bewildering slowness for Ludovico Il Moro Sforza. However, he endured his exile at the Dominican Monastery in Pisa with the patience for which he was well-known. The sun rose and the sun set. Animals snorted, whinnied, barked, and mooed. Children played. Old men and young men moved at a snail's pace throughout each day. Ludovico watched and listened. Even his heartbeat seemed to slow. *Will it never end, this monastic life,* he wondered. Each day he received messages, letters, and memos of all kinds, reading each with great eagerness, then letting the missives drop to the ground.

He appeared to be waiting for word of some kind, but word of what?

The remainder of each day he spoke to no one. He went for long walks, sometimes running barefoot along the beach, unrecognized. At night he went to inns along the waterfront and took up with young women. His body hardened, and his spirit too.

At times he dreamed of setting sail to faraway places then remembered that he had a plan, a goal, a vision.

One night as he was going out for an evening of carousing, he found William dismounting his horse and walking toward him.

"William, amico! You have come to see me. To dispell my dreary frustrations, eh?"

"I have indeed," William laughed, despite his tiredness.

"But you must also have some news of some kind, eh?"

William shrugged, doing his best to shake off his extreme fatigue.

"I know you are exhausted, amico. Come, we will get something to eat. News can wait."


The two of them dined on calzone and *gambretti di mare* at an inn near the bay. A young man not much older than the two of them sat down at the table next to theirs. After several rounds of good Pisan wine, they found themselves deep in conversation with one another.

A sailor born in Genoa, the fellow spoke at length of discovery. "One day I shall find a passage to the East, to which our own Marco Polo traveled," he laughed, "...by sailing west!"

"West?" Ludovico pushed his hand along the table as he drank some Spanish ale. "What lies out there but water, and then—?" His hand dropped off the table. "Will you not fall off the edge of the earth?"

Although exhausted from his journey, William appreciated the good fellowship of these two expansive young men. Moreover, it meant that he did not have to deliver the news that was the purpose of his visit—the death of Sforza Maria Sforza.

The sailor laughed. "Ah, no. You see the earth is round, sir. Round. Round as a ball of twine. Round as your head. Round as a cannon ball. Round as a lump of pasta before your mama starts to pound on it. Oh, yes. Round. That is why you cannot see beyond the horizon. No, sir." He picked up his flagon of Spanish ale. "I shall bring back a fortune, that I will."

"But have you not a great need of ducati to finance such a voyage?" inquired Ludovico.

"Aye, I have already asked the pope." The young man gave Moro and William a weary look. "He laughed at me. I tried to see King Ferrante in Napoli, but he would have nothing to do with me." The sailor turned sad. "Same thing in Milano. I was to see the duke, Galea—"

"Galeazzo Maria Sforza," interjected Ludovico.

"Aye, that was him, but then he died and the other fellow—"

"Simonetta," added William in a quiet voice.

"Aye, yes, that's him. Say, you know these things. You are educated men, eh?"

"Milano is my home," said Ludovico finishing up his ale. "You know, your story is really quite wonderful."

"Aye, but you don't believe a word of it, do ye?" the sailor asked through bleary eyes.

Picking up Moro's flagon of ale, the serving girl offered to bring another, but the young prince declined.

"On the contrary sir, I do believe you," he grinned at the sailor. "So I tell you this. One year from this date, if you go to see the duke, you need not worry about Simonetta. The duke will see you, and you will get your money."

The sailor threw back his head and laughed. When he stopped, he put a heavy hand on Moro's shoulder, staggered to his feet, kissed the young prince on the forehead then continued to laugh. "I love to hear you talk, Signore, you sound like you know what's going to happen in Milano."

Moro sat clear-headed and quiet. "I do." He got up from the table and clasped the man's hand in friendship. "Had I the time and inclination, I would join you in your *expeditioni*. It sounds like an adventure not to be missed."

The sailor gave Moro an appraising look. "Well, sir, the clothing you wear isn't much to recommend you, but from the way you talk, I size you up as a man of means." He clapped Moro on the shoulder. "Perhaps you would like to come aboard, invest in my enterprise, and share in the wealth...bring some o' yer wealthy friends."

William interrupted the seaman. "My friend, I wonder about one thing. You say you are from Genoa, but you speak English with us as if you were born in a seaman's village in England— Portsmouth, Yarmouth or Falmouth."

"Ah, I have been many places in my life," the sailor mused. "Many years I spent in the bars at just the places you named. Too many perhaps. But now I live again. Sail with me, lads."

Moro gave him a warm smile then turned to William. "What a fascinating idea!" Then he shrugged. "Ah, but I have my own voyage to consider." He stared out the window. "It may take me to the depths of hell, or to the gates of heaven." He turned to the sailor, extended his hand, and clasped the other's arm in friendship.

"Do not forget. One year from today." With that William and Ludovico strolled toward the doorway of the inn. As he pushed the door open, Moro stopped and turned around. The sailor lifted his pint of ale in salute. Moro waved and ambled into the golden sunlight, William right behind him.

Outside, William and Ludovico turned to the west and gazed at the sun sinking toward the horizon line of the bay. The sun's golden rays shimmered off blue and white wavelets that shone like a sheet of glass stretching outward to infinity.

*What if the sailor is right?* William thought. *What if there is no edge. World without end. Amen. Perhaps God is infinite as well, and man's possibilities are equally so.* He felt himself in a state of growing excitement as he stared out toward the horizon. He had discovered something this evening—something about the world—something about possibilities. William made a decision.

"Amico. About the news I have—"

"Yes, my friend."

"My uncle sent me to find you, to tell you two things." He paused to let the news sink in. "My uncle sends his deepest regrets, as does First Secretary Simonetta, and I as well...."

Moro's face turned white with fear. "Ascanio? He is—?"

"No, not Ascanio." William shook his head. "Sforza Maria. Natural causes it appears. I am deeply sorry, amico."

The young prince stared at his friend. "Sforza Maria? Dead? How could that be? He has the heart of a lion!" He leaned against a wall then put a hand to his head. "Sforza Maria? My best and dearest friend." He shook his head, disbelieving. "We should not have been apart like this...we should have been together." He sighed. Then an expression of deep resolve crossed his face. "We should be together." He turned in William's direction. "And the rest?"

William rubbed his chin, not quite sure if he ought to give out the news that his Uncle Branda had told him. "My uncle mentioned, almost in passing, that Firenze and Napoli are now at war. Trivulzio departs for Firenze with much of the Milanese army."

Moro's eyes opened wide. "He told you to tell me this?"

"Not at all," William replied. "It was almost in passing. But it seemed as though he wanted you to know."

Moro and William walked toward the monastery, saying nothing for quite some time. Finally, Ludovico broke the silence, murmuring as if to himself. "Poor Sforza Maria. I will miss him dearly. Perhaps....what if I were to finance this man's voyage? And those of other adventurers? Why not? Sooner or later, someone will discover something new. It is in the nature of things." Moro ambled up the wide streets of Pisa with William, lost in thought.

When they arrived at the monastery, Moro returned to his cell with a certainty he had never before experienced, as if God himself gazed upon him, looking over his shoulder, uncovering the proper path for him to follow. He went to see the Mother Superior and obtained a room for William.

As the two men said good-night, William handed Moro the note given him by Bishop Branda, then went to his room and fell asleep without undressing.

Returning to his modest cell, Ludovico sat down on his cot and took out the note that William had passed to him. The handwriting belonged to Countess Beatrice d'Este Sforza, Tristano's widow. His heart began to pound in his chest. He tore open the seal. His heart began to pound in his chest. Surely this was the moment.

---

*Dearest Brother,*
    *We long to see your face. Bona and I both agree that without seeing your face soon we shall go a bit mad. I trust you feel the same way.*
                    *Your loving sister,*
                    *Countess Beatrice d'Este Sforza*

---

Moro fairly leapt off his small bed. *Yes, yes, yes!* He yelled without a sound escaping his lips and jumped up and down.

He hurried to the window, peered outside and gazed at the setting sun. *A domani.* He paced the room until late into the night, then slept in fits and starts.

Early the following morning he dressed quickly, visited the

kitchen, drank the cow's milk, and ate the porridge laid before him. After the brief meal he hurried outside. The stirring he felt in his stomach seemed almost unbearable. As he mounted the horse that he had been given and rode toward the middle of the town of Pisa, his heart raced. *Soon Trivulzio marches to Firenze, leaving Milano wide open to attack. Can I raise an army in time to take advantage of Simonetta who only looks for enemies to the south? Time will tell.*

He cantered past the bell tower noticing that it had a slight lean to it. *I wonder how long it will survive at such an angle?* He smiled. *Like Milano without Trivulzio's strong right arm to protect it.*

Eventually he found the small house belonging to the Neapolitan ambassador and knocked. In short order, he was shown into the ambassador's study. A few moments later a small man still in his nightshirt came into the room.

"*Buon giorno*, Messere Ludovico," the small man yawned and rubbed his tired eyes.

"*Buon giorno*, Messere." Ludovico extended his hand. "You may tell his majesty, King Ferrante, I am ready to march."

The ambassador looked amazed. "Ready? At last?" Moro's head bobbed up and down. "The king will be most pleased to hear from you. He has been hoping to hear these words for some time." The little man reached for some papers and began to fumble through them. "I must—I mean, perhaps I ought—" He appeared confused. "No, no, I must set sail, myself." He patted Moro on the sleeve and disappeared from sight, then returned. "No, no, I will send a messenger. But we have funds. We have funds, yes we do." He smiled. "Yes."

William awoke that morning long after Il Moro had arisen, his head still spinning from the drinking and exhaustion of the night before. Moro came by and enjoyed William's company as the musician ate breakfast.

"I must get back on my horse this morning." William confessed as he rose from the table. "The trip over the mountains to Milano will take two days." William gathered his things, and the two men walked to the stables behind the monastery. "I'm sure I will see you before long," William grinned as he mounted the horse.

Ludovico smiled up at his friend. "Those who have been loyal to me, like yourself, will be richly rewarded in the not-so-distant future."

William noticed Moro's good humor. He thought this strange for a man who had just been told of his beloved brother's death. 'I will see you before long' also seemed a strange good-bye for a man consigned to this monastery as if it were a prison.

Moro gave William an informal but distinctly military salute.

The musician felt that old, familiar sensation in his spine—the sensation of danger—as he rode away.

One cool and cloudy morning, a few days after returning from Pisa, William awakened to find a message nailed to his door. He opened it. The message from Simonetta told him to go to the castello's secret garden shortly after the sun reached its high point in the sky.

His heart leapt in his chest. Cecilia? He could not believe his eyes. Simonetta had done what he said he would do. His heart filled with gratitude. His imagination soared with thoughts of Cecilia and himself exploring the world together and spending endless nights locked in each other's embrace.

Then he realized that Simonetta had ordered him to the garden without specifying the purpose. His heart filled with dread.

Toward noon he dressed with a jaunty carelessness and shaved, then lapsed into a somber mood. *Can Simonetta possibly know the loyalty I feel toward Ludovico Il Moro?* He wondered.

He headed across the courtyard to the secret garden located on the moat level between the Corte Ducale and the western entrance to the castle. Oddly, he had not talked to Simonetta since his return. His uncle had told him it was not necessary since his mission to Pisa had only been to deliver the sad news to Moro. So he had no occasion to mention Ludovico's surprisingly good mood the morning of his departure. It still puzzled him.

Crossing the drawbridge, he headed toward the Corte Ducale. At the top of the stairs leading down to the secret garden, he paused for a moment as he caught sight of Cecilia playing the lute while several of Bona's damsels sang. His heart leaped. *How beautiful she is,* he thought.

William hurried down the staircase, missed a step and stumbled like a drunkard, lurching from one step to the next. The young ladies giggled as he bumped to a stop at the bottom.

Nodding to the others to leave them in private, Cecilia smiled at him. The girls twittered as they hurried up the stairs. William took her fingers in his hand, knelt and kissed the back of her delicate hand. *So small and soft,* he observed. "I have missed you, Signorina Cecilia. It quickens my heart to see you again."

"Grazie," she laughed. "Mille grazie." She beckoned him to sit beside her on the bench. He complied, gazing into her eyes which smiled back at him with great affection.

Her mouth appeared soft, liquid and inviting, her teeth unusually even and white. But it was the large, brown eyes that so captivated him, drawing him in, refusing to allow him his freedom. "My heart has been a block of ice, a cannon ball-sized lump in my chest since I first touched your lips with my own."

Cecilia threw her head back in laughter. "You are so *romantico*. I thought you English were supposed to be cold, Messere William. Frigid. Icy, like the fiords of the northern countries."

"I cannot speak for other Englishman, but those who would have the good fortune to meet you would find themselves all knotted up inside, in a quandary which they could not easily undo." *What are you doing?* He wondered. *You cannot be so intimate with a woman you hardly know.* He picked up her hand and held it. It seemed suddenly quite warm. He looked up to see her blushing.

"You are *impetuoso, amico,*" she replied softly. "*Molto impetuoso.*" She took her hand and touched his face. "*Moltississimo impetuoso.*" A sad look crossed her face.

He placed his hand on her cheek, its heat arousing him. Without quite realizing what was happening, his hand slipped behind her neck, drawing her closer. His lips enfolded her lips which yielded to his. He took her lower lip into his mouth, covered it with his tongue, running it over her teeth. She began to melt.

*Eeoowww!* Suddenly, a sound like that of screeching cat erupted from her as she broke away. Her breath came in short gasps, and her bosom heaved. She seemed quite annoyed as she recovered her senses, wiping her forehead with the back of her hand then waving her hand in front of her face to cool down. At length, she recovered her poise and sense of humor. "Messere William, you must behave yourself."

He started to move again toward her lips but she pushed him away, ever so gently.

"What is it, my beautiful Cecilia? What?"

She fanned herself once more, her face a mass of conflicting emotions. She touched her sore bottom lip. "You are such a passionate man. How can one woman contain you?" She tried to laugh, but seemed almost about to cry.

"What is the matter?" he leaned closer, imploring her with his eyes.

"It is impossible, William of the British Isles."

"Nothing is impossible, *cara mia*. I know you have the same feelings in your heart for me that I have for you. I can feel them."

She shook her. "Of course I have feelings for you. You saved my life."

He lifted her chin and smiled. "Gratitude? Those are the only feelings you have? Is that what you are trying to tell me?"

"*Si, si,*" she mumbled. "I mean no, no." Her shoulders slumped. "I feel many things. You have read Dante? Paolo and Francesca, the ill-fated lovers? I am so confused."

He put his arm around her. "It will all work itself out, my dear." She leaned against his arm for a moment.

"I know. I know." Then she sat up and laughed. "I must tell you, beautiful William, man of so many wonderful talents...musician, courtier—spy, even? Every woman in the court of Duchess Bona wants you as her lover. Every woman knows you travel to exotic places on Milano's behalf; everyone wants to know the secrets you possess."

"I know next to nothing, my dear. I am but a messenger, yet if some people in high places reward my small efforts as they have indicated they will, I believe I could support and take care of the woman of my choice."

Her eyes searched his with intensity. "You really mean that, do you?" He nodded. "Then I must tell you—" She put her head in her hands. "Oh, I hate myself for leading you to believe what cannot be." She turned to him and looked deeply into his eyes. "You are not alone."

"I am not alone? What does that mean?" William's mouth opened. His jaw went slack, and he could not say even one word for some time. She stared at her hands. He recognized that look. "Ah, I see. While I was gone—"

She shook her head. "No, even before. But we cannot speak of it, for he, he is not available, not yet. It is very complicated."

"He is a married man, a man of position?"

"No, nothing like that." Cecilia placed a finger on his mouth. "But his feelings for me, well, it is too early yet. But I am not free." She twisted her mouth up in a funny way. "I wish I were. If I were, I would choose you." She kissed his cheek. "I would choose you, William. What woman would not want to spend her days and nights with you?"

William's shoulders slumped. "I was away too long. I should have declared myself sooner, but I didn't dare. After all, I am but a musician. A court musician. What is that? You will marry a man with a position at court, perhaps some family wealth, a castle in the mountains, where the waters of the Ticino valley will float by."

She took his hand in her own. "My dear, there are others matters of equal concern. Not only for me, but for you."

He gazed into her eyes, a quizzical look on his face.

"What I say now, you must keep to yourself," she almost whispered. "Be careful. Be very careful in the months ahead. You have attached yourself to Simonetta, and he trusts you, and uses you. Others may desire to do the same."

"I don't quite—"

"Oh but you do, William. Think about it. When first you kissed me, I inquired from others who you were. I was told you were connected to Bishop Branda. Soon after, when he was at court, I talked to him about you. He worried that you were taking sides,

William. Against his advice."

"I am flattered you would go to such lengths." William leaned back on the bench. Despite the playfulness of the conversation, William sensed that a deeper meaning had begun to take shape. He had no idea what it was about, but he was alert to the something he could not see and could hardly sense.

"It is good of you to tell me what is real and what is fantasy, madam," he murmured, his eyes downcast.

She touched his wrist. "You went to Napoli to secure a moment to see me. Why would I not at least try to find a moment to talk to you?" She smiled. "If I am not your lover, not now, at least I am your friend. Perhaps more than you know." She took his hand in her own and stood. "Perhaps this would be a good time for you to go visit your uncle." William also stood. As she headed for the stairs, he took a step in her direction. She motioned him to stay then climbed several steps. She stopped, turned, blew him a kiss and put a finger to her lips.

William sat down on the bench. *Go see my uncle. What did she mean by that?*

From out of the shadows, a figure approached. William looked up to see Simonetta staring down at him. "First Secretary—?"

"Very touching, my young friend. Very touching indeed."

"You heard everything?"

"It was to be a private meeting, but I was gathering flowers around the corner. There is no other man in her life." Simonetta's expression betrayed no feeling, at all. "Of the rest, I could not hear. What did she say?"

The young musician glanced at Simonetta then looked away. "Oh, you know what women do—they try to let you down without making a scene. I know them well enough to know that they will always tell you what they think you want to hear."

Simonetta nodded in agreement. "Who can figure them out?"

"Yes, who can—" William glanced again at Simonetta, who seemed satisfied by what he had been told. "First Secretary, I hoped my meeting with her was to be private."

The old man nodded. "So it was intended to be. However, Duchess Bona is—well, puzzling to me. She is being excessively pleasant toward me these days. I had hoped to glimpse a clue from your conversation with the damsel. I mistrust a woman who is so compliant."

William laughed. "Well said, well said."

"I will leave you to your reverie, my young friend." He headed toward the stairs and then stopped. "You never discussed your trip to Pisa with me."

"Uncle Branda said you were satisfied with what I had reported to him. My apologies, Signore."

Simonetta thought for a moment. "Yes, of course. Sometimes I am forgetful. Age. All this intrigue is for the young." He snickered then turned serious. "You have been entrusted with very delicate matters. You and your uncle have proven very reliable. As a result, many good and worthy things have happened to the house of Castiglioni." Simonetta stood before him, a baleful expression on his face.

William was tempted to reply with humor and unconcern, as he had with Ludovico, but then he realized that the older man would not take it well. "I understand, Reggente. What you say is very true." He bowed to the First Secretary. Such a difference existed between old Simonetta and young Ludovico.

"*Pardonna mi,*" Simonetta frowned. "I don't know why I—" He appeared confused. "I forgot who I was, for a moment." Then his head seemed to clear, and he gave William a dour look. "Stay on your toes, keep your eyes open, report everything you see or hear."

He began to wander around the garden, lost in thought.

"First Secretary," William called out. His voice echoed across the stone walls. Simonetta stopped. "I would like to depart from the court for a few days...go to see my uncle. Cecilia says his health is a little...suspect."

The First Secretary nodded in agreement. "That will be fine. When you return, I think we will have another task for you." He bowed slightly. "Wish him well for me. I value his loyalty and his wise counsel."

William watched the old man climb up the stone staircase and disappear. *"I am interested in another man,'" she says. "'Cecilia has no other man, she is lying to you,'" he says. Whom should I believe? What would her purpose be in lying? Perhaps she's afraid that if she and I are too close I will discover something about Duchess Bona that will be of benefit to Simonetta? And the First Secretary? What's in it for him? Well, he is suspicious of Bona. Cecilia has access to Bona, perhaps he wishes me to spy on Bona through Cecilia? "You saved my life," she said. "Now I want you to do as I did, get out of Milano—be careful whose side you take.'" Do I believe her? Or do I believe Simonetta?*

A little hummingbird flew up to the fountain in the middle of the garden and dipped its beak into the water spurting from the cupid's mouth in the center of the bowl. Its beak caught in the rush of water, the bird toppled into the fountain. Able to right itself before a disaster occurred, it flew away in a hurry.

*Whom to trust?*

The affairs of court were entirely too perplexing, he decided. *I need to mount a horse and ride...ride away as far and as fast as possible.*

As he headed into the stables of the castle an hour later, he heard a muffled voice shriek, "Get off me! Get off me!"

He hurried into the stable where he found, in one of the back stalls, a large young man on top of a small boy, beating him with one fierce blow after another. The large young man had his pants down around his knees. William knew what that meant. *Damned filthy buggerer.*

Two quick steps and he grabbed the larger fellow by the collar, wrenching him off the victim. "Get the hell off the boy!" William whirled him around, slapped him several times, recognizing him as Bieko, the thief—the kid who had crept up to his bed when he first arrived at the castello and tried to steal the coins under his greatcoat.

Bieko recoiled—his face filled with rage and frustration. "This is none of your business, bastard!" he snarled.

The younger boy rolled out from under the older youth.

Bieko swung a heavy fist in William's direction.

The Englishman side-stepped the blow and hit Bieko square in the mouth. The young man doubled up in pain, putting a hand to his bleeding mouth. William smacked him again with a fist to his nose.

Tumbling backward, Bieko fell against the stable wall. He picked himself up, feeling his nose and mouth. "Damn, you filthy whore, you've broken my nose! I'll kill you for that!" Fury glowed in his eyes as he seized a bridle hanging from the wall. Before William could move, Bieko lashed out with it and hit the side of William's head with the metal bit.

William fell backward. *Shit!* He screamed to himself. Everything around him seemed to spin. Bieko pulled out his knife and drove it toward William's prone figure.

At that moment, the boy grabbed Bieko's booted foot, twisting it enough to throw him off balance. He shouted at William, "Signore! Signore! Get up!!"

Bieko kicked the boy away and turned toward William. When

Bieko came at him a second time, William dodged the knife, grabbed the young fellow's arm and bent it backward over his knee. Bieko's wrist snapped.

"*Aaaaaiii!* You bastard! You've broken it!" The ragazzo clutched his wrist, hopping up and down in pain. Gradually he pulled himself together and glared at William. "You musicians! You think you are so important!" He spat on the straw under his feet. "You think the world cannot live without you." He shook his head in disgust and spat again. "You, with your benefices, your estates, your fancy clothes, your incomes from every parish in the duchy." He took a step forward and snarled. "You caused Duke Galeazzo to be murdered! That's right. All that wealth. All those positions that should have gone to the nobility. But did they? No, they went to people like you!" He paused to catch his breath, still holding his broken wrist.

William took a step in his direction. Bieko backed away.

"Le Gran Batard had the right idea. '500 ducati to the man who ends the life of my wife's murderer.'" He pointed an accusing finger at William. "That would be you, Signore, and I for one will be very happy to see you dead and the reward in my hands." He turned and shuffled off toward the entryway of the stable. Then he stopped, turned around and hissed, "My advice to you—watch your back, every moment of every day." He disappeared into the sunlight at the door of the stable.

William shuddered at the mention of Count de Rupefort's name, Le Batard. He remembered only too clearly the hatred in the man's eyes when they met in Savoy years earlier. *Bieko knows about le Gran Batard's threats. I wonder who else knows?* Once again he shuddered then pushed his fears out of his mind.

He turned to the boy who was no more than ten or eleven years old. "Are you all right? Did he hurt you?"

The boy curled up in a ball, holding himself tight, pushing back the tears.

"What was it all about?" William's voice was soothing, encouraging.

"They make you give them money, some of the older boys. If you don't have any, they beat you, make you steal for them—" Tears came to his eyes.

"Or..." Again William's voice was soft, encouraging.

"They will put their thing in you." The boy began to cry.

"Did it ever happen to you?" William asked.

The boy shook his head. "But I have no more money. My friend, Ottobono, they did it to him. He had to leave the court. I heard he went crazy." The boy shook with sobs.

William helped him to his feet. "You'll be all right. I will see to that."

The boy brushed the hay and dirt from his shirt. "Thank you, Signore. I don't know what would have happened to me if you hadn't come along."

"From now on, if you are in any trouble you come see me, or my uncle, Bishop Branda. We'll take care of it. You need not be afraid."

"Bishop Branda?" The boy looked up wide-eyed at William. "He is a very powerful person. More powerful than Bieko's family." He continued to pick the dirt off his shirt and again looked up at William. "I am Tolentino. Giovanni Tolentino. I know you. I have seen you in the chancery where I work."

"How do you do, Giovanni." The two of them shook hands.

"You are a good fighter. Where did you learn that? Can you teach me?"

William and young Tolentino stepped out into the sunlight. "My brother was a midshipman in the English navy. He had learned to fight, and he taught me." William paused for a moment. "Perhaps you can help me, Giovanni." The youth nodded. "I need to know what people at court are saying. What rumors are going around. I don't care if they are true or not."

A little smile crossed Giovanni's lips. "You are the musician, yes?" William said nothing. "The lady, Cecilia...." William's eyes opened wide. "They say she, she likes someone a lot. She talks about him all the time."

William's heart leapt. "All right, Giovanni," he laughed. "Now clean yourself. From now on you are working for me." He handed the boy a few scudi. "Keep your eyes and ears open. But tell no one that you are my eyes and ears, understand?" The boy nodded his head and thrust the coins in his pocket. "Now I need something to eat. I am very tired from giving that cow a good beating, and I will be embarking on a long trip."

The youth bowed and ran away. William looked up. In the shadows of a doorway, he saw Bieko and several boys watching him.

*Well, here is more trouble,* he murmured.

William ambled off to the servants' dining hall where he found food to fill his hollow stomach.

*Bieko is far larger and stronger than he looks,* William thought to himself as he ate. *And much less of a fool than he pretends to be.* Pieces of things were falling into place, but not clearly so. Moreover, his disappointing conversation with Cecilia had left him without energy. For a moment he thought about going to the ducal chapel and listening to the singers. Then he remembered no singers or instrumentalists remained at court.

He went to his room and took out a bottle of good Lombard wine. It felt good to think about the past—about his parents, about Caroline, about the caves of his youth. He missed his father and mother, and most of all, his brother, Adrian. His thoughts went to his uncle. Stoic, good-natured, thoughtful. The man seemed to have no ambition except to serve Milano. Yet he had no wife to support him in perilous times, no children to enjoy or watch grow up. *At moments like these*, William realized, *it would be entirely satisfying to have a devoted and delightful wife at my side.* Surely his uncle must have felt that need.

Or was it that he had never asked his uncle about these very personal concerns. William realized he had much to learn about life, much to learn that had nothing to do with ambition, fame, or power.

He got to his feet and went once more to the stable. The long ride to Castiglione Olona would clear his mind.

# 8

## *The Ambitions of Ludovico Sforza*

*A Valley*
**TERDONA, ITALIA**
July 1479

"**L**et Il Moro choke on the hairballs of my cat!" muttered an elderly peasant.

All around, the ragged figures of weary youths and dour old men rested on their pitchforks, axes, and pikes, hiding from the sun in the shade of the mulberry trees dotting the hillsides. The dusty road leading from the port city of Genoa inland to Milano seemed endless. The march across the Apennine Mountains had been long and tiring, and the men were spent and irritable—even rebellious.

"Where's the paymaster?" grumbled a thick-bodied Sicilian, one of the few wearing a helmet and carrying a sword. "No pay, no fight." Like the other soldiers borrowed from the ranks of the king of Napoli, he had seen many battles and knew the futility of fighting without pay.

Others in the tattered army of 8,000 turned and listened.

"No more promises," grumbled the elderly peasant. Dressed in old clothing and carrying nothing but a rusty axe, he spat in the direction of a figure who sat on his horse high above them on the ridge of the hill, a figure silhouetted against the fierce blue of the Lombard sky.

"No pay, no fight!" a pimple-faced young man carrying a pitch-fork yelled.

"Si! Si!" the others shouted in agreement.

At that moment, a young man in a uniform galloped over to them. "What's going on?" Ibieto dal Fiesco, the tall, young commander of the tiny army questioned. His straight posture and handsome face, marred by a nasty scar across the forehead, bespoke a man of authority. As Ibieto glared down at the men, they turned very quiet. "Speak up!" he demanded.

"Where's the pay we've been promised? I see no money," grumbled the Neapolitan soldier, realizing that Ibieto dal Fiesco was but one man and they were hundreds.

"It's in Il Moro's pocket!" shouted another man suddenly emboldened.

"Yes! That's right!" shouted another. "In Ludovico Sforza's pocket."

"No pay, no fight!" the Neapolitan sneered, throwing down his sword and helmet.

Capitano dal Fiesco gazed down at the farmers, old men, vagabonds, and borrowed soldiers. He could barely contain his fury and contempt. *Well, they have little to gain or lose by standing and fighting.* Unlike them, he had much to gain or lose, for he hoped to regain the power and position his family had lost to Simonetta's allies in Genoa. *If Moro is successful, well then, nothing stands in the way of fulfilling my own ambitions.*

He put a hand on his sword then thought better of it. After all, these men far outnumbered him, and he would need their good will in the hours to come. He glanced up the hill at the silhouetted figure of Ludovico Il Moro, then flicked his horse's reins and began the slow ascent to the high ridge where Ludovico sat on his horse staring out into the abyss.

Ludovico Il Moro's jaw had a firm set to it and his dark, wary eyes had a very determined cast to them as well. Sitting on a horse next to Il Moro Pier Francesco Pontremoli also watched.

Below the two men and to the east, a line of soldiers snaked its way up through the mountain pass toward him—enemy soldiers.

A grim smile came to Il Moro's lips. "Let us go, my good horse," Ludovico muttered, urging his horse farther up the hill, seeking another perspective. Soon a battle would take place, a battle that would define his future.

At the crest of the hill, Moro glanced over his shoulder at the ragged little band of men resting at the bottom of the western side of the hill. A sad look spread across his face. *What a pitifully small number*, he thought. From the corner of his eye, he saw dal Fiesco and his horse making their way up the hill.

The look on Moro's face became harder, tougher. His friends at court had assured him that Simonetta was too concerned about the movements of Sanseverino's army which had departed Venice and the king of Napoli's approach to Firenze to worry about Ludovico's little army.

But what a risk he, Il Moro, was taking. *Il Tiempo.* The uncertainty of time—and fate.

When at last he had been ready to leap at opportunity, certain that time and fortune were on his side, his instincts had proven to be correct. He had captured several small cities between Genoa and Milano with little opposition. Patience, always his strength, had paid dividends.

These last few months, the smile had never left his face. His army's sense of purpose had been awakened by that smile. Who cared if the pay was poor and conditions miserable? Ludovico was on the march.

But now, as he peered down at the enemy, doubts assailed him. *Perhaps I was wrong, wrong to think that Simonetta could not fight on more than two fronts. Wrong to think friends at court would create a surprise without its being whispered to the wrong people. Wrong to think myself a worthy heir to so great a prince as my father, Duke Francesco?* A dark mood descended on him. He wondered if he had a place, a purpose, a destiny.

At his side, Pontremoli patted his horse. "Your father would be proud of this moment."

Ludovico grunted. Having demonstrated the way to wrestle a state from its ruling family by means of cunning and force of arms, his father had spawned a host of imitators—Sanseverino, Trivulzio, and of course, young Ludovico himself. Edgy laughter played around the corners of his mouth. "He would, wouldn't he?"

"*Imitazione* remains the highest order of flattery, my lord," repliedPier Francesco.

Ludovico stared down at the enemy, now dismounted and sharpening its pikes. He watched men-at-arms mill about, shouting, cursing, and grunting, weighed down by lances, heavy armor, and chivalric tradition. His own force was less than a quarter the size of that forming into an assault line below. The danger was very real.

"Would that your father was at our side—even if it were just his ghost," muttered Pier Francesco.

Ludovico cast a mocking glance in Pontremoli's direction. His mind drifted back to stories told to him as a child—how his father had besieged the city of Milano after the death of Duke Filippo Visconti, Ludovico's grandfather. Now Ludovico sat in the saddle ridden by his father, grasping the very sword worn by his grandfather, Duke Filippo Maria Visconti, poised to take back for the Sforzas the city which so loved Francesco. He raised his head to the sky above.

The figure of Ibieto dal Fiesco, commander of Ludovico's tiny army, loomed up beside them. The man had about him a quiet reassuring confidence. His dark moustache drooped as he gazed down at the array of troops poised to attack from the eastern side of the hill on which they stood.

Pointing to a slight ridge several hundred feet below their position, he said, "That is where we should meet them." Then he pointed to a grassy knoll closer to their position, a little ways below them. "However—"

"Yes?" Ludovico questioned.

Gazing at young Sforza, dal Fiesco weighed the depth of Ludovico's ambition—and whether the youth's promises of riches and steady employment were anything more than promises.

"Messere Ludovico," dal Fiesco began, with some hesitation in his voice.

"Si, si, Capitano—" Ludovico encouraged him. "Go ahead."

"*Eccellenza,* the men refuse to meet the enemy without payment. For two weeks they have been fighting without pay." Ibieto paused then continued. "Moreover, they are frightened. The reputation of Capitano Trivulzio is well-known. They fear for their lives."

Ludovico reflected on these words. In battles such as this, the usual strategy called for a few men-at-arms—the skilled, much-heralded knights like himself—to be unhorsed, captured and ransomed. Infantry on each side did little more than rescue downed men-at-arms who had been unhorsed. The battle would end there.

But this situation was much worse. Simonetta's fury and sense of betrayal toward Roberto Sanseverino was very intense. Capture was out of the question. Hanging was the only alternative.

"They outnumber us five to one," dal Fiesco confided to young Ludovico. "Simonetta has offered thirty scudi to any man willing to fight us. In one day two hundred men put down their plows and joined him. We have only some 8,000 left."

Ludovico nodded and gave a sidelong glance to Pier Francesco Pontremoli who untied a small sack from the back of his saddle and handed it to Ludovico. "Show these to our men and tell them that I will increase their pay to thirty-five scudi to be paid after the battle." Il Moro drew out a handful of coins and handed them to dal Fiesco.

The young commander examined them. Each coin was a gold ducat worth half a month's wage for a commander like himself. Now smiling broadly, he exclaimed, "They will be content, *Eccellenza*. I can assure you of that."

He turned his horse and descended in the direction of his men.

Pontremoli gazed at Ludovico. "Enough to pay an army?" he pulled out another handful of coins, each old and practically worthless.

"When dealing with snakes," he grinned, "it is only necessary for the tongue to breathe in the scent of its victim. Its eyes are worthless. Dal Fiesco is firing up their imaginations with thoughts of the gold that lies within the walls of Milano. Their imaginations are fired by what he has seen."

As the heat of the afternoon waned, several dozen knights rode up the eastern slope of the hill toward Ludovico's small band of defenders. Simonetta's forces wore the Sforza-Panigarola lion and viper emblems and royal blue colors over their armor. The flags of Ercole d'Este, Duke of Ferrara, signaled his command of Simonetta's forces.

Behind the men-at-arms, a thin line of lightly armored soldiers using pikes as weapons started walking up the hill. In the rear, bowmen fitted arrows to bowstrings.

Sforza turned in his saddle and looked down the hill to the west. He saw dal Fiesco urging his men up the hill, his most loyal soldiers arrayed behind the tattered recruits so they could not escape. At length, all of dal Fiesco's men reached the ridge.

"Make ready!" dal Fiesco yelled to his archers.

"Let them come to us, Capitano," Ludovico remarked softly.

Dal Fiesco gestured for a group of well-armed men to come closer. "You men are to protect Messere Ludovico." They nodded their heads. "Wherever he goes, you protect him. Thirty extra scudi to each of you if he comes out of this battle unharmed."

"Thirty scudi and a chance to join the ducal guard if we are successful!" shouted Ludovico. The men began to laugh and joke.

Pontremoli lifted the colors—Ludovico's mulberry-colored flag with its viper and shield emblem on it. Ludovico raised himself up in his saddle. "In the name of the duke, my father!"

Capitano dal Fiesco thrust his sword forward. "To the house of Sforza!"

The men on the ridge chanted, "Sforza! Sforza!"

The duke of Ferrara's army labored up the hill, finally stopping some twenty yards from the Sforza army. The knights on horseback threw their visors up and gestured toward the top of the hill. Slowly, the pike-bearers moved forward.

A rain of arrows fell on the small band poised at the top of the hill, and a few men dropped to the ground.

"Now!" shouted dal Fiesco. Ludovico and dal Fiesco spurred their horses on. Their men leapt forward. In a moment, they were on top of the forces in blue.

Ludovico Il Moro swung his sword at two men who went down at once. Dal Fiesco felled a knight with a thrust of his sword to the groin.

Several of the men in blue fought their way toward Ludovico, but his defenders headed them off. Again and again, the duke of Ferrara's soldiers regrouped and ran toward Ludovico. Each time Ludovico's loyal guard closed ranks around him.

Ferrara's forces gradually disengaged and backed down the hill. The first battle had been brief. Now it was over. Ludovico's army remained intact. A fierce yell emerged from the lips of his soldiers. "Sforza, yay!"

Galloping up to the young prince, dal Fiesco extended his arm to Ludovico.

"Dama Fortuna smiles upon us, does she not?" Ludovico grinned broadly.

"Tomorrow will be different," dal Fiesco frowned. "Fresh troops under the Marquis of Mantua are on their way. The Marquis is a first class condottiere and will pursue us harder than has Duke Ercole."

A mysterious look played across the handsome features of young Ludovico. "There is an excellent chance that we shall fight no more, yet victory shall be ours."

At dusk, Trivulzio and a dozen soldiers clattered along the cobblestone streets of Milano. Erect on his black Arabian charger, Trivulzio was in an ugly mood. The orders recalling him to Milano from Firenze annoyed him, for his army had just made a fine tactical thrust into the middle of the forces of the king of Napoli, much to the relief of Lorenzo Il Magnifico. He was frustrated, hating with all the furies in hell, to give up the advantage he had fought so hard to gain.

He arrived at the castello, its fortified walls bristling with cannon. Guards came to attention as he galloped over the drawbridge and trotted through the main portal into the courtyard. As he dismounted, Simonetta appeared. The men embraced and retreated to the shadows of the courtyard.

"Moro is in Tortona with an army," muttered Simonetta. "Sanseverino, damn his soul, has filled his head with foolish visions."

Trivulzio nodded.

"Sanseverino and his army of Venetians in the East will cease fighting once Ludovico bends to our will," Simonetta suspected. "You must negotiate with him immediately then return to Firenze. I want this war over."

Trivulzio bit his tongue and said nothing.

At the door to his apartment in the castello, Trivulzio found Zimarro "Bieko" del Corte waiting for him. The young man bent Trivulzio's ear for a few minutes, then the soldier sent him away. As Trivulzio changed his dirty battle uniform for a fresh Milanese outfit, he gave one of his guards an order to carry out.

The guard entered the ducal chapel where he found William practicing as he did every day at this hour. The guard informed him that Trivulzio wanted to see him. Puzzled, William put his instrument away and followed the guard to Trivulzio's apartments.

"*Buon giorno*, Capitano," William bowed as the door opened, and the soldier stood before him.

"And to you as well." Trivulzio did not smile as he motioned William to a chair "Sit, *piachere*. I only have a moment. Ludovico is in Tortona."

William's heart leapt in his chest. *So the rumors are true. Moro is making a move.* "I have just had a conversation with Zimarro 'Bieko' del Corte. He accuses you of making unmanly advances toward him. What do you have to say to that?"

William felt Trivulzio's stare. It was worse than a priest's before confession. "I found him attacking young Tolentino of the chancery staff, and I cuffed him a bit."

"It appears you broke his nose, his wrist, a few teeth and left him with a black eye," Trivulzio continued, impassive and apparently objective. "His father is one of Simonetta's most trusted counselors."

"If I found him attacking another one of the ragazzi, I would break more than that. And I don't much care who his parents are!" William's quiet but intense tone of voice surprised both William and the Regent of Milan. "If you have any doubts, get young Tolentino in here and ask him where he got all the cuts and bruises on his face and body."

Each man stared into the other's eyes for a moment.

Then a hint of a smile crossed Trivulzio's rugged features. "I have heard rumors of buggery going on inside these walls. In fact, I have had to clout a few of these young people myself. Duke Galeazzo Maria served as a poor model for them." Trivulzio seemed distracted and far away. "I meet with Ludovico in a few hours to persuade him to put down his arms. You know him well, as I do. What are your thoughts?"

William remained silent. Trivulzio had never asked his advice before and he didn't want to overstep his position, or betray his friendship with Ludovico. Yet he intended to be truthful. "If I may be frank, Reggente, Ludovico Il Moro is now a much tougher opponent than he was in the recent past."

Trivulzio's eyes widened with curiosity.

"The deaths of his beloved brothers would have caused him enormous pain and suffering six months ago. When I met him in Pisa a few weeks ago and informed him of the death of Sforza Maria, he hardly seemed to notice. He seemed to have other things on his mind."

"I thought as much. Thank you. Very helpful." Suddenly Gian Giacomo gazed at William, as if seeing him for the first time. A sly smile came to his lips. "Pack what you need. You will be riding with us." He motioned to a guard. "Find a *tenente's* uniform for Messere William. Ludovico trusts you. Perhaps we can shake his certainty a little." He continued to grin, quite pleased with himself. "Oh, and your pay as a tenente will be three ducati per month— in addition to your pay as a musician." He chuckled to himself.

Two hours before midnight, Trivulzio and eight lancers rode into Ludovico's camp in Tortona. Experienced soldiers among Ludovico's followers ceased what they were doing to gape at the legendary commander whose gaze was fixed on an unknown point. Trivulzio smiled to himself—he knew that one glance from him and two dozen more of Ludovico's troops would desert by the time the sun reached the horizon.

Riding next to Trivulzio, William Castle now wore the uniform of a Milanese lieutenente. He felt both uncomfortable and excited. He feared that Trivulzio was going to use him to create a sense of betrayal in Ludovico. Still, he felt a measure of pride in wearing this uniform. He knew it was foolish, but somehow he felt a link to the past—and to Duke Francesco. Despite the late hour, he was alert to anything that might happen.

Outside Ludovico's tent, Trivulzio dismounted and stood at attention. Men nearby gawked at him, open-mouthed. "The hero of Vercelli," one elderly man whispered to a boy of fifteen.

"That's him—he out-fought and outsmarted the pope and the king of Napoli near Firenze," a filthy youngster in farmer's clothing remembered.

"I hope he is not going to fight against us," declared a large, fat, middle-aged man, his hands shaking as he wiped the sweat from his brow.

Pontremoli emerged from the tent. At the sight of William in the uniform of Milano, a look of shock crossed his face. He bid Trivulzio and William Castle enter.

Inside the tent, Ludovico bowed slightly. "Trivulzio. I am delighted to see you." William knew this to be a lie. Trivulzio knew it was a lie as well. Since childhood, the two men had been bitter rivals. Trivulzio had been a fine athlete. At the court of Duke Francesco, he had been the one who caught the eye of the old general, who knew future military talent when he saw it.

Ludovico had been a great favorite of the old duke as well, but, as the third son, little chance existed that he would ever rule. However, the duke recognized his son's great ability to read the intentions and hopes of those around him from a look, a sigh, or a feigned smile. He asked his young son what he thought about the people who came to court—ambassadors and passing royalty as well as local nobility come to celebrate Christmas and Easter. He had been pleasantly surprised at how observant young Ludovico was.

"And our friend, the Englishman, newly risen in rank." Ludovico's good nature betrayed no shock at the sight of William in uniform, no discomfort at facing his chief boyhood rival and one of his closest friends, in the uniforms of his enemy, the Milanese army. "Let us celebrate your rise in rank." He ordered a steward to pour glasses of wine for the guests. The steward hurried to do so.

William was surprised to see how good-natured and confident Ludovico appeared.

"It has been a long time since we have seen each other." Trivulzio smiled and waved toward the tent opening. "This morning you defeated the forces of Duke Ercole." A consummate military man, one who never revealed an advantage, Trivulzio would not allow his tone of voice to reveal his disdain.

Ludovico shrugged. "We were fortunate to have the summit of the hill behind us. Come, a toast." He raised his glass. "To better days ahead." The three drank to his toast.

*Ludovico appears to have learned his father's lessons well.* William observed.

Trivulzio gave Ludovico a stony look. "The First Secretary asks you to join him in fighting on behalf of Lorenzo Il Magnifico, whom the pope and the king of Napoli have plotted to kill.

As he listened, the expression on Ludovico's face remained fixed. Finally he spoke. "I have the highest regard and the greatest love for Lorenzo Il Magnifico."

Trivulzio leaned forward. "The First Secretary urges you to abandon this foolish course of action. Any success on your part will undoubtedly be accompanied by the most outrageous treachery on the part of Capitano-Generale Sanseverino."

Ludovico smiled. "From childhood we have played together, Gian Giacomo. We learned our grammar together and the arts of war. Having served my brother, Duke Galeazzo, we have each suffered exile for it. Under Simonetta, Milano is a festering sore, a realm lacking perspective or purpose. I beg you, Gian Giacomo, join us in restoring the luster of the Sforza name to the duchy."

Trivulzio fell silent. William imagined he could hear Trivulzio's thoughts —*such ambition from a pampered boy who knows nothing of the arts of war, much less running a state. Yet to offend him would be dangerous for he has many friends. And, in truth, lo stato di Milano is wretched. Simonetta is old. But is Ludovico the one to change all that?*

A hard smile came to Trivulzio's lips. Choosing his words carefully, he continued. "I serve the government of Milano and the duke of Milano, your nephew. Think about this course of action. Your forces are meager, your men ill-paid. Already you have lost two brothers in pursuit of this dream of yours."

Ludovico stared into Trivulzio's unblinking eyes. "Neither of us would be here now had my brother ruled with the wisdom of my father. Now Simonetta makes the same foolish mistakes, alienating the citizens of Milano."

Trivulzio shook his head, back and forth, and threw up his hands. "No, no. The king of Napoli supports you only to distract us from the defense of Firenze," Trivulzio continued. "Soon he will desert you as well. The First Secretary has authorized me to forgive the treasonous acts you have engaged in if you return to Milano with me, at once."

Ludovico replied with stony silence. Trivulzio had a reputation for speaking the truth no matter the consequences—to trusted ally or implacable foe. The young prince shuddered for a moment at the thought of meeting this man in battle. *Yet, if all goes well, that will never happen.* "I rejoice to see you, Gian Giacomo." The young rebel voiced his answer in a husky whisper. "But your return to Milano wedded to the banner of Simonetta leaves my heart heavy."

The soldier stared at the wall. His young rival's gift for shaping ideas was equaled by few men, the soldier admitted to himself. He raised his wineglass once more. "To the memory of your father, the great Duke Francesco."

Ludovico raised his glass, "To the memory of my father." The two men clinked glasses.

Trivulzio stood up, excused himself, and left, along with 'tenente William Castle.

With Pontremoli at his shoulder, Ludovico watched through the open tent flap as Trivulzio and William climbed onto their horses. "Trivulzio aches for the reins of power as most men would lust after a well-proportioned woman," Ludovico murmured. "All his energies are devoted to it. His mind is filled with it every moment, even when he is waging war." He glanced at Pontremoli. "The question is..." Ludovico turned back to view the figures galloping off into the darkness. "Can those ambitions be harnessed to our purposes?"

On the way back to Milano, Trivulzio felt uneasy. His mouth had turned dry, a sure sign that something was taking place—something of which he was only dimly aware. *Ludovico appeared far too confident for a man in his position—8000 ill-equipped, badly trained, and inexperienced farmers facing 20,000 battle-hardened veterans.* Gian Giacomo knew that the Marquis of Mantua would destroy Ludovico's little number the next morning, and that brought a satisfying warmth to his innards. But somehow, he had to find out what lurked behind these vague suspicions. "What do you make of that little encounter, William?"

The musician shrugged. "You would think he would be frightened by the prospect of tomorrow's actions. But he was not. Not in the least."

Trivulzio nodded his agreement.

A full moon flitted in and out of clouds encircling Milano. The cathedral bell signaled late Mass. At the instant of its tenth ring, a coach passed between the Duomo and the Palazzo Arengo and made its way up the street, past stables and inns, past houses of ill-repute and vegetable stands. As the moon broke out from behind a cloud, the coach pulled up to the Castello di Porta Giovia's entrance and stopped.

The guard, a boy of nineteen girded by ill-fitting armor, barred the way with his lance. Behind him several other guards stood ready.

"Who goes there and for what purpose?" the boy shouted up at the carriage driver.

"Countess Beatrice, sister to Ercole, Duke of Ferrara, commander of the forces of Milano, replied the driver, an elderly man with one eye missing. "To see Duchess Bona. It is urgent."

The boy peered inside the coach. In the dim light he saw the face of a handsome, regal-looking woman in her late forties.

"Pass," he said and stood aside. The coach rolled into the inner courtyard.

Not far away, in the chancery, Simonetta stopped pacing the floor. Trivulzio stood at the window.

"Unshakable? Moro was unshakable?" Simonetta could not believe his ears as Trivulzio ended his report. "Bah! It is all because of General Sanseverino!" The old man shook his head in anger. "Never! Never have I known such a troublemaker." He heaved a sigh and turned to the soldier. "He speaks nothing but foolishness into the willing ears of young Ludovico whose appetites are whetted by the sounds of words that please him."

"Moro appeared eager and confident, *amico*," replied the soldier gruffly, thrusting out his jaw.

Simonetta shook his head in disgust. "The last thing I want to do is behead any of the sons of Duke Francesco. But Sanseverino!" He threw up his hands. "That is another matter!" He turned back to the soldier. "Thank you for your report. You may return to camp now."

Trivulzio got to his feet. "I serve you best by remaining in Milano, Governatore."

The old man raised his hand. "No, no. Your place is with our troops in Tuscany where the danger is greatest. There is no danger here." He showed the younger man to the door. "Good-bye, compare."

The soldier's rugged features gathered into a frown. "May

Dama Fortuna look upon us with favor." He disappeared through the door.

In her apartment on the second floor of the tower which bore her name, Bona, the beautiful Duchess of Savoy, looked out upon the city from her window. She felt troubled. For one thing, the gay round of fetes and musical evenings no longer filled her days and evenings as it had when her husband, the duke, lived. For another, her sexual yearnings seldom found fulfillment with the young men she entertained.

Behind her, Antonio Tassino reclined on her bed, eating grapes. Half-dressed, he bid her come to him. She did. He then kissed the curve of her bosom and murmured, "Is the beautiful duchess sad this evening? Has her lover not filled her with exquisite pleasure?"

"Yes, yes, of course, Tonio," She smiled absently and caressed his hair.

"Then what troubles her?"

She gazed at him. "You have no idea at all?"

The handsome young man stared at her with a blank expression on his face.

"When a woman has been at the side of a man of great power, and he is taken from her in the full bloom of his manhood, a woman feels it in her soul."

"The duke, your husband, was a man much disliked by the citizens of Milano, was he not?" He dropped a grape into his mouth.

"No, they loved him," she replied.

"Is it not true that he ordered his artist to decorate the halls of the Castello di Pavia all in one night, on pain of death?" He leaned over and caressed her shoulders.

"He was much possessed by the idea of perfecting the castello. That is true. But the decoration was completed."

"Was he not cruel and unjust in many w—?"

"Yes, yes! It is true," she interrupted, her voice irritable and raspy. "But never was he a tyrant to his wife. He desired me at all times in his own wolfish way. I miss him terribly."

The young man kissed her shoulder. "You are a woman fit for a king," he replied in a distracted voice. *Now is the time to plant a seed*, he thought to himself and smiled.

"You heard about the omen that three ravens flew above the duke's head just before he was assassinated?"

The duchess nodded.

"In the kitchen, where much is known and I am well-connected, rumor has it that there were four ravens."

She gave him a puzzled look.

"Your minister, Simonetta, was rumored to have been a part of the group of plotters who assassinated the duke at the church of S. Stefano."

She appeared stunned and bewildered.

"You didn't know that?" He touched her hair tenderly. "I believe they are right."

Hot, angry tears came to her eyes.

Countess Beatrice's coach rolled across the courtyard and came to a stop at the foot of the great tower where the duchess kept her apartments. Tristano Sforza's elegant widow stepped down from the coach and walked with serene grace the few steps to the guard at the entrance to the tower.

Tassino heard a knock at the door, opened it, and a page whispered to him. He nodded then turned to Bona. "One moment, my dearest," he whispered, blowing her a kiss.

Still half-dressed, in a dark hallway lit only by large torches which cast great shadows on the cold stone of the walls and ceiling, Tassino looked around. A velvet-gloved hand beckoned him into the shadows. Tonio followed the hand into the darkness. With the outline of her face barely visible, Countess Beatrice took something from inside her cloak and handed it to him. "This is but a small reward," she whispered. The sack jiggled with coins.

"I guarantee nothing," muttered Tassino, hiding the sack inside his jacket. "But she is softening."

"Under Ludovico's tutelage, the young duke will assert his rights," murmured the woman. Tassino led her toward the door to the chambers of Duchess Bona. "Simonetta believes he is God himself," grumbled the young man, "refusing to allow my father to become guardian of the treasury. Huh!"

Hearing a tap on her door, Bona stopped her pacing about. The door opened. Before her stood Countess Beatrice d'Este, her sister-in- law.

"Welcome, dear sister." The two women embraced. After seating themselves, Bona poured her friend and sister-in-law a glass of mulberry wine.

Countess Beatrice raised her glass. "To the fine wine of Lombardy. No wine anywhere compares to the mulberry of Lombardy."

"Indeed, yes." Bona gazed out the window, distracted.

"How do you fare these mournful days?" Countess Beatrice wondered aloud. "Your voice has lost much of its song since—"

"—since my dearest husband was torn from my side. From that moment to this, I am but an empty shell." Tears welled up in Bona's eyes.

The older woman took Bona in her arms. "There, there, sweet sister. It is already two years since I lost my Tristano, and I am desolate myself."

"My husband, the duke, valued Tristano beyond words, dearest Beatrice," Bona wiped her eyes. "When last you were here, you promised a way out of this hell—no one is my friend except the young Englishman. The minister keeps my son from me. All my old friends ignore me—"

The countess gazed into the eyes of her friend. "Simonetta holds the reins of state very tightly. Reins which ought to be in the hands of others, most notably, those who cherish you."

"Would that it were true," answered Bona. "My days in this fair city seem endlessly grey."

Tristano's widow rose, walked around the room, seemingly lost in thought, then turned back to her friend. "There is a way, but you must act now."

Duchess Bona turned from her view of the city and stared at the countess.

"You mean, the way of Ludovico and Ascanio?" Bona looked alarmed. "I, I don't—"

"Time and again Tristano told me that Ludovico would accomplish things that no other man alive could accomplish." Beatrice took Bona's hand. "He trusted and admired his younger brother completely."

Bona twisted her handkerchief in distress. "I have come to hate Simonetta, it is true. But I just don't know.... If only I were sure—"

Countess Beatrice listened, a tiny, reassuring smile crossing her lips. "If I bring you a man whom everyone trusts, a man who is prepared to assure you that all will be well, would you then do as we have talked about—open the garden gate, allow nature to take its course?"

Bona could only give her a blank stare. Finally she nodded, 'yes.'

"Bring in the damsel, Cecilia Gallerani," Beatrice suggested.

"There is work for her to do."

Bona stared at her sister-in-law, astounded at the request. She stood up, went to her desk, picked up a small bell and rang it.

A moment later, Cecilia appeared. The young woman curtseyed followed by a questioning look.

The duchess waved to Countess Beatrice.

"Go to the apartment of Bishop Branda," Beatrice directed, her voice soft but the tone of her voice resolute. "Confirm that the young man we have talked about will do as Il Moro wishes."

Cecilia nodded and disappeared out the door.

Moments later, Countess Beatrice descended the staircase and came face to face with the young guards. "My dear man, Duchess Bona asks you both to go to the ducal kitchen and fetch us something to eat, and while you are there, partake of some wine and cheese yourselves. We need to be alone for a little while."

The guards took the pass signed by the duchess and hurried away.

Inside the bishop's suite in the Corte Ducale, the bishop huddled together with William and Cecilia Gallerani.

"Will you do it?" Cecilia asked, gazing in William's eyes.

The bishop shook his head back and forth. "What you ask is impossible. Detection would mean the end of everything."

"I understand," she replied. "Moro understands. But it is his only hope."

The bishop shrugged and turned to his nephew. "It is your decision."

William gazed up at the ceiling, pressing his forefingers together. "In my heart I know the cause is just, but Simonetta has been helpful to me, personally—for the most part. I would have a great deal of difficulty knowing that I had betrayed yet another person who had been good to me."

"So the answer is 'no'?" Cecilia touched his arm, softly, with a gentle urgency.

The bishop leaned toward his nephew. "Certain death awaits us all if anything goes wrong."

William got to his feet and paced about the room. "Nevertheless, Il Moro is the only one who has a vision for what a state can be, what it should be."

Cecilia got to her feet and headed for the door, followed by William and the bishop. "Then I will tell him you will be there—"

Bishop Branda hurried to the door, intercepting her. "This cannot be decided on the spur of the moment."

William also followed her as she opened the door. ""I have so much I wish to say to you, Cecilia, my dear, sweet Cecilia."

Cecilia touched his cheek with genuine affection. "There will be plenty of time—later." She slipped out the door.

"You are sure about this. Not just blinded by love, or lust, or idealism," the elderly man wondered.

William shrugged his shoulders, not at all sure himself.


Countess Beatrice's coach waited at the foot of the steps of Bona's tower. Cecilia Gallerani hastened from the Corte Ducale to the coach and slipped inside while the guards were still absent from their duties guarding the tower. The driver whipped the vehicle into motion. It rumbled around the courtyard and headed out the main portal. From out of the darkness, another rider raced after the coach—Gian Giacomo Trivulzio.


The coach headed east toward Ferrara, the home of Countess Beatrice d'Este Sforza. Before long it stopped at a roadhouse. Tristano Sforza's elegant widow got out and stretched her body while the driver went inside for some refreshment. He brought back a small meal for the lady.

Trivulzio watched at a distance. He did not see the coach door closest to the building crack open and a figure dressed in black slip into the darkness.

Countess Beatrice climbed back into the coach, and it drove off toward Ferrara. Trivulzio followed for several kilometers then decided to abandon the chase.

At the roadhouse, Cecilia picked up a horse which Countess Beatrice had left for her. She galloped all night across the plains of Lombardy, circled around the encampment of the duke of Ferrara at daybreak, and trotted into the Sforza camp half an hour later.

She snuck into the tent of Il Moro, approached him and whispered in his ear. "It is done. He is willing."

Il Moro rubbed the sleep from his eyes. In a moment, he was instantly awake. "He is willing? Really? I can't tell you what—"

She put her fingers to his lips, sneaked out of the tent then rode all day back the way she came, until at last she again appeared at the villa of her parents.

While her father was hard at work, Cecilia crept into his office, went over and sat on his lap, almost asleep. Facio looked up.

"Hello, my dear."

She yawned. "Papa, you know that I would never willingly put either you or mother in danger, don't you?" Again she closed her eyes.

"What are you talking about, child? What are you up to? Does it have to do with the presence of Ludovico Il Moro in this house?"

She smiled but said nothing, then brought his hands that en-folded hers to her lips. "Sometimes we must take risks in order for great things to happen." She kissed the top of her father's head once more. "Tomorrow
morning I must be up when the cock crows." She turned and left the room.

A few moments later, she fell into the bed that had been hers since childhood and entered the world of dreams.

As the sun rose on a new day, Bishop Branda awoke early and went downstairs to the small kitchen of his suite of rooms. A ser-vant put together a quick breakfast of eggs and pane. An hour later, William awoke after a fitful night's sleep and staggered into the kitchen where his uncle ate breakfast.

Bishop Branda smiled at his nephew. "A good night's sleep, nephew?"

"About the same as the night I spent in the *prigonia* of King Ferrante," William answered, remembering that most horrible of experiences.

The bishop waved his napkin. "So far you have landed on your feet, my son. Your time in the *prigonia* in Napoli was good for you—a reminder of the price you pay for showing your hand too openly, or for failing to understand the nature of those who op-pose each other, while holding you hostage to their ambitions."

William reflected on these words. "Wise words to the innocent. I will continue to be careful, Uncle."

Later that morning, Bishop Branda left his suite and went to Bona's apartment in the tower that bore her name.

Bona was surprised to see him. "You," she said, at first amazed but slowly pleased to see him. "I had not thought you supported

Il Moro…openly."

He smiled. "Not openly. But entirely, yes."

Half an hour later he returned to his own suite of rooms. He slipped inside and looked around for his nephew who sat at a window reading a book.

"Come!" whispered Bishop Branda. "She is ready."

William gave his uncle a wave of his hand, picked up his trombone then hurried out the door and down the hallway.

Branda watched the retreating figure, a frown spreading across his brow. "Yes, my boy, for the love of God, show some care in what you do. And may all of the angels in heaven follow your every move."

Some time later, the duchess heard a knock at the door. "E-e-enter" she stuttered.

William stood smiling before her, his trombone case in one hand. "Our duchess wishes some diversion?" He bowed to her.

She swept him in from the hallway with surprising force. He almost stumbled, and the two of them burst into laughter. "Yes, my dear. Play your beautiful music for me." She plopped down on the divan as he prepared his instrument.

Cecilia appeared in the background. William noticed, giving her a wan smile. She gave him a slight, playful curtsy.

William picked up his horn and played a few notes. Bona stopped him. "Make my cares go away, Englishman, yes. More important, be my friend and listen to what our damsel, Cecilia, has to say." Her wide, soft eyes seemed scared and excited.

He stared at her wild, almost desperate expression. "Perhaps it is something I should not know." His eyes gleamed. "Or perhaps it is something I already know.

144

Cecilia approached. "Whatever I tell you," she said, "will change your life forever, and mine as well." The two turned to Cecilia, who took a seat on a foot-stool, leaned close to them, as if the walls had ears and proceeded to tell them about her midnight mission to Ludovico Il Moro Sforza at his encampment and Il Moro's plan to rescue Milano from the clutches of Cicco Simonetta and Gian Giacomo Trivulzio.

As William listened to the daring plan, his jaw dropped in amazement. It was daring…and foolish…but just might work. If it did not, he, Cecilia, his uncle, and Il Moro would all hang from one of the portals of the castello. He tried not to think about that possibility, listening instead to the part he had been asked to play. A substantial part. Perhaps the most vital part.

*God help me,* he said to himself, as if he were being dragged into one of the rings of Dante's Inferno. *God help me.*

# 9

## *The Secret Garden*

*The Apartments of Bona of Savoy*
**CASTELLO DI PORTA GIOVIA**
MILANO, ITALIA
September, 1479

**"I**t is up to you, William. Il Moro will tap on the door each of the next three nights. You are the only one who can accomplish this." Bishop Branda spoke softly as he, William, and the Duchess Bona huddled together in her apartment.

The Englishman glanced from the bishop to the duchess. "Do I have a choice?"

The bishop nodded. "You do, of course. But if not you, we will have to find someone else—" Branda gave out a sardonic laugh. "One of the damsels, perhaps."

Shocked at the thought of Cecilia going to the secret garden in the middle of the night, William shrugged his shoulders. "If it looks possible, I will do what I can, if not...."

Bishop Branda nodded, understanding that in matters as dangerous as this no guarantees were possible. He stood up and patted William on the shoulder. "You must get some sleep. Be alert for the ringing of the bell of the Duomo—"

After returning to his tiny room, William decided to inspect the castello's grounds—and perhaps the secret garden whose door led to the moat where Ludovico would soon be waiting.

He skirted the parade ground which stood empty and silent in the moonlight, walking from shadow to shadow, listening, watching, alert to any sound or movement. But he saw nothing—until he had returned to within a few yards of his room.

He was about to step out of a shadow when he saw a figure move through the doorway and into his room. "Damn!" he muttered. The figure reappeared for a moment and turned toward him. The moonlight revealed the face of Bieko. "Damn! Damn! Damn!" he whispered again and again, watching as Bieko disappeared into the night.

William remained outside his room for a full half hour then made his way to the door. He slipped inside his dwelling, lit a candle, looked around, then went to the small table beside his bed. Sure enough, the small pouch with four ducati inside—the one the duchess had given him—was gone. Fortunately, he had recently handed his uncle the remaining monies she had given him so the thief had gotten very little. But it unnerved him to realize how closely Bieko was observing him.

He took off his clothing and lay down on his bed. Soon he was fast asleep.

At the sound of the three bells, William awoke, alert and ready to act. On first impulse, he dressed and prepared to hurry to the garden. But then he stopped himself. *Where was Bieko? Who might be with him?* No, he decided, Ludovico would have to wait. William reasoned that he would certainly have to take care of young Bieko, the thief and spy. He fingered his dagger as he thought about the ragazzo de camera and sat down on his bed. *Be careful,* he reminded himself. *Do nothing foolish that would endanger the plan that your uncle has so carefully put together.* Fully dressed but quite exhausted, he went back to sleep.

The following day, Ludovico Il Moro and young Galeazzo San-severino waited at their camp, trying to relax by getting some sleep. Lookouts indicated that the enemy appeared ready to attack, but for whatever reason, they did not. Ludovico guessed that the Marquis of Mantua had not yet arrived. He ordered his fifty best cross-bowmen under the command of Ibieto dal Fiesco to intercept the marquis and cause as much delay as possible.

Dal Fiesco was only too happy to take action. Inactivity was the curse of his existence.

For Ludovico, the waiting proved difficult. Thoughts raced around in his head. By the following morning he would be in a position to rule Milano—or he would be dangling from a hang-man's rope. He kept a low profile all day long. Without doubt, some in his camp were spies working for Simonetta. *We must not raise suspicions.*

At midday, William left his tiny room and went to the chancery. Simonetta was absent, as William had suspected. At Simonetta's age, the old man took a long nap during the middle hours of the day, even in cold weather.

No one at the chancery paid any attention to William. After all, he visited there quite often, relaying messages and conferring with Simonetta and Trivulzio. Occasionally, he had been seen chatting with young Tolentino. Several young scribes noted the famil-iarity of the two and supposed that it was a typical friendship of an older mentor and a younger boy. No one knew that William had saved Giovanni's life and honor.

After looking around for a moment or two, William motioned to Tolentino who got up and met him in the hallway outside the chancery. "I need you to follow that bastard Bieko tonight." William told the boy, handing him several soldi. "He stole money from me last night. I will be with the duchess most of the evening, or with my uncle. If you see him following me, or entering my room, come tell me, no matter how late the hour."

Young Tolentino bowed. "Anything you say, Signore. Whatever gets that bastard in more trouble is worth the effort."

In his encampment several hours ride on horseback from Milano, Ludovico lay on his cot staring out at the stars which shone all across the sky. The moon appeared as expected.

Galeazzo Sanseverino made his way to Ludovico's tent. The young leader of the Sforza clan got to his feet and readied himself for action. The two young men clasped arms and embraced one another. Galeazzo went to the tent exit and spoke to the guard. "Bring up our horses" The guard hurried away.

For the next few hours, Ludovico and Galeazzo rode across moonlit valleys and onto the plains of Lombardy surrounding Milano.

At a small farm northwest of the city, Ludovico and Galeazzo met with its owner—a loyal supporter who agreed to drive his wagon into Milano with Ludovico and Galeazzo hiding beneath the wagon's load of hay. If all went well, the farmer would stop near the castle. Ludovico and Galeazzo would climb out under cover of darkness and find their way to a little used bridge across the castle's moat, under which they were to wait. A door would lead them into a secret garden. William would be waiting on the other side of the door to let them in. That is, if all went as planned.

When the bell in the tower of the Duomo struck the hour of ten in the evening, William roused himself from his bed at his uncle's apartment, crept outside and slipped through the shadows to the stairs which led down to the secret garden below. He glanced around and saw a guard staring at him. He nodded to the guard who stood at the entrance to Duchess Bona's tower some distance away and glanced around. The Corte Ducale was otherwise deserted. He looked hard into the shadows but could see no movement. *Perhaps Bieko was only interested in the money after all.* William knew the guard would be wondering what he was up to. He had a ready answer to that question.

He crossed the path that led to the tower and approached the guard. "I am looking for a ragazzo named Bieko," William muttered in the darkness. "Have you seen him?"

"No, Signore," replied the guard. "I have not. Should I tell him you wish to speak to him if I do see him?

"No, no. This is not something I wish him to know about. The youth stole something from me." He balled up his fist.

The guard did his best to suppress a smile. "Very good, sir. My lips are sealed."

William took out a few scudi, stuffed them in the guard's pocket and proceeded up the stairs to the suite of Duchess Bona.

Knocking on the door, he heard a muffled voice command him to enter.

Inside he found his uncle tending to Bona who lay prostrate on a couch. Several damsels also tended to her. He took his uncle aside and explained his hesitation.

"We must go forward tonight," Bishop Branda whispered, as he gave the duchess a reassuring smile.

A knock at the door startled them. Branda hurried over and opened it. Tolentino stood in the darkness. Branda ushered him inside, and he went over to William.

"Bieko has been following you all evening, Messere Castle. When you went to the stairway, he was watching. He almost caught me watching. I thought I was going to die."

"Good for you, Giovanni. Good for you. Where is he now?"

"He is waiting for you in your room."

"Is he alone?"

"As far as I could tell, he was alone."

Giving him a pat on the shoulder, William spoke softly. "Very good. You may go now. Get some sleep."

The boy disappeared into the gloom of the staircase.

William sat down to think things through.

Branda's voice interrupted his thoughts. "More difficulties?"

The musician nodded his head up and down. "Bieko, one of the ragazzi di camera, has been following me. He has a grudge to settle. Last night he stole some of my money. Tonight he waits in my room."

"I will have him arrested—"

"No, no." William waved his hands. "That would cause more trouble …and wake up everyone. No, I will deal with this."

Nearing two o'clock in the morning, the hay wagon concealing Ludovico and Galeazzo Sanseverino lumbered up to Porta Nuova, the northernmost entrance to the walled city of Milano.

"Halt," the guard ordered.

The wagon came to a stop. Several troops encircled the wagon. One stuck a pike into the hay.

Another looked the driver in the eye. "Destination?"

"Palazzo Marliani," the driver yawned.

"At this hour of the night?" The driver shrugged. "All right, pass."

As the wagon rolled forward, the guard signaled two horsemen who lingered in the shadows.

Beneath the hay, Ludovico peeked out the back of the wagon

and saw the horsemen following as the hay wagon rolled forward. "Messere," he whispered.

"Si, si," replied the driver.

"We are being followed. Do not go to the castello." Ludovico brushed the hay from his mouth. Galeazzo suppressed a laugh. "Take us to Signora Marliani's palazzo."

"*Dove lo palazzo?*" The driver whipped the horses onward.

Ludovico gave him directions as he continued to watch the horsemen.

The wagon moved slowly toward the middle of the city of Milano. After a quarter of an hour, they stopped at the entrance to the Marliani palazzo. Its windows were dark, and nowhere could any signs of life be seen.

Down the street, the horsemen waited and watched.

The driver climbed down from his perch and rang the bell at the gate.

A candle flickered in a second story window. A moment later, footsteps came toward the gate. "Si, si, what is it?" a female voice asked.

"Someone important to see Lucia Marliani," the driver murmured.

"I am Lucia," the voice replied. "Who is it? What does he want at this hour of the morning? I am not expecting anyone."

In his uncertainty, the driver walked back to the wagon and explained the situation to Ludovico.

"Tell her a member of a family as out of favor as her own wants to restore what is owed her," Ludovico whispered from beneath the hay. "And tell her to hurry."

The driver cast a nervous glance down the street where the horsemen waited. Then he returned to the gate and explained who the important person was.

As he spoke, the horsemen moved their horses closer to the wagon. "Please, madam, hurry. Our lives are in danger," said the driver, doing his best to keep his hands from shaking.

On the other side of the gate, the voice was silent. The three members of the Lanze Spezzate cantered up the street, moving ever closer.

"Tell whomever you are hiding to go away," she said at last. "It is freezing cold and I'm going back in—."

"Signora—" the driver croaked out a hoarse whisper. "It is Ludovico Sforza himself. He begs you to help him."

"Nonsense, it is not Ludovico."

The driver watched the approaching soldiers, frozen to the spot.

"Do something!" whispered Ludovico in a voice almost loud enough for the horsemen to hear. "Tell her she wears an ankle bracelet inscribed, *"Amore, Galeazzo."*

The driver hurried to the gate and repeated what he was told. Just as the soldiers pulled their horses to a stop behind the wagon, the gate opened and the driver urged the horses forward.

Standing in the moonlight, shivering despite the heavy coat she wore over her nightgown, the dark-eyed, alabaster-skinned, extraordinarily beautiful Lucia Marliani waved to the horsemen.

"Let us see once more what you have there," one of the soldiers ordered as the wagon passed through the gate.

"No, no. Go back to your duties, Signori. It is late and we are all tired." Lucia pushed the gate closed and locked it. The soldiers stood outside the gate unsure what to do. After all, the Marliani family was well-known in Milano.

The driver of the hay wagon whipped his horses and wagon up the circular entry way to the palazzo then pulled around to the side of the palazzo clothed in darkness. Ludovico and Galeazzo climbed out of the hay. Lucia walked up the path and watched them climb out of the hay wagon. She stared at them in astonishment.

"Moro, dear Moro! God in heaven, what are you doing?" She hurried them to a door in her palazzo.

Inside the building, the two young men picked the straw out of their clothing and laughed.

"Moro, I cannot believe my eyes," Lucia whispered.

"Yes, dear Lucia," Ludovico smiled with great affection, picking the last of the straw from his clothing. "It has been years since we have spoken."

She drew him closer and wrapped her arms around him. Tears welled up in her eyes. "It has been too many years...." She gestured toward the palazzo.

For the first time, Ludovico noticed that the palazzo which his brother, Galeazzo, had given her was practically empty of furniture and furnishings.

"Duchess Bona petitions Simonetta every week to recover objects Galeazzo gave to me with no result. Soon I will have nothing—not even the palazzo."

He leaned down and kissed her. "I will see that everything comes back to you. I promise." He grinned in the darkness. "Tonight we enter the castello through the secret garden. We have an ally who is close to Simonetta and therefore above suspicion. Before dawn, he will help us inside the castello. Then we will hasten to the quarters of Duchess Bona and the young duke. With them in hand, we will force Simonetta's surrender. Trivulzio is out of the city and poses no threat. If all goes well, we will possess Milano by first light, as did our father twenty-five years ago."

The plan's simplicity and attention to detail brought a smile to

Lucia's lips. "You found me and loved me and I loved you—and it was so simple." She smiled wistfully at him. In the moonlight, the curve of her sumptuous bosom heaved. "Then your brother, the duke, had to have me—"

"Who can say 'no' to a duke?" He kissed her again, this time even more deeply. "Now, my dear, we must be off." He looked around. "The soldiers are suspicious, I'm afraid, but there is another entrance, if I remember correctly."

"Si, si." She took him by the hand and led him out another door and they passed into a small, empty stable.

Galeazzo Sanseverino followed close behind them. "I will unhitch the horses," muttered Galeazzo, "and bring them around." In a moment, Galeazzo returned with the two horses from the hay wagon. The two men found a saddle in the stable. Ludovico threw it over the back of one horse and cinched it in place. He glanced over at Galeazzo Sanseverino.

"I need no saddle." Galeazzo placed a bridle over a horse's head. The two men led the horses toward a back gate, out of sight of the horsemen who lingered at the front gate.

Opening the creaky old gate, Lucia poked her head out. The little used back street was empty. Ludovico gave her one last kiss then mounted the saddled horse. Galeazzo threw himself onto the other horse, and the two men raced off into the darkness.

Lucia gave them a small wave of the hand. "God be with you," she murmured, turning back to her deserted palazzo.

The two young men maneuvered through the streets of Milano with care, moving slowly from one shadow to another until they were well away from the palazzo. Then they galloped away, picking up speed until they flew through the streets. Several times they met groups of soldiers who were startled at the sight of men on horseback streaking past.

As they neared the castle, they slowed the horses.

A figure moved out of the shadows and into the street, blocking their path. "Please sir, a coin for a homeless man."

Ludovico started to push his horse past the man then thought better of it. He stopped, reached into his pocket, withdrew a coin and tossed it to the shaggy-looking beggar.

A torch on the wall of a nearby tavern cast a beam of light on Ludovico's face as he leaned down. The beggar gasped. "Sforza! Come to claim his throne he has." He began to dance and laugh. "Haaaaaa haaaa!!"

Ludovico smiled and pressed his horse ahead into the darkness.

Several heads stuck out the windows of nearby buildings. "Shut up, you fool, quiet down!"

A woman holding a broom came out a door and swatted him with it. "Fool!" she shouted.

The beggar continued dancing in the street. "Sforza is coming! Sforza is coming!"

Standing at the door to the bishop's empty apartment, William wiped the sweat off his brow. With no idea what lay in wait on the other side, he opened the door slowly, and entered the darkened room, a hand on his dagger. He paused, waited and listened. At length, he could tell the room was deserted. If Bieko had been there, he was now gone. *Thank the Lord.* He lay down on his bed and was soon fast asleep.

When the bell in the bell tower of the Duomo struck midnight, he roused himself, dressed and picked up his trombone. Duchess Bona's apartment offered the closest, safest haven for the short walk to the garden.

Tying up their horses at the entrance to the hunting park which stretched out from the western entrance to the castello, then hurrying through the park's many trees, Ludovico and Galeazzo made their way to the ruins of an old outer wall of the castle and a portal no longer in use. Moving across a rotting drawbridge spanning the moat, they came to an iron portcullis that sealed the ancient portal. They descended the rocks beneath the drawbridge until their feet touched muddy ground just above the waters of the moat.

After searching for a several minutes, they found the small door they sought. Ludovico tapped on it several times. No answer. Ludovico tapped again. Still no answer.

Inside the Corte Ducale, a guard rested his back against the wall of the entryway to the tower of Bona of Savoy. Half asleep, he listened to the sweet sounds of William's trombone, eyes closed, a smile on his face. When the music came to an end, the guard played the tunes over in his mind. When William descended the stairs of Duchess Bona's apartment, the guard gave him a smile and a salute, then closed his eyes once more. He opened them again as William turned toward the Corte Ducale. He found it strange that the musician would be walking toward the ducal court at such an hour instead of the musician's own modest quarters. "Ducal business, eh signore?" he murmured as the Englishman passed.

William paused in the darkness and turned toward the guard. "Exactly right, Sergeant. Ducal business." He glanced up at the window of Simonetta's apartment. A light was on. "The First Secretary is up late tonight."

"He hardly sleeps these days," answered the guard.

"You look as if you could use a little sleep yourself," William joked with the sentry, then followed the path to the stairs that led downward to the secret garden.

On the other side of the door to the secret garden, sitting on his haunches close to the edge of the water in the moat, Ludovico Il Moro tapped at the iron gate again and again. For a long time there was no answer. One last time, he told himself and tapped again. His knees were beginning to ache and his back, too.

*How odd*, the guard thought to himself as he observed William standing at the stairs to the secret garden. *The ducal quarters are on the floor above.* He started to follow the musician then thought better of it. He would get in trouble, big trouble, if he left his post.

At the top of the stairs William turned around. He saw the guard staring at him. He skirted the stairs and entered the Corte Ducale. *No, tonight was not to be the night.* He sighed and headed to his uncle's apartment to report what had happened. He hoped Ludovico would not be exposed for too long. Another hour and it would be daylight.

Ludovico tapped at the iron door one last time. Still no answer. "That's it," he murmured to Galeazzo Sanseverino. "No one is coming."

Galeazzo wondered where they ought to go now.

Somehow, Ludovico realized, they had overlooked this contingency. *What fools we are*, he murmured to himself. "Tonight we improvise."

With the light of dawn beginning to cast away the darkness, the two men headed toward the streets of Milano, its industrious people already hurrying this way and that at the early hour.

Dressed in peasant garb, with Galeazzo hunched over to

disguise his great height, they moved in the direction of a nearby church. Several times they had to retreat into the shadows of doorways, as mounted soldiers patrolled the streets. At last they reached the church of Santa Maria della Grazie and eased themselves inside, looking around to see if anyone noticed them.

"I recollect," Ludovico whispered, "that the brothers of this order complained to Simonetta that this church's organ needed fixing. Perhaps..."

They went in search of the organ loft and soon found themselves in a musty room that had not been used in some time. They lay down on the floor and went to sleep.

# 10

## *A Second Try*

*Bishop Branda's Apartment*
**CASTELLO di PORTA GIOVIA**
September, 1479

Avery tired William Castle awakened the next morning. Having slept little, he found himself with a splitting headache. He went to the servants' quarters for something to eat, concerned about Ludovico's safety—at the same time wondering if he were doing the right thing by waiting so long to help young Sforza. After filling his stomach, he returned to his room and slept for another hour.

Late in the day, bells rang throughout the castello. Ludovico's small army had been defeated by the troops of the Marquis of Mantua although Ludovico Sforza had not been found. Most members of the court assumed that he had fled south to Pisa, or even to Parma, although everyone imagined that Pier Maria Rossi, Lord of Parma, would rather hold him for ransom than offer him refuge. No matter, the rebellion had ended.

William went to see his uncle. Together they decided that both of them ought to spend time with the duchess, knowing how high-strung she could be.

Indeed, they did find her distraught, her speech rambling. Branda put her to bed and insisted that none of her damsels tend to her—after all, she might easily reveal the secret that she, Bishop Branda, William, and Cecilia shared.

After dinner, William went back to Bona's apartment, trombone in hand. He played for several hours—until his lips felt raw. The duchess seemed much soothed when she went to bed and insisted that William stay and hold her hand. He looked in on his uncle who lay on a bed, asleep in one of the other rooms—intent of staying as close to the duchess as possible. He returned to the bedroom of the duchess, lying on her bed, holding her until she fell asleep.

When the bells in the towers of the nearby churches signaled the midnight hour, he arose, slipped out of her room and descended the staircase. One hour to go. He needed some rest.

Standing in the hallway outside the door to his uncle's empty apartment, William wondered what lay on the other side of the door. Yes, Bieko could easily have three or four good-for-nothing friends waiting for him inside. But he guessed Bieko wanted the grudge to end swiftly and silently with no one the wiser. He extinguished the torch outside his room.

Bending down, he pushed the door open, barreling his way into the room. A body hurled past him, rushing toward the space where he would have been had he stood still. William stuck his foot out, and the figure tumbled to the floor, banging the door closed. The moonlight sliced through the darkness and, for a moment, illuminated Bieko's face contorted in anger, a dagger in his hand.

William kicked in the direction of the fellow's crotch and connected. *Ahhhh!* Bieko yipped. William flung him on the bed, covering his mouth and clutching his windpipe before the surprised *ragazzo* could speak. Bieko clawed at William's hand, but the musician hung on like a tiger, as if its teeth had clamped on the neck of its prey. Before long, the young man went limp. William started tore up a bed sheet, intending to tie up the youth and stuff a large wad in his mouth.

At that moment, the bell of the Duomo rang 1:00 a.m. *Damn, Ludovico will be at the door in a moment.* He hesitated. The prudent thing would be to tie up Bieko. But if it took more than a moment, Ludovico might be discovered. William didn't dare be late. Not tonight. He got to his feet, bent down and tore a single strip from the bedding. He bound Bieko's hands behind his back then stuffed a wad of bedding in the mouth of the unconscious assailant.

At the door he listened for any sign from the hallway that someone had heard the fight. He cracked the door open. The hall appeared to be deserted. He picked up his trombone and headed out the door.

Hovering in the darkness before he risked going to the stairs to the secret garden, he watched the guard at the tower of Bona of Savoy very carefully. Very soon he determined that the man was drunk. Apparently withLudovico's army defeated and the threat ended, his commander had ordered a double ration of ale for every man in the castello.

Staying in the shadows, he slipped over to the secret garden staircase and scurried down the inner staircase to the garden below. As he descended the stone staircase one quick step at a time, he found himself slowing to a halt. *Why are you doing this?* His head ached and his stomach churned. Sweat soaked his shirt. *This is not your affair. If Ludovico is captured, he will hang, and so will you. The First Secretary has been good to you, even if he has used you to further his own ends. You betray his trust. Why do this?* He turned and retreated several steps up the staircase.

Once again he stopped and gazed down at the tiny garden. Somehow, he could not abandon Ludovico and his cause. Ludovico had a quality about him that made William and many others want to see the young prince succeed. Moreover, Simonetta was old and Trivulzio self-serving. Milano under Trivulzio's rule would continue to be austere and mean-spirited. Ludovico represented a new age, a new freedom.

So many reasons to plunge forward; so many reasons to go back the way he had come. Ah! For several moments, he stared down at the little garden below him—a descent into his destiny. How often he had stood at the edge of the cliffs of Dover and gazed down at the waters of the channel. What would it be like to leap into the murky waters below? Now, he knew the feeling—the dread and the excitement.

He descended the stairs a few steps then looked behind himself, at the Corte Ducale. One last glance. Suddenly a figure came toward him. William slunk back into the shadows and watched as the figure approached. *Good Christ, it's Bieko.* William stayed in the shadows as the ragazzo looked around, peered down into the small garden but saw nothing. He disappeared from sight. William knew it was time. He emerged from the darkness.

With one last glance around the staircase, he plunged downward into the gloom. He fancied that he heard a tapping coming from the door that led to the moat. There was another sound, too. He listened. A faint howling from the bowels of the castle—some prisoner begging for his life in the deep recesses of the dungeon— came to his ears. William shivered.

At the bottom of the staircase, he stopped and listened again, then slid into the shadows, slipping a hand over his dagger. He waited, he watched. No one came.

Stepping out of the shadows, he approached the door to the moat, wondering if anyone could be on the other side. He waited and waited. No tapping. Finally, as he was about to leave, he decided to tap. At first, nothing. He tapped again. Nothing. One more time. And then he heard it—a slight answering tapping on the iron grating outside. Again he hesitated. *This could be the most foolish thing you have ever done, William.*

On the other side of the door, Ludovico tapped at the iron gate. Ah, yes! An answering tap. His heart leapt. *Oh, my God!* His temples began to throb. His throat went dry. Would he find Simonetta and his men on the other side waiting to arrest him? *My God, what foolishness...to expose myself like this.*

The tiny door squeaked open, just a crack. A man's voice whispered, "Moro?"

"Si, si," replied Ludovico. By now he had been in the night air for some time. His hands were turning blue and his feet were already numb in the November air.

The small door opened wider. Ludovico faced the young Englishman. "God love you, my friend," whispered the young prince as he crawled through the small space in the open door. Galeazzo Sanseverino followed.

In the darkness of the secret garden, Ludovico and Sanseverino shook hands with William. "I prayed for your safety," the musician whispered.

"Our prayers have been answered, good friend," replied young Sforza.

He looked around the small, dimly lit garden. No one else appeared. "Thank the lord," he murmured. "Now we must find my nephew and Duchess Bona."

"I will take you to them." William motioned for Ludovico to follow him into the gloom.

William crept up the stairs into the patio of the corte. With Il Moro and Galeazzo Sanseverino remaining in the shadows, he crossed the path leading to Bona's tower and approached the guard, humming a little song, appearing a little tipsy. He drew a bottle out of his coat and handed it to the guard. "Join me, my friend. Piacere. Let's have a little fun." He moved slightly so the guard's back was to the path from the secret garden to the tower.

In the background, Ludovico crept toward the entryway to Bona's tower and the suite of rooms within as William and the guard enjoyed the bottle of ale.

Bona paced the floor of the living room of her apartment, her face flushed with anxiety. Bishop Branda sat in a chair nearby. When she heard a little knock at the door, she jumped in the air, startled. Bishop Branda went to the door and opened it. Ludovico Il Moro stood in front of him. The two men shook hands as Il Moro entered the apartment.

The duchess hurried to her brother-in-law, her last hope for tranquility. "Moro!" she exclaimed. She hugged him with all her strength. He released her and gave her a winning smile.

In the darkness of an adjacent room came another voice. "What is going on?" whined a small, sleepy voice. The boy entered the room, rubbing his eyes. He recognized Ludovico. "Uncle, uncle!" he cried, ran to his beloved Ludovico and embraced him.

"Gian Galeazzo, my fairest nephew. What a fine boy you have become," said Ludovico, patting him on the head. He bent down, picked up the boy and enfolded him in a warm embrace. "I am here to take care of you. Everything is going to be alright," He murmured in the boy's ear. The boy gave him another hug.

William and his uncle smiled as they watched the reunion of the Sforza family.

Moro smiled at his sister-in-law. "You must have used all your charms for Simonetta to allow you to keep the boy over night."

The beautiful young widow shrugged, doing her best to suppress a smile. It was, after all, her private secret.

Ludovico's small party descended the stairs of the tower. She met the two guards and ordered them to assist her. After a moment of uncertainty, they fell into step with her, Ludovico Il Moro, Galeazzo Sanseverino, William and Duke Gian Galeazzo. They hurried the short distance to the Rocca, entered the building and walked the short distance to the chancery office where they knew they would find First Secretary Simonetta.

At the door to the chancery, Il Moro turned to William. "It would be well for you to disappear now. Return to your quarters. Your life is precious to us both. It will be best if others know nothing of how much you have helped our cause."

William grinned. "I was thinking the same thing." The two men embraced. William hurried down the hall and disappeared around a corner.

In the candle-lit gloom of the chancery office, First Secretary Simonetta poured over reports from the eighty ambassadors the duchy employed. Though well past seventy, he worked with the zeal of a man half his age. He had devoted most of his adult life to the well-being of the duchy and had overseen the peaceful transition of government upon the deaths of two Sforza dukes. He intended for disorder to have no place in the duchy so long as he lived.

Even at this early hour of the morning, Bartolomeo Calco, the second secretary, and a few scribes worked nearby.

The First Secretary heard a knock at the door. "Enter," Simonetta muttered.

A chamberlain walked through the doorway. "Duchess Bona

wishes to speak to you, Messere."

"At this hour?" He frowned.

Bona of Savoy marched into the room. From the shadows behind her, Ludovico and Sanseverino appeared.

Simonetta's eyes danced from one to the other. "Chamberlain, call—"

With a deft move, Ludovico drew his dagger, backed the chamberlain against the wall and put the blade to his throat. The man went limp. Young Duke Gian Galeazzo followed Ludovico into the room.

Bona turned to Simonetta. "It is no use, First Secretary. It is Ludovico's time."

Glancing around himself, seeking help from one direction or another, Simonetta inched a hand to the hilt of his dagger. Ludovico gave him a deadly, commanding look. The old man froze in place. Then a look of defeat slowly crossed his face. He released his grip on his dagger and raised his hands.

Young Duke Gian Galeazzo stepped to the side of Ludovico, who placed an arm around the boy's shoulder. Ludovico's eyes softened.

Simonetta let out a great sigh, part despair and part relief. "The state of Milano welcomes you, Messere Ludovico. Everything will be done as you wish." He bowed slightly before Ludovico.

Behind Simonetta, Bartolomeo Calco put down his work, got to his feet and walked to the group, a smile on his face. "Bravo, Ludovico Il Moro." He began to clap his hands. "Bravo Il Moro."

Simonetta turned pale. "Bartolomeo—you—all this time?"

The Second Secretary nodded. "I am afraid so, my friend." Calco bit his lip. The decision had not been an easy one for him. "I know you will think I have betrayed you, but it is not so. Our loyalty is to Milano and the legitimate government of the duchy.

It is time for the reins of government to be placed in the hands of those who most deserve it."

Ludovico looked from one man to another and boomed out a laugh. "Well said, counselor."

Each secretary, scribe, and page began to applaud. Ludovico gave Calco a friendly clap on the shoulder. Savoring his triumph, he marched to the window.

In the courtyard below, a throng of people had gathered. Cries of "Sforza, Sforza!" and "Moro, Moro," drifted up to him. "The beggar wasted no time," he murmured, pleased. He turned to Calco. "You told us they would be loyal, and you appear to be right. We thank you for that." He gave Calco a little bow.

The Second Secretary gave him a little bow in return. Ludovico patted him on the shoulder, laughing and smiling.

As he gazed out on the throng, his glance came to rest on the face of the beautiful Lucia Marliani, who smiled up at him.

Simonetta turned to the chamberlain. "Give the order to all the troops— Ludovico has returned. Henceforth, he will act as *Reggente* for Duke Gian Galeazzo."

The elderly First Secretary leaned over to Ludovico and whispered, "The late duke, your brother, intended for you to govern as regent for the young duke, along with Trivulzio."

Ludovico patted the First Secretary on the cheek, gloating for a brief moment then turned his winning smile on Calco. "Minister Calco, our beloved brother thought well of you." Calco bowed once more. "Henceforth, you will assume the duties of First Secretary. I welcome you to my inner circle." The two men shook hands.

Simonetta eased over to Bona. "Most illustrious Duchess," he whispered, "do you not know what you have done? I will lose my head and you will lose your state." Bona looked away in stony silence.

Half an hour later, at a tavern near the Duomo, a thin, tired-looking soldier hurried in and collapsed. "Moro is back. He has the castello."

The young men in the tavern turned to him, stunned. Then they leapt to their feet, raising their flagons of wine. "To the Sforza! Long live the Sforza!"

One young man grabbed the pretty, dark-haired, dark-eyed serving girl. "Here's one for Ludovico!" He pulled down her blouse and planted a big kiss on her breast. A pained look crossed her face. The young men began to bang their flagons together. "Sforza! Sforza!"

People everywhere flocked to the streets. "Sforza returns! Moro is here."

The people of the city danced in the streets, all moving toward the Castello Sforzesco—the Castello di Porta Giovia.

The serving girl left the inn by the back door and hurried down an alley.

Hearing the shouting, Ludovico returned to one of the chancery windows. At the sight of him, a roar went up, sending a great wave of energy flowing through him. He opened the window and climbed through it onto a ledge. His figure silhouetted by the moonlight in the night air, he grasped the window frame and hung far out over the sill, dangling in mid-air over the moat below.

The crowd roared its approval. "Moro! Moro! Moro!" continued in waves throughout Milano.

"*Viva Milano!*" he shouted, waving. He noticed that Lucia had disappeared from sight.

"*Viva Milano! Viva Milano! Viva Milano! Viva Milano!*" They shouted back.

"Viva *la pace* Milano!" he yelled.

The crowd shouted back, "Viva la pace Milano! Pace! Pace!"

"Viva la casa di Sforza!" he bellowed at them.

"Viva la casa di Sforza! Viva la casa di Sforza! Viva la casa di Sforza!" they chanted.

"Viva l'Italia," he shouted back.

"Viva l'Italia! Viva Milano! Viva Sforza!"

He waved and they waved back. A great, expansive feeling filled his heart as he opened his arms to them. Their adoration lifted him up—he felt himself soaring over the countryside.

"Moro! Moro! Moro!" They chanted.

It was for this moment that he had waited, watched, and plotted. He climbed back inside the room, flushed with excitement. "Summon all the ministers," he said to Calco, who stood just inside the window. "Tonight we begin the greatest age in the history of our fair city—and our *Caro Italia.*"

One by one, the members of Simonetta's staff as well as Bona of Savoy's ladies-in-waiting filed into the Sala Ducale, where the business of state was conducted and the place where the duke slept.

Ludovico stood by his nephew, ten-year-old Gian Galeazzo, Duke of Milano. At his right hand, Bartolomeo Calco appeared. In the background stood Galeazzo Sanseverino. Il Moro gazed at several of Simonetta's chief bureaucrats—Second Secretary Marchesino Stanga; Chief of Antiquities and Public Works, Jacopo Antiquario; and Head Ambassador Erasmo Brasca.

His eyes then took in the young women of Bona's court, one silver-haired beauty in particular—the one with especially warm, dancing eyes. As he gazed at her, Cecilia Gallerani seemed to suppress a smile. The warmth of her eyes made him feel alive. A burning sensation shot through his body as he gazed at her. *Courage and beauty. High birth as well? A mistress? A consort, or more?*

He walked over to the ladies-in-waiting and greeted each one. "Such beautiful women. You are like those maidens of the sea who used to drive sailors mad as they sailed around the boot of Italia."

Each of the young women tittered at his flattering words. As he came to the silver-haired beauty, he stared into her eyes. A hint of a smile now flickered across her face.

She gave him a long, knowing look as if she saw his future unfolding before her. A loving sweetness came up from the depth of her being, emanating through her eyes and filling him with her devotion.

"You have succeeded, as we all hoped you would." Her voice had a lilt to it, as if each word were played on a *lyra de braccio*. He nodded. She smiled, her mouth widening until her fine small teeth gleamed in the candlelight. "You see before you a maiden of the sea, my lord—" she whispered. "...a Circe."

Ludovico laughed, then wrenched his gaze from her face and addressed the men and women gathered around him.

"Gentlemen and ladies of the court. We are all concerned for the well-being of our duchy." Ludovico examined each person's expression for sympathy or hostility. "Be assured that any man or woman who is loyal and works hard for the state will be amply rewarded. As of this moment, Bartolomeo Calco will be First Secretary, Jacopo Antiquario and Marchesino Stanga, my Second Secretaries."

The courtiers turned to look at each other in surprise, and relief. The continuity of government was assured.

"You have nothing to fear so long as you remain loyal to the crown of Milano. If any man does not serve well the duke of Milano or myself, I will not hesitate to dispatch him."

Ludovico motioned to the young duke at his elbow. Each man in the room bowed, and the young boy bowed in return. The introductions finished, the courtiers all left the room. Moro signaled for Calco and Galeazzo Sanseverino to remain.

Moro motioned them to a desk where he took out a piece of paper and began writing. Finishing, he sealed it and gestured to Sanseverino. "Notify your father that we wish him to return to Milano at once." Galeazzo Sanseverino's face broke out in a wide smile. "We will create a *condotta* which will give Capitano-Generale Roberto Sanseverino command of all Milanese troops as soon as he is available. Show this letter to anyone who questions your authority."

Then the new ruler of Milano turned to Calco. "As to the fate of Trivulzio...." He paused, lost in thought. "I have the highest regard for his military prowess." The room fell silent. "On the other hand, he and Simonetta were close." Again he trailed off, wondering, weighing. Finally he turned to Calco. "Order Capitano Trivulzio to return to Milano. We will discuss his fate."

Calco bowed. "It will be done immediately, *Illustrissimo.*"

Ludovico savored the word, the first time he had been addressed as *Illustrissimo,* the word reserved for the most powerful and most potent person in the duchy. It warmed him, like bathing in a pool of honeyed nectar.

Shortly thereafter, Ludovico, Galeazzo, Bona and the young duke walked to up to back to Bona's chambers. Climbing the stairs, Ludovico entered. He embraced his nephew, Gian Galeazzo. "Now you are in the hands of those who love you."

The boy threw his arms around his uncle. "I always hoped you would come."

"And so I have." Ludovico put his arms around the boy and kissed his forehead. "And nothing will ever pry me away from you." Ludovico escorted the boy to his bedroom. The boy's mother watched, her face wreathed in smiles, as Gian Galeazzo climbed into his bed.

"Since we do not yet know whom to trust," counseled Il Moro, "I am ordering everyone out of these chambers tonight except for you, the boy and myself." He turned to the boy. "If you become lonely—or fearful...." Ludovico drew on a cord at the side of the bed. "...just pull this cord, and I shall come to your aid." The boy nodded and pulled up the covers.

"Good night, Uncle."

"Good night, Gian Galeazzo." Ludovico leaned down and kissed the boy on the forehead once more.

In the Corte Ducale's suite of rooms occupied by royal counselor Bishop Branda, Count of Castiglione, the elderly statesman sipped a glass of fine Lombard wine and stared into the fire.

Across the table from the bishop, William sat in a chair, leaning back, also sipping a glass of wine.

"We have done exceedingly well, Nephew," mused the old man. He raised his glass and toasted Il Moro for the umpteenth time that night.

William raised his glass as well. "We have indeed, Uncle. We have indeed."

"Who knows what the future hold for us, but especially you—with your youth and energy?"

By now the two men were tired and a little drunk. The hours preceding Il Moro's triumph had been tense and uncertain for each of them. Now, with a successful conclusion to all their efforts, they were exhausted, yet filled with a sense of hope—for themselves, for the court, for the city and for the state.

"Yes, how I wish I was twenty years younger," the elderly man mused. "Or even fifteen." He and his nephew chuckled at the concessions. The bishop took one last, long sip of wine and got to his feet. "Now it is time for an old man to rest." He put his wine glass on the table and sauntered in his bedroom. "Good night, Nephew."

William remained at the table content to savor the night's work, wondering what the future held and hoping for a happy conclusion to his attraction to Cecilia Gallerani. He felt that Il Moro would surely help him in this effort. He got to his feet and went to a window, peered outside for a moment then slumped down into the small alcove below the window. He put his feet up and folded his arms across his chest, savoring the events of the past two days, reliving each moment with a resounding sense of satisfaction. Soon he was fast asleep.

# PART II

# 11

## *Trivulzio Surprised*

*A Military Encampment*
**FIRENZE, ITALIA**
January, 1480

A cold wind blew through the encampment as dawn broke on the tiny Milanese army set up on the Arno River near Firenze. Men in tattered clothing huddled around small fires. For most, the cold seemed much too bitter for sleep. They sat close to the warmth of the fires, blankets drawn tightly around themselves, sharpening the edges of their pikes and swords. Clattering hooves in the distance warned of fast-approaching horses. The soldiers glanced at one another. Perhaps Trivulzio returning from meeting with Lorenzo de' Medici? Or the forces of Pope Sixtus IV?

The men reached for their pikes as a lookout rode through the camp. "Trivulzio returns!" he shouted. "Trivulzio returns!"

In an instant the half-asleep soldiers staggered to their feet, all thoughts of cold melted away like snowflakes on hot coals. Trivulzio! Their leader. The finest, most courageous soldier Milano had seen since the death of Duke Francesco. His feats were legendary among his soldiers.

"Have you heard how Trivulzio scaled the wall at Vercelli and defeated the Burgundian army, all by himself?" Each new recruit was told the story of his determination.

Trivulzio, the captain of the Ducal Guard, rode into camp, sitting tall on his horse, a grim smile on his face, jaw thrust forward. With GioAntonio Rebucco at his side, Trivulzio brought his horse to a stop and gazed with affection at each man.

"*Uomini di Milano*, it is done. I have been chosen to head the armies of Milano…and Firenze."

The men returned his gaze with uncertainty, understanding nothing.

Trivulzio smiled. "Your rations will improve. New clothing will be provided."

The men broke out into broad smiles.

"With our Milanese forces now combined with those of Firenze, the pope's troops will cross themselves over and over, praying they will get back to Roma safely, and the forces of King Alfonso will scurry back to Napoli like rats."

The cold, tired men began to wave their pikes.

"You will be home for Easter."

The ragged army broke out in cheers, and a chant began. "Trivulzio! Trivulzio! Trivulzio!"

In the midst of the shouting and cheering, a rider galloped into camp. He found an officer and handed him a dispatch with the ducal seal on it. The lieutenant hurried to Trivulzio and saluted. The commander eyed the seal and motioned Rebucco to break the seal and read the message.

As Trivulzio's close friend read the dispatch, his shoulders slumped. "I do not believe this. It simply cannot be true."

"You cannot believe what?" growled Gian Giacomo.

Rebucco looked up, a sick look spread across his face. "Simonetta." He struggled to speak. "Out."

"Que?" Trivulzio took a step toward Rebucco, his brow furrowed.

"Ludovico Il Moro Sforza now rules Milano," Rebucco whispered. He handed the dispatch to Trivulzio. "The little duke has made him regent. Simonetta is a prisoner and you." He shook his head.

Trivulzio's jaw clamped shut like the bottom half of an iron mask. "The devil you say," he cursed through clenched teeth, and turned to the young messenger. "What in the name of God happened?"

The boy recoiled in fear. "The duchess—" Sweat poured off his forehead. "The jealousy of Tassino...of the First Secretary's power...played a part, or so I have heard." Trivulzio waved him off, handed the dispatch back to Rebucco and motioned for him to read aloud.

Rebucco began to read silently. A great sigh escaped from his lips. Then he read the last line of the dispatch.

> *"Ludovico Sforza, Regent to Duke Gian Galeazzo Sforza,*
> *Commands Capitano Trivulzio to return to Milano at once—"*

Trivulzio's lifelong friend looked up at Gian Giacomo, an expression of dread in his eyes. "My stomach is tied in knots, Capitano—"

"Damn Sforza trickery!" Trivulzio's eyes blazed with fury. "And Simonetta's stupidity. I lose my dream and perhaps my head!" His voice choked with emotion. "Tricked." His thick shoulders sagged. Then he stood erect and declared, "If I could draw a line down every street in Milano, ending in the figure of Ludovico sitting in his chambers in the castello, do you know what word would echo through the streets?"

Rebucco looked bewildered.

Trivulzio laughed. "Betrayal. That is the one word we would hear spoken over and over. Betrayal. His trickery will haunt him to the end of his days. And Milano as well." He motioned for the lieutenant and GioAntonio to follow him. The three men disappeared into Trivulzio's tent.

In her dingy little hovel down by the canals, the young servant girl from the Crown Inn grabbed up her few belongings, took her fourteen-year-old brother by the hand and pushed him out the door and into the sunlight of a beautiful, crisp January afternoon.

"Why are we leaving, Carlotta?" the boy asked his sister.

"Shhh. I will tell you soon, Antonio." She marched him up the alley and into a street.

Just then a dozen soldiers galloped past them. Carlotta, the young girl, got a fleeting glimpse of the leader, a man with steely grey eyes and a jutting jaw.

"Trivulzio," she murmured to herself as she mounted an ox cart and pulled her brother up beside her.

Antonio, hearing her words, looked up at her. "Trivulzio?"

She smiled grimly as she clucked the oxen forward. "Trivulzio. A great leader. He rides back to Milano—perhaps to his death."

"Why, Carlotta?" asked the boy.

"Well, after the death of Galeazzo, Simonetta made Trivulzio guardian to the duke's son, Gian Galeazzo, who is about your age. Now the Sforza brothers have gotten rid of Simonetta and one of them, Ludovico Sforza, made himself guardian to Gian Galeazzo. Trivulzio is in danger."

"Are we in danger, Carlotta?" Antonio was fascinated with the story. His sister shrugged. She hurried her little brother into a waiting cart and whipped the oxen into motion.

"Keep quiet," the old crone in the back of the wagon yawned, awakening from her nap. "You fill the boy's head with strange stories and his heart with fear."

Antonio smiled. "I am not afraid."

In this way, the young son and daughter, as well as the mother of the deceased court painter, Alessandro Grumello, left their home near the canals of the Navaglio and headed south to Napoli and the waiting arms of her family near Otranto on the Adriatic Ocean. Fearing that a return of the Sforza family to power meant a return to the bizarre behavior of Galeazzo Maria, the three members of the Grumello family left behind the stench of Milano far behind in favor of open farmland and ocean breezes.

In the late afternoon breeze, Milanese troops marched back and forth across the courtyard of the castello. Capitano dal Fiesco reviewed the troops, shaking his head in disgust.

At his elbow, William stood watching the soldiers.

"So, Master William, soon you will be playing your instrument for our new regent?" dal Fiesco asked. "Life returns to the court of Milano."

Careful not to reveal his part in the coup that had just taken place, William did not smile. He merely shrugged. "I look forward to this new page in the history of Milano, Capitano. On it will be written many wonderful things, if that is what you are asking." He wondered if he sounded like any other court sycophant— optimistic, but a little too much performance beneath the good feelings. He hoped so.

"Ah, you court people," dal Fiesco sighed.

Galeazzo Sanseverino, the younger son of Roberto Sanseverino, galloped up to William and dal Fiesco, dismounted and bounded up the steps of the reviewing platform, a smile on his face. Towering above the others, eighteen-year old Galeazzo resembled his father in his height and light skin, but had a grace absent in the elder Sanseverino. "William! God love you!" He exclaimed, shaking William's hand. He turned to dal Fiesco. "What think you, Capitano?"

"Of the troops?" dal Fiesco asked, gazing out at the soldiers. "For the most part, a poor lot. The government spent little on the defense of the castello. Trivulzio's troops in Firenze are probably much better."

Galeazzo Sanseverino nodded in agreement.

At that moment, Ascanio Sforza, youngest of the brothers to Ludovico Il Moro, galloped up and dismounted. "Good afternoon, my friends."

Dal Fiesco bowed to young Sforza, as did Sanseverino and William. "Ah, Bishop Ascanio," purred dal Fiesco. "Congratulations are in order. Have you spoken to your brother, Ludovico?"

"That is the purpose of my visit," smiled the young man who had kept out of sight until the castello had been wrested from the hands of Cicco Simonetta and fully secured.

"The Sforza shall rule for a hundred years," added Capitano dal Fiesco. Such flattery was uncomfortable for him, yet he knew that to sing the praises of Ludovico was important.

A wide smile spread across Galeazzo Sanseverino's handsome, laughing face.

"Ah, Capitano dal Fiesco..." Ascanio grasped the man's hand. "...my thanks to you for I have heard that you held the forces of the Marques of Mantua at bay until Ludovico's plan bore fruit."

"I had little choice, and honestly, less faith." Dal Fiesco's mouth twisted up in a slight half-grin. "Moro is a very clever young man. But never did I believe that he would win over Duchess Bona or her lover, Tassino, to our cause."

"Moro knew how desperately Tassino sought rewards for his family," Galeazzo smiled. "He hoped his father would become guardian of the treasury, and Simonetta stood in the way."

Dal Fiesco glanced up at Ascanio. "Your brother will bring great things to the duchy of Milano."

Ascanio did a little dance and threw his hands in the air. "No more exile! No more worry about currying favor with the First

Secretary. An easy chair, a few books and some wine—that is all I ask." He walked across the parade ground in the direction of the rocca and the Corte Ducale.

"Too soft," dal Fiesco muttered once Ascanio was out of earshot.

Galeazzo nodded. "And Ludovico? Soft like Ascanio? Or brave and wise, like his father? Or like Galeazzo Maria, cruel and stupid beyond measure?"

Dal Fiesco watched Ascanio disappear beneath the portal that led to the Corte Ducale. "Time will tell." He turned toward Galeazzo, sizing up him up for a moment. "You will do well at this court. If Duke Galeazzo valued a man for the strength of his wrist and his stomach, Reggente Moro appears to esteem the man with the gift of humor, courtesy, grace—a man who remains observant at all times, like Rolando and the knights who surrounded Charlemagne."

William chuckled at hearing dal Fiesco wax poetic. A lot of what the English would call "tossing around hog droppings" would be flying around the castle for the next few weeks until Ludovico settled on which families had proven most loyal to him and which would be exiled. He imagined that Trivulzio would be hard hit—that his lofty ambitions would not fare well with a rival who was younger, smarter and more visionary than Trivulzio, if less experienced in warfare.

Galeazzo Sanseverino also smiled. He intended just what dal Fiesco had observed—to lead Ludovico's court in celebrating the ancient courtly traditions of grace, eloquence, and joy. A fine dancer, a superb tournament knight, a witty member of any group, and a man of courage in any battle, Galeazzo intended to exercise his considerable will power in bringing the court of Milano to life. Bowing to Capitano dal Fiesco ever so slightly, Galeazzo turned and walked away.

Following the young giant with his eyes, William sensed that Ludovico would be far more entertained by the young warrior than by himself, a foreigner, a musician, a 'nobody.' He sighed. *Oh, well. Ferrara and Naples were again adding members to their choirs. Why not?*

Sitting in the Sala del Asse reading correspondence, Ludovico glanced up as Pontremoli entered. "Bishop Ascanio," announced the older man. Ludovico nodded and Pier Francesco disappeared, returning in a moment with Ascanio.

"*Mio fratello!*" Ludovico embraced the younger Sforza. "A wonderful day, is it not?"

"A day to be relished!" smiled Ascanio. Pier Francesco returned with glasses of wine for each of the three of them. Together, they raised their glass. "To the reign of Ludovico, visionary heir to our father!" toasted Ascanio, grinning from ear to ear. "A great day in the history of our family—in the history of our duchy, and of Italia." They drank up.

Ludovico reached out and took his brother's hand, released it, and raised his glass of wine again. "To our beloved brothers, Ottaviano and Sforza Maria, who died fighting for our place in the long line of our forebears who ruled this *stato magnificato.*" Ludovico shook his head with an almost childlike awe as he soaked up the truth of the moment—every stone, every blade of grass, as well as the hearts and minds of the thousands of Milanese within his sight belonged to him, to do with as he pleased.

Ascanio gazed at his brother, who seemed lost in thought. "If Galeazzo Maria took this same opportunity as license to glut his senses, our father took it as a solemn responsiblity."

"Such understanding does you honor, brother," smiled Ludovico, raising his glass once again. "And now I offer a toast to you, dear Ascanio. Henceforth you shall be known…" Ludovico drained his glass. "…as Archbishop Ascanio with all the rights and duties thereof."

Ascanio's face flushed with excitement.

"And one day—" Ludovico leaned forward, his eyes narrowing, sweeping his hand before him as if the world were being laid at Ascanio's feet. "—another hat, one with a more appealing color."

"*Cardinale…*" murmured the younger Sforza, rolling the words around in his mouth, as if each syllable were a sweet-tasting grape. "A triumph for *la familia.*"

A knock at the door interrupted their celebration. "Enter!" Ludovico commanded.

William Castle walked in and bowed. "You sent for me, Regent Moro?"

Ludovico motioned him to a chair. "William, you must know that this is a great day for *la familia Sforza*, for Ascanio and myself." Il Moro and Ascanio took a seat. Pontremoli retreated to a corner.

"I understand," the musician smiled. "Could it be any more wonderful?"

"*Essactamente!*" Ludovico poured a glass of wine for William and handed it to him. "We toast our success and honor you for your loyalty, your ability to stay in the good graces of all concerned. You have rare talents. We plan to make use of them. You do honor to your family, particularly our most loyal friend, Bishop Branda." He raised his glass and drank. William and Ascanio did the same.

Red-faced from a little wine and much praise, William stared at the floor. "I…I…thank you. I did what I felt was the right thing to do."

Il Moro got to his feet and paced the room. Moro pursed his

lips, then spoke. "From Bellinzona in the North to the shores of Sicilia in the South, we contend with families that control and distribute the wealth of Italia as they please. For us to accomplish our ends, we must control who has the power in each state, where we can. Venezia will never be our friend. Firenze will always be our friend. The Neapolitani...well, they are Spanish; they are inconstant."

Ascanio and William saw what appeared to be a new face of the young ruler—the sober visionary who looked far into the future.

Ascanio watched the rays of light through the window play with the angles and the filigree of his cut-glass goblet.

"If we control the papacy," continued Ludovico, "we control the destiny of the peninsula."

"The papacy?" Ascanio's eyes filled with wonder. "A week ago, you slept on the ground, wondering if you would survive the night." He chuckled. "Now you think about the papacy—and how to control it for years to come, eh?"

Ludovico's eyes burned with intensity yet his smile remained soft and amused. He ambled to the window and gazed out over the city below him. "Nothing is to hold us back from our highest ambitions, *fratello mio,*" he murmured in a half-whisper. "To rule Milano has always been our destiny." Il Moro approached Ascanio and William, laying a hand on the shoulders of each man. "Fix your gaze on the stars, *amici,* for the comet's path is the one we shall follow."

"I cannot even begin to guess what you are talking about," replied Ascanio in an amused, mocking tone, for he knew only too well what Ludovico had in mind.

"Ascanio the First—Pontiff of all Christendom," whispered Ludovico.

The youth grinned and leaned toward his brother. "...and Ludovico I, king of Northern Italia." His eyes glittered as he savored the ring of his words.

William could hardly believe his ears. Here in this room the first brick had been laid for a history-making change in regimes, more momentous than he could have imagined. *Will Ludovico be able to realize such vast dreams?* He studied Ludovico for a moment. *God in heaven, he certainly has the look of someone who can do so.*

He thought for a moment about the past—the civilizations long gone that had died for one reason or another, usually for lack of a vision that would secure the well-being and yearnings of all the people contained within its borders. *Can Ludovico protect his duchy from the wolves that gnaw at its edges?* William had no answer to that question, but suspected the next few years would provide him with a visible answer. He hoped Il Moro would be up to the task.

Ludovico walked the two men to the door of a side room. "We will talk more of this later. Meanwhile, keep your ears open. I am expecting Gian Giacomo any moment." He pursed his lips. "He has some explaining to do if he hopes to keep his head on his shoulders." The two men went inside the room. Ludovico kept the door to the room slightly ajar.

As he walked inside, William pondered the question— what can Il Moro do about Gian Giacomo Trivulzio? On the one hand, a valued and highly effective military man but on the other, a faithful advisor and friend to the disgraced and displaced Simonetta... as well as the arch enemy of General Roberto Sanseverino, Il Moro's friend. *Time would tell.*

In the vast courtyard of the castle, Capitano Gian Giacomo

Trivulzio and a small band of Milanese soldiers cantered beneath the main portal and entered the castle's parade grounds.

Standing near the entry portal, Ibieto dal Fiesco glanced in the direction of the captain of the ducal guard. "Now there is a man whose life hangs by a thread."

Galeazzo turned and observed Trivulzio. He shook his head. "Ludovico will not rush to punish him."

Dal Fiesco glanced at the young officer, then turned his gaze once more to Trivulzio who cantered around the parade ground and headed toward the Corte Ducale.

The older officer leaned toward young Sanseverino. "Follow Ludovico, Galeazzo. Learn all you can from him. But remember this…." He put a fatherly hand on the young man's shoulder. "Cunning in a world of mistrust survives only if the sword behind it is strong."

Galeazzo gave the older man a slight bow. "I shall remember."


Arms folded across his chest, Ludovico stood at a window of the Sala des Asse, gazing at imagined mountains to the north of the city.

Pontremoli entered the chamber and announced, "Capitano Trivulzio, Lanze Spezzate."

Ludovico Il Moro nodded. Pontremoli disappeared, returning with Trivulzio, who bowed to the man who had replaced him as regent. The soldier's face looked tired and heavy.

"*Buon giorno, Capitano.*" Ludovico waved Trivulzio to a chair, noticing the soldier's bloodshot eyes. "You appear to have slept little."

"*Buon giorno, Illustrissimo Messere,*" replied the soldier. "We were in battle with the pope when the news—the welcome news of your return to Milano—came to us."

Ludovico noticed that Trivulzio's face and body betrayed no fear, no concern, no caution, although his life hung on the next few words he uttered.

He searched Trivulzio's eyes for a clue to the man's feelings and intentions. *If he betrays even a hint of ambition, jealousy, pride— anything other than a desire to serve the duchy, I shall hang him alongside old Simonetta.* But the captain's eyes remained dark, fathomless pools— neither hostile nor inviting. *Dangerous, yes—sinister, no. Certainly a good man to have on one's side.*

Ludovico broke the silence. "We know that you have served our family well, Capitano." The regent considered the value of this man so beloved by the soldiers of Milano. *To whom does he owe his loyalties?*

"Thank you, Messere." The captain observed the regent closely. After all, Ludovico knew quite well how reliable a friend he had been to Simonetta. "I look forward to continued service to the duchy."

"That is what we are here to discuss," answered Sforza pointedly. "The duchy needs the allegiance of all the great families."

"No one opposes the Sforza." Trivulzio betrayed no emotion with his words.

"Your prowess on the field of battle is legendary," Ludovico probed, "and any oath of loyalty to which you swear is taken with great seriousness."

"I have sworn fidelity to the duke of Milano. That sacred trust has never changed, nor will it." Trivulzio's eyes were hooded and wary, for clearly Ludovico held the soldier's life or death in his hands. Trivulzio sat and listened. Usually he was in command of every situation. Now he was not. It was time to listen.

*How easily I could have killed him.* A voice spoke to Trivulzio, deep inside his brain. *Had Simonetta but listened to me and allowed me to take command of Duke Ercole's troops, I would have defeated Moro in Tortona without difficulty, or dispatched him in the tent when the two of us were negotiating. Moro's troops quaked in their boots at the sight of me. It was all within my grasp!* Trivulzio sighed. Old Simonetta wanted no violence. And the Milanese troops in Firenze certainly needed his leadership. *But the price to be paid—my head?!*

"Your lordship is a man of great *virtu* and *potere*," Trivulzio said. "I would honored to serve you and the duke." Trivulzio bowed slightly. *Bah!* He raged in his head. *This is a sick, stupid little game. Yet, a game of life and death it is.*

Ludovico stared into Trivulzio's eyes, making every effort to discern how the soldier felt about Fortune's betrayal. But Trivulzio showed no dispirited emotion. *Perhaps he is simply the first-rate military man that all in Milano knows him to be.* Ludovico extended his hand in friendship. "Thank you for coming to see me, *Capitano*. You need rest. I urge you to return to your home in Mesocco, enjoy the warmth of your family and regain your energy. Your wife, Marguerite, is a fine woman."

The soldier grasped the hand and returned the firm grip. *So Il Moro has not yet decided my fate,* he said to himself. *So be it.* He tapped his heart two times in salute. Moro returned the salute as Trivulzio turned on his heel and walked out the door. For the moment he lived; his head remained firmly attached to his shoulders.

Behind the door in the anteroom, William listened to Trivulzio's words. Ludovico had asked him and Ascanio to stay for a reason. Without doubt, between the three of them, they held Trivulzio's life in their hands.

In the flickering candlelight of the hallway outside Ludovico's chambers, Trivulzio murmured to Rebucco, "Our heads are safe for now." Trivulzio put an arm around his friend. "What's more, I wager I shall be Duca di Milano within the year."

Rebucco grinned.

In the antechamber where William and Ascanio sat, Pontremoli peeked his head into the room and nodded to them. The two men got to their feet and walked into the Sala del Asse.

Ludovico motioned for them to take a seat, then leaned back in his chair and nodded toward a map of Lombardy and Emilio-Reggio. "As soon as we can get the pope and King Ferrante to stop fighting the Florentines, we need a military force to go to Parma. The de Rossi family has been at the throats of other noble families there. We need a force to go there and make peace—bring back de Rossi's head if necessary." He turned to Ascanio and to William. "What do you think? Can we trust Trivulzio? Or Captain-General Sanseverino for that matter?" He sat down and gazed at his two friends.

Neither William nor Ascanio offered an option.

Moro threw his hands in the air. "Very well. It is a matter for us to think about." He got to his feet and nodded toward the anteroom. William and Ascanio returned to the adjoining room.

Others would be interviewed this day, all of whose loyalty had to be questioned.

The Castello of Porta Giovia—with its thirty-foot-thick, red-brick walls —offered protection against almost anything man or nature could throw at it. Inside the courtyard, odors of horse manure and hay filled the air, along with the midday smells of vegetables and beef simmering in large vats just inside the open kitchen doors.

Roberto Sanseverino, newly arrived from Venice, slid his vast, dark bulk from his horse and hit the ground with a surprisingly light touch. With slitlike eyes and a face as flat and forbidding as a fortress wall, he strode over to his son Galeazzo and dal Fiesco, welcoming them with affectionate hugs. The Captain-General caught a glimpse of a smiling Trivulzio astride his horse, circling the parade ground on his way out of the castello, Rebucco at his side. The general's eyes narrowed, sensing that his enemy had somehow won Ludovico's favor in jousting for positions of influence at court.

The older Sanseverino frowned and turned to the other two men. "How is it that Trivulzio always lands on his feet?" He shook his head at the sight of Trivulzio, returning the waves and salutes of the Milanese soldiers marching in the courtyard. "He is more popular than anyone in Milano, save Ludovico, and last week he was the enemy of the Sforzas." The captain general grunted his disapproval. "Duke Francesco would never have tolerated such arrogance." The others muttered their agreement.

General Roberto gave each of them a wary smile, remounted his horse and clicked the beast around the parade ground as he headed for the Corte Ducale and the chambers of the regent.

At the door to the Sala del Asse, General Sanseverino knocked. It opened and he faced Pontremoli who smiled.

"*Buona sera*, Pier Francesco," the general muttered. "Please tell the regent that I am here and would like to confer with him." Pontremoli retreated into the room.

Inside, Ludovico got to his feet. "Welcome, welcome, my friend!" he declared, embracing the older man.

The eyes of the tough-looking soldier crinkled up in a wry, cunning, half-smile. "My congratulations, Messere Ludovico. You have achieved the impossible without the exchange of a single blow."

Ludovico Il Moro's eyes filled with good humor. "Tassino's ambitions were well-known, and Duchess Bona's yearnings as well. It took no great cleverness to turn them to our purposes."

Sanseverino gave him another wry smile. "It appears as if you are relishing the evening meal as the rest of us sit down to breakfast." Ludovico laughed. The condottiere cleared his throat. "You know, *Illustrissimo*, I am not a political man—" Ludovico suppressed a smile. "But we must speak to the fate of First Secretary Simonetta…and the other who served as *Reggente* to the duke, Captain Trivulzio."

Il Moro gazed at the soldier with cool, searching eyes.

"He has many friends in Milano," the soldier continued. "Each carries a spear easily planted in your side." The general shifted his vast bulk in his chair and leaned toward the youthful ruler. "Your father would never hesitate to sacrifice the life of one man to secure a stable realm for the many."

Noting the icy edge to the man's voice, Ludovico listened for the meaning behind the words. *So he brings up my father who married into the ruling family of the Visconti only to have to fight his way into Milano to claim his legacy—ah, perhaps Sanseverino has his own designs on the Duchy of Milano.* Ludovico smiled at the officer.

"There is truth in what you say, my friend." He stopped and turned to Sanseverino. "However, the same might be said of my appointments —Calco, Stanga and Antiquario. He stared at the soldier quite intently. "The integrity of these men is not in question."

Sanseverino straightened himself in his chair. "No, of course not, Illustrissimo." For the first time, his voice had a pleasant, even humble note to it. "Were Simonetta executed, and Trivulzio exiled, a clear message would be sent to everyone that the regent is a man of great *potere,* and he who would think of rebellion or assassination would do so at his own great peril." The soldier suppressed a smile. *Simonetta, his enemy, humiliated, vanquished, perhaps soon to be executed.* Yet his face betrayed no emotion. "Trivulzio is a man of enormous ambition." He shrugged. "Of course, I need not remind his Excellency of that fact." He opened his hands to the son of Duke Francesco whom he had followed well and faithfully for many years. "I can only advise caution in dealing with a man with such yearning."

Moro got to his feet, shook hands with the soldier and gave him a warm smile. "Thank you, Captain General. I will give your wise advice careful consideration."

Pontremoli appeared and showed Sanseverino to the door. The soldier bowed in Ludovico's direction and disappeared into the dark hallway. Ludovico stared at the open door and the darkness beyond, well aware of the forces swirling around him, each member of the court uncertain about his or her place, including the intense hatred between Simonetta and Sanseverino and the fierce ambitions of Trivulzio and his faction. The general was quite right—Trivulzio bore watching. Any hint of disloyalty or excessive ambition and Trivulzio must reined in, or more.

*Intrigue—playing one faction against another—is the game you have enjoyed most since childhood, like throwing meat to dogs on a tether to see which one will reach farthest and hardest for the prize. Trivulzio and Sanseverino. Each will fight hard to rule Milano in the years to come.* Ludovico glanced upward. Strange shadows played across the ceiling. *Keep them busy and away from Milano,* he reminded himself. *As your brother did with you.* He smiled with satisfaction, ignoring the chill wind blowing down the hall and into his chambers.

In the small room where the two of them sat, William faced Ascanio. "How do we judge Trivulzio against Sanseverino? How do we make such judgments?" William's tone of voice was light-hearted, but there was an edge of honesty to his voice. "I would hope no one would lose his head."

Ascanio gazed out the window then put a finger to his nose, flattening it, and a thumb and middle finger to each cheekbone, pulling down the flesh of each cheek. "I am Roberto Sanseverino and I wish to be duke of Milano." The picture and sounds were completely absurd—and very much like Sanseverino.

William doubled up in silent laughter. He had never known this side of Ascanio.

Dropping his hands from his face, Ascanio became deadly serious. "If anything happened to the Captain-General, his many friends—Pusterla, Borromeo, Marliani, even your uncle, would announce their unhappiness in the same way that Galeazzo learned of it—at the point of a dagger." Ascanio half-shrugged and half-laughed. "Then where would we be? Down to the last brother?" Again he raised and lowered his shoulders with a laugh. "The same is true of Trivulzio." He shrugged. "One brother," he said, almost to himself.

William pretended not to notice the last statement. But he was shocked. One day after achieving this enormous victory, Ascanio himself seemed to be calculating his chances of succeeding to the throne of the Duchy of Milano. It was a painful moment of understanding, seeing more of the depth of men's ambitions—even his own—and how dreams and reality can become indistinguishable. It left him disillusioned and fascinated.

Not far away, in the rochetta, the Castello's inner fortress, Antonio Tassino, the carver at the royal table who had worked his way into Bona's affections and her bed, raced up the stairs and pounded on the door of the Sala de Tesoro.

A guardsman appeared from the shadows and blocked his way. "Go no farther, sir."

"The duchess wishes me to bring the Balabass ruby to her!" Tassino's voice was shrill and excited. He tried to push his way past the guard, who was immovable. "She wants it now!"

From a room to the side of the treasury, a small man with long white hair limped over. "What's going on here?"

The guard turned to him. "Messere Eustachio, Messere Tassino has indicated—"

"The duchess wants her ruby," interrupted Tassino.

The fiery little Eustachio drew himself up to his full height. "You tell the duchess that I served the duke, his lordship, Galeazzo Maria, who died three years ago this month. When her son Gian Galeazzo is invested duke of Milano, I will serve him." He drew his sword and shook it in Tassino's face. "No one, but no one, goes in that door, unless he is the duke of Milano."

"Stupid little scum," Tassino seethed. "You were to be replaced." He ran down the stairs and disappeared from sight.

That evening, when all was quiet, Il Moro walked the halls of the Corte Ducale. He came at last to a small room which he seldom visited in recent years, a room in which he had spent many happy hours talking to his father.

Il Moro entered the small room, lit by two candles—a study lined with suits of armor placed in niches in each wall. The armor belonged to the Visconti dukes—his grandfather Filippo Maria and his great-grandfather Bernabo Visconti. Two other niches contained a suit of armor in one and a ceremonial helmet and shield in the other. All had belonged to his father. The ceremonial helmet and shield displayed, in low relief, a great battle in the manner of the Romans.

Bending to one knee in front of his father's battle dress, Ludovico folded his hands together in prayer and closed his eyes. Opening them, he gazed at the visor of the suit of armor as if his father were contained within. "Solemnly, I do swear to uphold and defend the body and the spirit of our beloved Milano against all who would take our liberty from us. This I swear on my life." He continued to stare at the helmet as if to bring his father to life, long enough for the old duke to guide his son through the trials that would come soon enough.

*"No one—nothing will ever take this away from me,"* he murmured in a barely audible voice. A hard, cold, intense look crossed his face. *The duchy is mine, and I shall give it up for no one or nothing on this earth.*

# 12
## *In Search of Direction*

*Corte Ducale*
**CASTELLO DI PORTA GIOVIA**
MILANO, ITALIA
February, 1480

L udovico stepped into the cool sunlight of the small courtyard of the Corte Ducale, strolled to a bench and sat. The regent motioned for Calco, who had been following close behind, to sit down beside him. "*Per favore,* you were saying—"

The minister took a big gulp of air. "Venice is Milano's sworn and eternal enemy. The Venetians hunger for more territory. Its desire for more markets for its goods is unending. Unfortunately for them, the Turks have blunted their expansion to the East, so...."

"My father stayed on good terms with the Venetians," Ludovico recalled.

"The Venetians feared him. They hoped a weak ruler would succeed your grandfather, Filippo Maria. However, after Filippo Maria married into the Panigarola family, your father had the strength to bend the duchy to his will once old Duke Filippo Maria was out of the way. The Venetians were mightily vexed."

"You know this how, Minister?" Ludovico probed.

Beads of sweat stood out on the little man's forehead. "I cannot say, Governatore."

Ludovico recoiled. "You cannot say? Either you are ill-informed and have no answer, or you are protecting your sources. Which one is it, Minister?" There was more than a hint of annoyance in his eyes.

"I do not have all the answers at my fingertips, *Illustrissimo*. But I will endeavor to get them for you within the hour."

Ludovico eyed him closely. "Not only will you have the information I seek, you will have it on the tip of your tongue at all times. Is that clear?" Calco nodded. "Whatever information you deliver must be verified by a second source before it is given to me. I encourage rumors, half-truths, and innuendos—but they must be separated from facts, conversations, statements."

"Very well, *Eccellenza*. I will instruct the staff of the chancery."

"And all others who work for us. We will meet again at three o'clock this afternoon," the young regent instructed.

Calco bowed and hurried away.

As Calco disappeared in the direction of the rochetta where he kept his offices, Ludovico Il Moro saw William Castle standing a respectful distance away. Il Moro motioned him over. William approached and started to bow. Ludovico raised his hands with a smile. "No, no, *amico*." He extended a hand and spoke in a soft voice. "You are too much a friend to treat me with undue respect. But for your efforts, we might be floating in that moat outside the wall—with our heads stuck on a pike."

William shivered at the thought. They shook hands and sat down. "I'm happy it ended as it did, *Eccellenza*."

"Are you? Well, I truly hope so. You took an enormous risk on our behalf." He was silent for a moment. "Simonetta treated you well?"

William shifted uncomfortably in his chair. "He was like a father to me."

"Yet you betrayed his trust?" Ludovico squinted at the young man.

"I...it seemed...when I—" the musician stammered. "It is true. I did. Do I feel less honorable? I knew that sooner or later I would have to choose sides. While Simonetta appeared harmless, Trivulzio was far more threatening. The choice was simple—would I want Trivulzio to rule Milano, or yourself?"

"Trivulzio was more threatening?"

"So far as I could tell, yes. Although he probably did not make any significant decisions, still he had an impact. Whenever I appeared before the First Secretary, Trivulzio was always present."

Moro nodded his head up and down. "An important piece of information, my friend. You have been of great value to us. You have every right to expect a reward. A substantial one. You have but to name it." The musician fell silent. "Don't be hesitant, amico. I know that Simonetta offered you Castello di Vezio in Varenna for the services you rendered him." William was surprised by this revelation, even a little shaken. "Perhaps I should offer you another castle nearby, Felino, near Parma, perhaps. Would that be the proper act of gratitude?"

"Varenna and Felino—" William turned the word over in his mouth several times. "Both are places of unsurpassed beauty." His words came out slowly, as if to do otherwise would appear greedy. "*Certamente,* each of us would like to believe that he can return to some place that offers him nourishment and safety."

Ludovico smiled. "Then it is done."

"But more than obtaining a fine piece of property, the greater reward would be to help build something here in the ducato, Eccellenza—perhaps help you rebuild the court in some way, bring back the musicians, the dancers, the artists who fled during the regency of Trivulzio and Simonetta."

"I hoped you would assist me in doing exactly that. We need people of talent and intelligence, people who can perform dual roles as artists and ambassadors."

The young Englishman's face lit up in a big smile. "First and foremost would be to seek the return of Josquin, the singer and composer. Your brother Ascanio and I have been lamenting his absen—" William stopped in mid-sentence. He saw that Ludovico was already immersed in other thoughts—and now waited for him to leave. "Thank you, Eccellenza, thank you for your kindness, for your consideration."

Getting to his feet, Ludovico embraced the musician. "One day Milano will rival ancient Athens, and you will be able to boast to your grandchildren that you were part of its rebirth." William bowed and hurried off while Ludovico returned to his reflections.

At the appointed time that afternoon, Calco and Ludovico met again. Even before the pleasantries were over, Calco unburdened himself of the mountains of information he had gathered in the past five hours.

"Mocenigo, the doge of Venice, was a wealthy merchant and friend of my father's. Years ago, before he became doge, I heard him and my father discuss this matter. I had to consult with my brother to see if my memory was correct."

"Not enough." Ludovico shook his head. "I want secret dispatches about the doge and his *consiglio*." He reached into his pocket, took out a gold ducat and flipped it in the air for his minister to catch. As the coin twirled to a stop in his First Secretary's hand, Ludovico continued. "People in high places can be separated from their deepest secrets with the use of the proper coin. Now then, Roma...." Ludovico took the coin from Calco's palm and stuffed it back into his pocket.

The thin shoulders of the First Secretary sagged. "The papacy is even more vexing. I cannot begin to tell you. Each new pontiff has been worse than the one before. Our current occupant of the papal chair, Sixtus IV, acts as if he were an equal to the duke of Milano, the king of Napoli, and the doge of Venezia. Clerics throughout our land call for reform of the Church but della Rovere, Pope Sixtus IV, ignores their cries and simply goes about acquiring land for his nephews."

"Facts, minister. New facts. What you tell me, I already know," Ludovico huffed.

Calco was gripped with fear. "The pope is no immediate threat to ourselves except that he courts the doge of Venezia." The minister paused, watching Ludovico, who stared into space. "This we know from your niece, Caterina Sforza-Riario. She is very reliable."

Ludovico sat up, ears pricked, for the first time all day. "Good. Good. You have finally told me something I did not know. Go on, about the Fiorentini. Lorenzo Il Magnifico has forever been a friend to Milano. We will speak of him another time. Now, about Napoli—"

"Ah, Napoli," Calco pressed a hand to his forehead. "Were the king and his son more reasonable, less temperamental, the peace of Italy might be maintained, with some prospect of success. Ah, well, kings...."

Ludovico laughed. Calco, too, when he realized he had made a joke.

"You fear the Neapolitani?" Ludovico squinted.

"I fear their instability. They are of Spanish-Moorish blood. Hot tempered. They humiliate their friends and never forgive their enemies even if it would be to their advantage to do so. Duke Alfonso, your sister's husband, is worse. A very angry man. We shall rue the day he becomes king, mark my words. Ambassadore

Stanga tells us these things in his report."

"Consider them marked, Minister." Ludovico smiled. Calco relaxed his grip on his cane. "And Francia, the land of Jean d'Arc? I am so long out of touch, wandering the countryside." His eyes flashed with anger.

"The French have been so busy with the English and the duke of Burgundy that they have been no threat. Your father always felt that alliances with the French kept them on the other side of the Alps only because each time they turned to look southward, the English would spit on their backside."

"Yes, yes…and the Turks?" Ludovico's eyes narrowed.

The First Secretary ran his hand through the thin strands of hair left on his head. "The Sultan of Turkey is a threat. He is well-armed. He will keep the Venetians and the Neapolitani busy."

"So, as long as Venezia, Napoli, and the papacy are otherwise occupied they pose no threat to us?" the young regent probed ever deeper.

Calco nodded his assent.

"And ourselves? What have we been trying to accomplish?"

A self-effacing man, Calco looked skyward, his lips tightening. "I am not quite sure, *Reggente* Moro. Secretary Simonetta discussed little of this with me. But I would say that we were seeking to get along with everyone. We have sought no new territory. Since the time of your father's death, there has been little war because we did not impose ourselves on others." He searched Ludovico's expression for a sign of his feelings, wondering if his answers had satisfied this young man of twenty-five, suddenly one of the most powerful men anywhere in Europe. Without thinking, he rubbed his throat below the Adam's apple, as if a noose were tightening around it.

A chuckle welled up from deep within Ludovico. "Well told,

Minister. Well told. Before long we shall have a long talk about ourselves as protectors of Milano." Ludovico also wondered what the state of Milano intended to accomplish.

Hesitating, Calco spoke at last. "I shall endeavor to carry out your every wish, Eccellenza."

Ludovico held up his hand. "Minister, as regent of Milano, we have only to serve the duke. Address me simply as Messere Ludovico or as Reggente."

"Of course, Reggente."

"One thing more." Ludovico put his hand on Calco's arm. "Remember what my grandfather, Filippo Visconti, once said: 'I care less for my body than my soul, but I put my government before either.' Bring me all the correspondence from our ambassadors to France, the papacy, Napoli and Venezia for the years since my father died." Ludovico got up and disappeared into the Corte Ducale.

A few moments later, Calco entered the chancery. Jacopo Antiquario, Minister of Public Works, and Marchesino Stanga, the Superintendent of Finances, waited for him. The two men nodded to a valet, who poured some wine for them.

Stanga waved his hand for the valet to leave. "So tell us, Bartolomeo, what think you of this young man, this Ludovico?"

"Just tell us, do we lose our heads as poor Simonetta is sure to do?" interjected Antiquario.

The three men laughed. "Actually," Calco mused, "He is no different than he was as a youth—always cordial, never angry, always thinking several steps ahead of everyone else."

"How so?"

"I told him of the circumstances with the states around us. He replied by asking to see all diplomatic correspondence since the death of the duke, his father. Thirteen years of correspondence." The three men looked at each other in awe.

"Rulers do not pay such attention to the past," muttered Antiquario.

"It reminds me of a time when Ludovico was about fourteen years old," mused Stanga. "Galeazzo was about to put to death a man-at-arms who had made a small error of protocol. The boy learned the facts and interceded, but the duke merely laughed at him. Thereafter, I recollect Ludovico saying, "I shall get to know men so well that the decisions I wish them to make will be inevitable by the time they make them."

"What do you suppose the young regent wants?" Calco glanced around the room. "Wealth? Fame? Expansion?" Antiquario looked mystified.

"Our survival may well depend on knowing the answer to this question," Stanga reflected.

The others agreed. In a few moments they left the room.

Calco had already begun gathering the correspondence demanded by Ludovico.


In his candlelit chambers, Ludovico sat at a dining table laid out with damask cloth from the Middle East, silverware from 14th century Ferrara and goblets from Denmark. The serving table was laden with a sumptuous feast of seafood broth, cuts of pheasant, duckling and deer meat, vegetables, numerous cheeses, and a variety of wines.

As Pontremoli poured him a glass of wine, Ludovico heard a knock at the door and leapt to his feet. Pier Francesco put the bottle of wine down, went to the door, and opened it.

Cecilia, the silver-haired beauty, stood in the doorway. Slim, coy, and radiantly beautiful, her eyes danced with pleasure. Her lustrous, silver-blonde hair was coiled and held in place with jeweled inlaid laces that seemed to dance in the candlelight. She gazed at Ludovico with amusement, not the awe he expected.

Smiling slightly, he took her hand and kissed it. "I have been seeking you." He did his best to conceal his insatiable urge to touch her, to cover her soft skin with kisses. He took her hand and escorted her into the room.

"And so you found me," she whispered, her eyes bright and playful, as if tossing out a challenge.

"You must have been intending to stay hidden, madam," he shot back, flashing a grin. Her breasts looked inviting, with just a hint of cleavage exposed.

"Ah, but it is Ludovico who stays hidden—spending all his time in the chancery reading dusty old letters," she answered.

*Coy, playful, seductive, she will be a delight,* he decided, throwing his head back with laughter. "Umm, you are indeed quick-witted." He showed her to a divan, and they sat. Pontremoli appeared at her side with a goblet of wine and a plate of biscotti. "Please try this." Ludovico leaned back in his seat, an expansive look to his face. "It is from the region near Gallerani."

"Ah, then you know my family name." Her smile was mischievous and showed fine, straight white teeth, unusual in a time when few men or women had good teeth. "But then Moro is reputed to be able to find out anything he wishes to know."

"Oh, am I?"

"Indeed."

"Not difficult. Your father was chamberlain to my father and served him well." He felt his face redden.

"And you expect all the Gallerani to serve you with equal devotion?" Her eyes grew cool and mysterious as she dipped a biscotti in the wine. "With all the perquisites that accompany such service?"

Sensing that she was changing the rules of the game, he frowned. Somewhere in the depths of his being, he recalled Lucia Marliani whose willingness to become mistress to Duke Galeazzo Maria brought her great wealth.

*She is not here for that reason,* he concluded. *What then? What does she want?*

"On the contrary," he smiled, "far from exercising loveless authority as did my brother, I seek to understand, at the feet of those who are more knowing than I."

She stared at him for a long time, still cool and mysterious. Slowly her expression softened. "I thank you for that." She became more serious and held out her wine glass, touching hers to his. She got to her feet, went to the window, and gazed out. "I hardly imagined that you would get the meaning of my words, Moro. Apparently, you have a gift for understanding."

Ludovico's heart leapt at her words. Clearly, she was neither intimidated nor flattered by his position. As he gazed at her, he sensed something strange happening, leaving him confused. True, he felt his pulse race at the thought of touching her, but something else was happening.

The young woman returned to the divan, sat down, leaned over and reached for his hand. Her lips were close to his, and her sweet breath filled his nostrils.

"What is it you want?" She asked.

He said nothing, answering only with a look filled with desire.

She leaned back on the divan, hands folded in her lap. "What I mean is, now that you have the power you seek, what you want to do with it?"

He gave her a long searching look and spoke at last. "I could give you an answer that would satisfy most people—" He stared off into the darkness, "—and might satisfy myself, for the most part." He turned back to her, leaned close, and slipped to one knee. "Perhaps you are my oracle and can tell me what I want."

Cecilia threw back her head in laughter. As he got up and sat next to her, she reached for a cushion and tucked it under his head.

He leaned back on his elbow and stared at her shapely ankle. He reached out and touched it. "In fact I am lost." He chuckled, in a hopeless, whimsical way. "I have gotten power—I have no idea what to do now."

"Ah, but you do. You do. Open your mind." She plumped up several pillows and reclined against them. Pontremoli came over to the two of them and offered each a pastiche of seafood in wine. She smiled at Pier Francesco then turned back to Ludovico, now mesmerized by the light dancing off the jewels in her hair.

"Anything you have ever wanted—your dreams, hopes, ideas— let them pour out."

He savored the shape of her lips and her mouth, took a sip from his wineglass then touched her ankle once more. Her eyes twinkled. He leaned over to kiss her.

Cecilia touched his cheek gently, kissed him on the mouth with cool, soft lips, and put a hand on his chest. "Speak to me," she whispered. "Open your mind, tell me what you want. Perhaps I can help you find answers you seek. If not, then being together is a waste of your time, and mine."

For several minutes he remained silent.

"Speak to me, Moro," she whispered.

"What do I want?" He stared out into the candlelit room. "I wish for darkness." He laughed slightly.

Cecilia went to the candelabras and blew out each candle in the room. She returned to him, took him by the hand and led him to the bed. She propped herself up against the wall and drew him down to her, letting him rest his head on her lap. She stroked his hair.

"Now what do you want?"

For some time he said nothing, letting the stroking of her soft fingers soothe and ease his concerns and fears.

"To fulfill my father's destiny."

"And...," She stroked his hair, one strand at a time.

"To be remembered—there were so many, twenty children, natural and legitimate—"

"And—" She leaned down and kissed his head, pulling him closer to her bosom. "How will you do that?"

His eyes closed, and he breathed deeply, as if asleep.

"How?" she asked. "What do you want? How will you get it?" His breathing grew still deeper and he slept.

"Repeat after me, 'What do I want? How will I get it?'"

"What do I want?" he repeated from a faraway, dreaming, wandering, asleep place. "How will I get...?"

"...it," she whispered, pulling several blankets around the two of them. She loosened her bodice and pulled his lips up to her skin so he could breathe in the scent of her skin as he slept. She rested her chin on the top of his head, smiled, and closed her eyes.

William lay in his bed dreaming of things to come. Already Ludovico had taken him into his confidence, seeing in him talents for subterfuge which he hardly saw in himself. Yet he realized that his father's position at the court of Edward IV had been hard won. His father was no fool. He talked constantly of the need to measure the consequences of one's actions. The lesson had not been lost on William.

Soon he would be taking title to the beautiful Castello di Vezio at Varenna and the smaller castle, actually a villa, at Felino. Unfortunately, Simonetta had fallen before the promise of a marriage proposal with Cecilia's family could be arranged. But Ludovico would intercede on his behalf. Of that he was quite sure. Little by little, he was becoming indispensible to the Sforza family, as his uncle had hoped. He smiled at the thought. Everything seemed to be working out the way he had foreseen. Before long, Cecilia would be his. Not just a dalliance or a few nights of passion or a fantasy long dreamed about. No, she would be his for life—the mother of his children, his heartfelt companion. Every virtue a woman could have, she seemed to possess. *You have done well, William. Better than you thought you could do.*

# 13

## *Simonetta*

*The Dungeon*
**CASTELLO DI PAVIA**
PAVIA, ITALIA
January, 1480

In the deepening shadows of the dungeon at Castello di Pavia, a single beam of light fell across the dusty face of the old man. He stared out the window, but his eyes appeared to see nothing, as if he had already departed to another life. He moved back onto the hard wooden bed and shielded his eyes from the light.

Standing in the darkness across the room, a thick book under his arm, Ludovico Il Moro Sforza studied the old man intently.

William stood next to him.

A few moments before, Ludovico had offered the old man his freedom in exchange for a token of some kind—a contribution of books from his library—but Simonetta seemed not to notice, as if his wits had already left him. Ludovico approached the old man and patted him on the shoulder, then turned to leave.

A sad smile made its way across Simonetta's face. He turned back to the young ruler of Milano and spoke, his voice hardly more than a whisper. "Your father once said to me, 'If I could combine Tristano's courage and good sense with Ludovico's vision, tact and understanding of people, I should have the best ruler who ever lived.'"

Ludovico retraced his steps and slid into a chair next to Simonetta's bed. He gazed at the ancient statesman.

"Yes," murmured the young prince. "I took it as a compliment, as I was only ten years old and Tristano, my natural brother, a man of forty."

*What does Simonetta want?* The musician wondered, looking for a hint of bitterness in Simonetta's watery blue eyes. There was none.

Speaking softly, Simonetta murmured, "When you cast about seeking an answer to the question, 'What will my reign mean to my family, to the Ducato and to Italia—ask yourself, 'What would Galeazzo Maria do in these circumstances?'"

"And then do the opposite," Ludovico laughed. "I know."

The creases in the old man's face deepened as the corners of his mouth turned up in a tiny smile. "You are a young man," he continued in a raspy whisper, "wise beyond your twenty-seven years, astute in your judgments of people."

Ludovico reached over and poured some water into a wooden bowl near the old man's side and handed it to him.

Simonetta took the bowl and drank. "You have had the finest models, your father, your brother, Tristano, the friendship of Lorenzo de' Medici. Find your own vision, your own stamp as the ruler of the duchy." Simonetta became very serious. "Your father's greatest problem from the beginning of his reign, and yours as well, is this—" He turned to face Ludovico, staring into the young man's eyes from far, far away. "You rule without legitimate title to the duchy of Milano."

Ludovico winced at the pain of this simple fact. "We are aware of that."

"Your father took title by force of arms," Simonetta coughed. "The Holy Roman Emperor, Fredrick II of Germany, refused to invest him or Galeazzo Maria with the title of duke." Simonetta became tight-lipped. "Therefore, your cousin, the duke d'Orleans, like yourself descended from the Visconti, believes himself more legitimate an heir to the title than yourself. Many will recognize it to be so, if it be to their advantage."

"Minister, I am aware of this," replied Ludovico, more tolerant than annoyed at this academic recitation of common knowledge. *It is even a little pathetic—an old man used to power wanting to keep giving advice.*

"Of course you are." A tiny smile cracked through Simonetta's leathery lips. "But there is something of which you are perhaps not aware." He reached toward the volume under Ludovico's arm. "I'm glad you brought it."

"Your library is chaos itself," Il Moro muttered as he handed the book to the old man.

Simonetta touched the gilded gold letters of the beautifully bound volume. Smiling sadly, he looked up from his pillow. "Until such time as the Holy Roman Emperor grants the investiture of Milano to the Sforza, this book will be your one best hope of convincing the great and the small alike that you rule by right of excellence as much as by blood." Simonetta tapped the cover of the volume and handed it back to Ludovico.

"*Commentaries...*" the young man read the title, a blank look on his face, ...by Giovanni Simonetta." Ludovico looked up. "Your brother, Giovanni—"

Simonetta nodded, now exhausted. He rubbed his eyes, gathering his thoughts. After a long silence, he spoke.

"This *libro* contains the life of your father, Duke Francesco, the situations he faced, and how he chose to handle them. It is not a biography, nor a history of Milano, nor a paen in praise of Duke Francesco of the kind written by parasites who surrounded the duke, like Filelfo." Simonetta took the volume once again, rubbing the dust off its cover. "It is an account of what actually happened—the noble and not so noble accomplishments of the duke. When it was finished ten years ago, it was the latest kind of humanist history, not written in the Roman style or with fanciful mythological, pagan, or biblical allusions like the tales surrounding the Visconti of a century ago. The models for this work were sound scholars and humanists like Leonardo Bruni of Firenze and Flavio Biondo of Forli, who sought only the truth of what happened in the past."

Ludovico smiled. "I will read it with—"

"The *Commentaries* tells what took place," interrupted the old man, his voice choking now, "as my brother and I saw it." Simonetta gazed at the cover of the book through a mist of tears. "We loved your father. We loved every moment of the life we shared with him."

Ludovico watched as the tender emotions left Simonetta's face, replaced by a harder, angrier expression.

"We can only hope that a work such as this will convince the doubters, the unruly barons in Genoa and Parma, that your father and the Sforza line are a gift from God and deserve their loyalty." He took the book from Ludovico and held it in his hands. "Such is our gift to you, Moro." He brushed away more of the dust from the name—Giovanni Simonetta.

"We shall value it, Minister. Be assured of that." Ludovico bent over the man, almost inclined to kiss the top of his head, as if it were his own father lying on the bed.

Something in all this gnawed at Ludovico, as if an emotion that he had never known before stirred within him. Sadness? No, he had known sadness in his life. It was something more—something so pure, so filled with light that he could not quite look at it.

Suddenly, a burst of light appeared from outside the dark dungeon so blinding that Ludovico could not see Simonetta's face. He could only hear the man's faint voice. "It was completed during the time of Duke Galeazzo, but he took no notice of it."

Finally the light softened, revealing the old man's face once more.

"I have said all I have to say, except this—trust not men-at-arms close to you. They will always shape invention and stratagem to their own purposes."

"You have never forgiven Sanseverino for opposing you."

"A dagger may come from any direction, Moro. Any direction at all." Simonetta closed his eyes. "This is the advice your father would have given."

Ludovico was moved by the man's concerns, touched at hearing again the words and feelings of his father. It occurred to him that Simonetta was the last and strongest link he had to his father. *How sad,* he reflected then reminded himself, *do not vacillate or be in doubt.* As he placed his hand on Simonetta's shoulder, the old man turned toward him and smiled.

"You will do well. I will tell that to your father when I see him." He inclined his face toward heaven.

A light went on somewhere inside Ludovico. *Of course!* Ludovico smiled at the old man, delighted to have learned his deepest need. *He seeks to be remembered.* He touched the old man's hand for an instant then rose from his seat. "Goodbye, Simonetta."

"Goodbye, Moro." Somehow, a steady light that shone through Simonetta's tired eyes. "May God and the *Dama Fortuna* smile upon you with glad eyes."

Ludovico turned and motioned William to the door. "And may God have mercy upon your soul," Ludovico whispered just loud enough for William to hear. He stepped toward the door, leaving the old man to the sad indignity of isolation and loneliness and death. William stirred in the corner and moved toward the door.

"You!" Simonetta fairly shouted out, raising his head off the pillow and pointing at William.

William froze in his tracks as if Christ himself had risen from the dead and made an accusation. He felt like Judas at the Last Supper.

"You," Simonetta repeated. His finger pointed at William as if thrusting with a bent sword.

Expecting Simonetta to launch into a tirade about loyalty and betrayal, William approached slowly, *I should never have come.*

The old man gazed at him for a moment. A beatific smile crossed his face. "Have a good life. A very good life." He fell back on his pillow, his eyes once more unseeing.

William wiped his forehead. *Have a good life. Was this the ultimate sarcasm, for which Simonetta was noted? Or did he mean it with some sincerity?* William was certain he heard tenderness in the man's voice. Or had he just imagined it?

In the courtyard of the castello at Pavia, William and Ludovico walked side by side.

"A very moving experience, Moro." William observed.

"It was. It was indeed." Ludovico chewed on his lip.

"I appreciate your trust in me, that you would want me there—" William stammered.

"I wanted to see how you and Simonetta would respond to each other." Ludovico's eyes twinkled. "The animal you deserted in order to saddle the larger, livelier beast."

William said not a word. What could he say? "He probably never knew what happened. One day he was at the ramparts of the castello, looking south, and from the west came a terrible wind. The next thing he knew he was in a dungeon."

"Sadly, it was the only way." Moro remained silent for the

moment. "No one worked harder to make the Sforza rule a success. Roberto Sanseverino's hatred of Simonetta is what doomed him."

Later that same evening, Ascanio Sforza made the sign of the cross and got up from his kneeling position in the ducal chapel of Pavia's castello. He left the chapel and wandered out into the courtyard, gazing across the garden in the moonlight. Everything was still.

"*Bona notte*, Archbishop Sforza," a voice whispered from the darkness. Ascanio turned and took a step toward the source of the voice. "No, no, come no closer. *Prego.*"

"Very well." The young archbishop gazed into the shadows. "If you prefer darkness, then darkness it will be. But I must know who you are." Ascanio slid away from the shadows.

"It would be best for me to remain unknown—for the time being at least," the voice replied.

"I see." Ascanio paused for a moment. Such a meeting could prove very dangerous. "I received a note saying this meeting is of the greatest importance to my future. How might that be so?" The tone of his voice dripped with skepticism.

"Ludovico is being secretive, with yourself as well as others. Is that not correct?"

"Perhaps, perhaps not."

"Under Galeazzo, you were more favored than at present—not by the duke so much as by the *popolo*. Is that not also true? The people were devoted to you."

Ascanio peered into the darkness. "The people of Milano have always loved us all. True, Galeazzo Maria was cruel and foolish, Sforza Maria was a pig, and now Ludovico has become—"

"Arrogant?" the voice replied.

The young cleric chuckled. "Well, but he has earned it."

"Ah, but were you not groomed to be duke?" asked the voice. "Were you not always the most cautious, most careful, least given to impulse?"

"I often wonder what my father was thinking—raising us as if each would rule—that we should devour each other alive?" He laughed to himself.

"And he made you a man of the cloth," added the voice quietly.

Agitated now, Ascanio turned to the figure. "I, who care less for religion than any man. Identify yourself, friend, for our conversation is turning —well, I begin to perceive a drift to your thoughts."

The shadowy figure moved closer. "No matter what your brother says, he trusted no one. He did not tell you about plotting with Countess Beatrice, did he?" Ascanio shook his head. "There you have it. A brother who will deceive those closest to him."

Ascanio gazed out over the soft, green grass aglow in the moonlight. For several minutes he voiced not a word. At length he asked, "I imagine you have a plan?"

"It is dangerous." The man leaned closer, revealing a pock-marked cheek.

*Who is he? And what a risk he takes!* The archbishop of Pavia thought, pacing back and forth. *What a risk I take for listening.*

"Go on."

"Have you funds to raise an army? Those who would help you have been taxed heavily and have nothing," the voice continued.

"I have nothing."

"Then you must raise the money." The voice dropped to a whisper. "When that is done, fly your pendant outside your chambers below the flag of Pavia from seven a.m. to eight a.m. each morning for a week. We will be in touch."

Retreating footsteps told Ascanio the man had disappeared.

Deep inside the castello, an iron gate leading downward to the dungeons stopped Trivulzio. The guard standing at the gate came to attention. "Good evening, Capitano." He crossed his pike in front of him in salute.

"Good evening, *Corporale,*" replied the jut-jawed officer. "I come to see Simonetta, the prisoner."

"Certo, Capitano. Prego. Your pass?"

"Since when does the Capitano of the Lanze Spezzate need a pass?" Trivulzio demanded, planting his feet in a defiant stance.

"Sir, these are the orders of Capitano-Generale Sanseverino. No one is to see the prisoner except Reggente Ludovico Moro, Messere Bartolomeo Calco, or His Grace, Archbishop Ascanio, unless by written order of the Capitano-Generale, or one of the above."

Trivulzio grunted, understanding full well that orders were orders.

"Sir, if I may say something," the guard spoke with care. "I saw the archbishop in the garden only a few moments ago. I am sure he will be happy to accompany you."

The soldier's body relaxed and a smile crossed his face. "Bishop Ascanio, of course. Please find him."

The guard hurried off.

Ascanio followed on the heels of the guard down the cold

stone staircase. As they plunged deeper into the bowels of the castello toward the dungeon, he had an uncomfortable feeling in his spine, as if this place of horrors could well be his final home. After his conversation in the garden an hour before, the darkness, the smells, the dull echoes of prisoners crying for help frightened him.

Up ahead he saw the face of Capitano Trivulzio covered with a welcoming smile.

"*Buona sera*, your Grace." Trivulzio offered his hand.

"*Buona sera, mi amico*," Ascanio replied, taking the soldier's hand in his own. He had always admired Trivulzio, always found him to be fair and honest, even if unpolished. "You wish to see Messere Simonetta?" A tiny nod of the *capitano's* head confirmed the answer. Ascanio addressed the guard. "Take us to the prisoner."

The guard opened the iron gate, and the three men descended further into the bowels of the Castello di Pavia.

At the door to Simonetta's cell, the guard rattled his keys until he found the right one, stuck it in the ancient oaken door and turned it until the lock snapped open. Trivulzio slid through the doorway without making a sound.

Inside the dank room, Trivulzio looked around and saw Simonetta lying on a bunk, his neck strangely twisted. He struggled to breathe, making short, choking sounds.

Often enough the soldier had known the stench and cold of a dungeon—he had put many a man in just such a place, and had used the rack more than once. Few men could stand such pain. *Actually,* he thought, *Simonetta looks better than I imagined. Although the man's skin is white as chalk, it is not yet the pallor of approaching death.*

"Padre—Padre Eterno—" the old man whispered through unseeing eyes.

Trivulzio pulled up a chair and looked into the face of this man whom he had known all his adult life, more of a father to him than his own father. Simonetta's ambitions were those of Duke Francesco himself and passed down directly to Trivulzio. Simonetta's loyalties had never been in question. Truly, a man of his word.

"No, my friend, it is I, Gian Giacomo." He leaned down and kissed the man's forehead with all the reverence that he would bring if the figure were Christ himself.

Simonetta's voice gurgled in his throat for a moment then Trivulzio heard a whispered rasp. "They said you wouldn't come. They laughed. 'Sanseverino is in charge,' they said. But I knew—you'd—"

The soldier put a finger to his lips. "Don't try to talk, mi'amico."

"Will it be soon?" The old man asked. "Tell me it will be soon—"

"Perhaps tomorrow or the next day. I want you to know that your family will be taken care of. I will see to that."

A wisp of light appeared in the cell as if the sun had somehow penetrated the thick walls of the castello. The old man turned toward it.

From the back of the cell, Trivulzio heard a shuffling sound. He looked over to see Ascanio shifting his weight uncomfortably.

The soldier turned back to the old man and whispered, "Can you hear me?" The figure did not respond. Trivulzio asked again. No answer followed the question. "Is there anything more that I can do for you?" Simonetta's voice was still.

Trivulzio was about to get to his feet when he felt a faint tug at his wrist. He looked down at the claw-like fingers scratching at his skin. He leaned closer.

"Take care," the faint voice whispered.

"I will, compare. I will be forever careful."

"Take care in whom you trust. Someday you will rule."

Trivulzio leaned closer still to the old man. "Shh.... Do not try to speak."

Simonetta's voice rasped on for a moment. There was more to say but his lips could no longer shape the words. The old man's eyes snapped open for a moment. "Take care—of....fish—" he wheezed. "B...bi..." His eyes closed again. Trivulzio put his ear to the old man's lips. "Bi—big—fish— eat—"

"—eat little fish?" asked the soldier.

Simonetta's clawlike fingers grasped at Trivulzio's arm. His head worked up and down. "Remember Bur—Burg—Burgun—" The elderly statesman fell back into unconscious mumbling. "Padre, Padre Eterno—"

He touched the old man's wispy white hair. Tears filled his eyes as he got to his feet and slipped out the door. Ascanio followed him out of the dungeon.

Trivulzio emerged from the underground, deeply moved by what he had seen. He wiped his eyes as Ascanio joined him.

"A great man, Simonetta," whispered the archbishop in a reassuring voice.

"Indeed," Trivulzio replied in a far-off voice.

"He said something about care or taking care of?" asked the younger man.

"Yes, I am not quite sure what he said. Something about 'big fish eat little fish,' and 'Burgun—.' I suppose he meant Burgundy?"

"Hmm, strange," the archbishop reflected. As they walked, Ascanio put a reassuring hand on the shoulder of the veteran soldier, a gesture which surprised Trivulzio.

Then he recollected that he had made just such a gesture toward Ascanio when both watched the funeral of Duke Francesco, Ascanio's father, more than ten years before. *This young Sforza has a great heart,* he reflected. *And a memory to match.*

"I'm sorry it had to end this way for our countryman," mused Ascanio as they reached the top of the steps of the dungeon. "Were his enmity for Sanseverino not so great, he would have come to a different end altogether, much as you yourself have eased into the new government so successfully."

The young man gave Trivulzio a wave of his hand and slipped into the darkness of the long hall. Trivulzio watched him disappear.

*Now there is a man who could be duke—were it not for my own ambition.*

# 14

## *Ascanio's Betrayal*

*Ducal Chambers*
**CASTELLO DI PAVIA**
PAVIA, ITALIA
March, 1480

Ten-year-old Duke Gian Galeazzo, members of the Sforza family, and their closest friends gathered for an intimate dinner in the ducal chambers of the castello. Ascanio, Duchess Bona of Savoy, the dwarf Falcone, First Secretary Bartolomeo Calco, William Castle, and his uncle, Bishop Branda, all joined in the celebration.

Seated next to his uncle, William laughed as Bishop Branda told him of his latest sojourn in France where he was resident ambassador to King Louis XI. William turned as the sounds of the two trumpeters at the doorway announced the arrival of the guests for whom they had been waiting— Ludovico and a mystery woman.

Ludovico strode into the room. At his side, a woman who radiated her love for him—and a woman enjoying her new position in life—Cecilia Gallerani.

Ascanio looked on, amused.

Bona of Savoy, a wicked smile on her face, seemed pleased.

Calco remained impassive.

Young Duke Gian Galeazzo appeared awe-struck.

William stared at the two of them. His mouth hung open, shocked at the sight of obvious happiness radiating from her.

*So that is where she has been.* A deep pain stretched from one side of his heart to the other. *William, you fool.* He remembered his father's advice: *Love them, enjoy them, leave them, believe in them but, for God's sake, do not think about them.* His mouth hardened.

He studied Ludovico's visage—penetrating eyes, a sensual nose and mouth, an alert, affable man possessed of an unusual ability to see into the heart of things.

The musician turned his gaze on Cecilia—her dancing eyes, her laughter. A splendid woman. *What would happen to her if something befell Ludovico Il Moro? Of course, I would be there to break her fall. But would she want that? Do you really have the means to care for the consort of a fallen hero? Do you really wish to devote your life to the repair of a broken-hearted woman?*

"You look so serious, Nephew," Bishop Branda grinned. "Why the long face?"

"A slight headache, that is all, Uncle. I thank you for asking."

After the sumptuous dinner, William paced the walkways of the castello's parapets for an hour. The pain in his heart seemed almost more than he could endure. Somehow she belonged to him. He knew it. *What had happened? How could she have abandoned him? How had she and Ludovico met? When? Where?* It must have been right under his nose. No wonder she had been so evasive. Right under his nose. He began to laugh. Mercury, the God of unpredictability, was at it again. *You think you have something that makes you happy and pffftt, it disappears.*

Little by little the pangs of jealousy began to eat at his soul— Sforza was not good enough for her. Sforza managed to obtain her heart by deceit and treachery, his calling cards. Perhaps he should simply pick up his knife at table and plunge it into Ludovico's neck. No, that would be foolish. *Why Ludovico? Why not me?* William began to see red before his eyes.

In the end, he decided not to do anything. Let time take its course. He would no longer be able to indulge in fantasies of making love to her, of seeing his yearnings fulfilled. He went to his new apartment feeling very sad. Very sad indeed.

When he looked up, he was surprised to see Bieko walking into the ducal gardens. He thought that Simonetta had sent the young man back to his hometown near Brescia. All thoughts of Bieko were soon forgotten as he became consumed again by images of Cecilia in another man's arms—and happy to be there.


The early morning sun warmed his face as William Castle stood at the parapets of his tiny Castello di Vezio overlooking the town of Varenna. *All mine!* He smiled to himself. Beyond the town below him, he could see the blue expanse of Lago di Como and the town of Bellagio which jutted out into the waters where Lago di Lecco and Lago di Como diverged. Across the water above the town of Bellagio, he could see the silhouette of the palazzo and the castello where Simonetta had first shown him this vision of beauty.

Despite his sense of satisfaction, a strange air surrounded him, as if something new had entered his life. *A yearning? No, I have felt that before.* He thought of his sweet Irish lover, Carolina, for a moment. Then the picture of Cecilia swooning in his arms snapped into his brain. He screwed up his mouth, resolving not to think about her anymore. No doubt it was loneliness which hung about him like a shroud, but it was more. He still felt puzzled and uneasy.

*Well, I have accomplished much. I have gained much. This magnificent castle. A vineyard. A small winery—and no woman with whom to share*

*it. Bah! You poor fool, you are thinking like a member of the fat Borgh-*
*ese. Satisfied with what lies in front of you, rather than scanning the hori-*
*zon for what lies ahead. That is what is taking place. Pointless, brooding*
*self-satisfaction. Why does the human animal feel such stupid things?*

Hearing footsteps, William turned around. An elderly man
approached. "Messere William, a man is here to see you." The
old man bowed. "Shall I bring him to you?"

"Does the man have a name, Vicenzo?"

"Si, si. I suppose he does." The old man's smile showed off
a mouthful of ragged teeth. "But he will not give it to me. He
says he is an old friend."

"Very well. Show him up the stairs."

The old man wobbled away and returned a minute later.
William squinted in the hot morning sun. His old friend, Mar-
tino Lactarella, hurried toward William, a big smile on his face.
"Look at you, amico, the master of all you survey, eh?"

"Martino Lactarella, you old devil," William grabbed his
friend, embracing him and wringing his hand until Martino
broke free. He noted that Martino had lost a great deal of
weight. "How did you find me?"

"I simply asked the first pretty lady at court where I could
find you. I was told that First Secretary had gifted this place to
you and that Reggente Moro had confirmed it—the Castello di
Vezio." Martino spread his arms wide and narrowed his eyes in
mock suspicion.

William laughed. "Services rendered. It is true." He showed
his friend to a small table that looked out over the lake. Vicenzo
appeared with a bottle of *vino*, some *fromaggio*, and *pane*. "And
what of you, amico? How is the court of Ferrara?"

"Exquisite, my friend. Duke Ercole is a great patron of the
arts. His daughters, although very young, sing and dance

beautifully. He has a superb library, a fine choir, and a mind filled with curiosity." Martino's thin, bony face turned serious.

"What is it?"

Martino produced a piece of paper and handed it over.

William shook his head. "Reading this Lombard dialect is not my strength."

The thin-faced musician looked around as if guarding a secret. "When I saw Archbishop Ascanio in Ferrara a few months ago, he insisted I come back to Milano, with a vague promise of commissioning a great work. I thought nothing of it. Just talk. But when I talked to him yesterday, he paid me handsomely, assuring me that the remaining seventy five ducati—"

"*Seventy-five ducati?*" William's eyes opened wide in amazement. "Seventy-five?"

"He said that within a few weeks he will be *inondata di ducati*. Those were his exact words. '*Inondata di ducati.*'"

"Perhaps his brother is going to give him a winery or some taxes of some kind."

The trumpet player twisted up his mouth. "No, no. It was the way he said it. The expression on his face and the look in his eye. In his mind, well, who is to say Ludovico is the one who should rule? I thought you would want to know. You have friends in high places, people who think well of you, people who would thank you for this information."

William stared up at the sky. "You are quite right. This is valuable information. Let me think about it." He clapped his friend on the back, picked up a bottle of wine, and poured a glass for each of them.

"I'm glad you came to me."

The two men raised their glasses of wine in toast to one another.

Deep in the bowels of the dungeon of the Castello of Porta Giovia in Milano, its dark walls illuminated only by torches, Ludovico, Calco, William, and two guardsmen walked toward a heavy-set man with a rough, handsome face, a generation older than the others..

"It is good of you to come in person, Antonio." Ludovico extended his hand.

"*Grazie, Eccellenza.*" Antonio Pallavicino bowed and kissed the ring on Ludovico's hand. "It is a matter which, as you might expect, required my personal attention."

They headed downward through a series of landings and doors.

A bone-shattering scream pierced the stillness as they approached an iron door thrown open by a soldier. They entered a room filled with torture instruments of all kinds.

William shivered at the sound.

In the middle of the dimly lit room, a man was stretched out on a table, his arms chained by the wrists to an axle revolving counterclockwise,
stretching his body. At the feet, his ankles were chained to another axle rotating clockwise, pulling his feet away from his body. He continued to scream.

"Is it the truth you speak?" A soldier leaned over the man.

"I swear I tell the truth," whispered the badly overweight peasant.

Ludovico held up his hand, and the soldier stopped cranking. "One more turn of the crank and the man's limbs will separate for all time." He moved closer and stared into the man's terror-filled eyes.

"I believe he tells the truth, Governatore," William observed.

"You spoke to him yourself, face to face?" Ludovico

demanded of the peasant.

"No, Excellency. But it is the truth. I swear it." Perspiration and blood trickled down the man's almost naked body. "I saw his ring. An archbishop's ring."

The regent turned to First Secretary Calco. "Write down his whole story. Perhaps the hand print of Pier Maria Rossi can be found in all this."

"Or someone closer," William murmured.

Ludovico raised his eyes to meet those of his friend. "Perhaps you are right. Perhaps it is someone closer."

"If it pleases your lordship," cried the man on the rack. "I am a poor man with a wife and three young sons. I did as he bid, believing it was in the duke's best interest."

Ludovico stared off into space. "After you tell us the full story, we shall weigh your future." He massaged the man's neck with his thumb, very gently. The man stared back at him in horror.

In the garden of the castello, Ludovico, Calco, and William digested what they had heard.

"I cannot believe my own brother—my loving brother Ascanio—could do this." Ludovico struggled to shake off his cloud of doubt.

Perplexed, Calco shrugged and said, "I have no way of understanding these kinds of things, Reggente."

Ludovico turned to William. "Is it beyond your understanding, William?"

William shook his head. "Not at all. I just recollected the last time I was deeply jealous of someone. It would not have been out of the question that I might betray them, even murder them. I didn't, of course." They all laughed.

"I am glad I have not been the object of your jealousy, my friend." Ludovico gave William a slight bow.

William chuckled. "I am equally glad, amico." His voice had a strange edge to it, an edge that no one else apparently noticed. The musician was glad of that.

Accompanied by First Secretary Calco, William, and four armed soldiers, Ludovico walked across the balcony of the rochetta and stopped at the door of the Sala del Tesoro. Its guardian, Signor Eustachio, hurried out of his room and unlocked the treasury door.

Once inside, Ludovico gazed around the room at the treasures of the duchy—the enormous ruby that once belonged to the Sultan of Turkey, Suliman the Magnificent; the sword of Charlemagne and stacks of gold ducati from the ducal estates.

"I assure you, Excellency, no one has been in here since yourself a fortnight ago," Eustachio rubbed his ear.

Ludovico pursed his lips. "Send in his lordship, my brother."

A moment later, Ascanio Sforza was brought in by two men-at-arms. The two men embraced.

"I almost never see you anymore, dear brother." Ludovico put his arm around the younger Sforza's shoulder. "Why so distant?"

Ascanio smiled, his face pale in the light of early evening.

Ludovico waved Calco and the four guards out of the room. "I hope you have been using your time to great profit." He picked his teeth, a tiger waiting for its prey to move. Ascanio looked up to see a hard-edged smile on his brother's face.

"Si, si, *veramente*." Ascanio retreated a step.

Ludovico picked up the sword of Charlemagne and ran its blade across his finger. "Though decorative, it still is sharp enough to draw blood. See?" He took Ascanio's hand and ran the edge of the blade across the palm, drawing a trickle of blood.

Ascanio pulled his hand away quickly, a puzzled, frightened look on his face.

Ludovico picked up the Turkish ruby. "Almost as big as a fist." He held it up to the window, allowing the light to shine through it. "They say this ruby tells the truth. Whomsoever it shines upon, their soul is revealed." He stepped out of the way so the light from the window shone through the ruby and onto Ascanio. "Of the many virtues important in a princely human, do you not think one is more important than all others?" Ascanio stepped out of the light, but Ludovico followed him with the ruby, reflecting light onto Ascanio's face.

"Perhaps so, brother." Ascanio put his hand up to the light.

Ludovico set the ruby back in its box. "I have always felt that first among princely virtues is *loyalty*." He sat on a gilded chair and leaned down, picked up a stack of ducati, and handed it to Ascanio. "For your loyalty and friendship, I had been thinking of giving you certain estates at Bergamo with an annual income of 2,000 ducati, as well as elevating you from archbishop of Pavia to cardinal of Milano."

Ascanio lurched backwards as if hit in the stomach.

Ludovico laughed. "But, in view of your tilt toward irreligious activity...."

Ascanio's face had turned white in the cold light of the room. He slithered toward the door where two men-at-arms barred his way.

"But we will have to devise a test of loyalty, yes?" Ludovico stepped toward Ascanio and put a hand around his brother's neck, his thumb resting on the windpipe just below the Adam's apple. Ludovico pressed slowly. His brother struggled to little avail.

Suddenly Ludovico released him. "You were away while we beheaded Simonetta."

Ascanio rubbed his neck. "I—I visited the duke of Ferrara," his voice barely audible.

"Just so, just so," mused the regent of Milano. "With the beheading of Simonetta, the old Ghibelline nobles have got their way— Sanseverino, Giovanni Borromeo, Pietro Pusterla, Antonio Marliani. They persuaded me to do it, and I went along with it. Perhaps they now have something else in mind, eh, Ascanio? To strike close to the heart of our family?"

Ascanio's eyes darted wildly. "This has nothing to do with me, brother."

"During your absence, there was a robbery of the taxes due the Lord of Parma, Antonio Pallavicino, who informed me the robber was caught." Ludovico grabbed the sword of Charlemagne. "The robber revealed to his lordship just who had hired him."

Ascanio cowered in the corner. "I am your most loyal servant."

Ludovico approached, sword raised above his head.

"What was the purpose of the robbery, brother? Why did you feel you needed money? What is your darker purpose, brother of mine?" Ludovico gritted his teeth and moved the sword slowly toward Ascanio's throat.

"I—I—just wanted a few more singers," whimpered Ascanio.

"Lies. Nothing but lies. Right to my face, you lie to me, brother. I know the men of this city. They wish to wrest the duchy from me, and you are their tool."

"No, Ludovico, I swear on our mother's grave!"

"I know these men, Ascanio. Everywhere our enemies set traps. And my own brother falls into one of them." He pressed the sword into his brother's side. "A wound, like that of our lord, Jesus Christus. How fitting." He gave the blade a quarter turn to the left, as Ascanio screamed. "Who was behind it, brother? Who?"

"Aahh!" moaned Ascanio, sinking to the floor. "It was dark, I didn't see!"

As he drew the blade out of the wound, Ludovico leaned down and whispered into Ascanio's ear. "Tell me or it goes back in."

"No, no! Please, no! It was a voice in the shadows! Have mercy, brother. I was a fool!"

Ludovico's eyes had turned from an angry black to a demonic red as he looked down on his brother. "The foul nobility of our duchy would like nothing better than for us to devour each other, setting one upon another until we are extinct. They shall not have that pleasure, beloved brother." He pressed the sword deeper, wrenching another scream from Ascanio.

Outside, Calco stood on the balcony, peering down at the courtyard below. Hearing the screams, he turned to one of the men-at-arms.

"Get a pail of water and a brush. We do not want the blood to stain the cobblestones."

"Yes, First Secretary." The man rushed off.

Inside, Ludovico continued to twist the sword in Ascanio's side.

Ascanio moaned, "I am dying."

Ludovico stopped the sword's thrust. "No, brother, you are

not. But henceforth, you are banished from the duchy of Milano. If, during that time, you prove yourself loyal and worthy, we will reconsider this sentence which we place upon your head."

Ascanio moaned, "You could always trust me."

Ludovico lowered the sword and knelt down at his brother's side. "It was so, brother. It was. And perhaps it will again be so. For life in our fair city will not be the same without you." He leaned down and kissed his brother's forehead. "In the meantime, you will be a man without a home. Leave here, and feel what it is like, for it is what I felt for so long—a prisoner of the king of France, thanks to our dearly beloved Galeazzo Maria." He tossed the sword aside.

Ascanio raised himself to a sitting position on the floor of the treasury gripping his wounded side, tears welling up in his eyes surrounded by unimaginable wealth, wealth that could help neither him nor his soul, for at this moment he felt what Ludovico intended him to feel—the sting of his betrayal. *God in heaven is this how Judas felt when he kissed our lord Jesus Christ and the son of God looked him in the eye knowing of his sin? What have I done? Lord God, do not forsake me in my betrayal. What has made me take leave of my senses, that I should betray my own brother—?*

On the balcony outside the treasury, Ludovico stepped into the glowing embers of twilight, motioning to Eustachio.

"Dress his wounds." The keeper of the Sala del Tesoro hurried inside the room. Ludovico turned to Calco and William.

"Our brother will be going on a mission to the duchy of Ferrara for a period of time. He would not, or could not, say who was behind the act of betrayal."

Slipping back inside the treasury, Ludovico watched as

Ascanio was carried out of the room. He listened as the guards clattered down the stairs at the end of the balcony. Then all was silent.

In the darkness of the room, he gazed out the window toward the city below. *Why would our most beloved brother steal from us that which we were born to do—rule the Duchy of Milano? He displays himself untrustworthy to ourselves who love him more than anyone.* He gazed up at the heavens, a deep sadness coming over him. "Do you, Dama Fortuna, continue to smile on our fair state, or is this a sign of some kind—an omen?"

Later that night, with the moon high in the heavens, William and Bartolomeo Calco stood at the door of the Sala del Tesoro. Two guards stood on either side of the door, unmoving, as if built of stone. Two other guards came up to relieve them. One of the soldiers brought a vessel of *Grappa Lombardo*, passing it from the minister to the musician.

"Thank you, Marcello. Thank you." Calco took a few sips and sighed with pleasure. The men guarding the door moved quickly across the balcony and disappeared. Marcello and his companion took their places by the door.

Calco peered in and then closed the door. "I cannot imagine how hungry our lord, Ludovico, must be," he muttered to William. "And still he grieves for the brother he has stabbed."

"He takes his brother's perfidy to heart," William observed.

A moment later, Ludovico came out of the treasury, his face tired, angry, and sad. "Who would go to such lengths?" he asked of no one in particular. He descended the stairs to the court below, followed by Calco and William.

The First Secretary stopped and turned to Ludovico. "One of my scribes heard Borromeo say to Marliani and Pusterla,

'How many more of these Sforza must we endure?' He did not hear the reply, but they all had a good laugh."

"Borromeo, eh?" Ludovico's eyes narrowed. "Well, well...."

A few nights later, Giovanni Borromeo rode back to his palazzo after dining with his good friend, Antonio Marliani. Suddenly, he was surrounded by a half dozen members of the ducal guard, who took the reins of his horse.

"What is this?" he demanded. The horsemen ignored his protests. "I shall report this to Ludovico Il Moro personally."

The guardsmen pushed him through a maze of streets to a building in a poor section of the city. They shepherded Borromeo up the stairs and into a dimly lit room. One of the men sat him down and handed him a sheet of paper. "Read this aloud."

"—*no matter what your brother says, he trusts no one. He did not tell you about plotting with Countess Beatrice of Ferrara, did he?*"

A soldier pressed his face into Borromeo's. "Did you say those words to Bishop Ascanio Sforza three weeks ago in the courtyard of Pavia, Giovanni Borromeo?"

"I did not!" replied Borromeo, leaping to his feet.

In the shadows, Ascanio whispered to Ludovico, "It is not Borromeo. I would have recognized the voice." Ludovico turned to Calco and shook his head.

Bartolomeo Calco stepped out of the darkness and into the light. "Good evening, Count Borromeo."

Borromeo leapt to his feet. "Messere Bartolomeo! Thank God you are here. These fools have just—"

"—helped us find you not guilty of high treason against the

state of Milano, of plotting with Ascanio Sforza to overthrow the regent of Milano. We thought we were about to exile you from Milano, confiscate your properties, and send you to the dungeon until we had extracted a confession from you. But it turns out the guilty party was someone else. Our apologies for disrupting your evening. Good night, Signore."

After Borromeo had been sent on his way, William took Ludovico aside, well out of the hearing of the others. "I have an idea."

Later in the week, Bieko was spirited off to an inn near the Castello di Pavia and made to read the same short speech.

This time Ascanio nodded his head. "He is the one."

Confronted with Ascanio's identification of him, Bieko admitted that Borromeo had been the person who hired him to separate Ascanio from Ludovico.

A rider galloped through the gates of the Trivulzio's castello at Mesocco which stood like a sentinel above the Ticino River.

Dismounting, the rider—GuidAntonio Arcimboldi—went in search of Trivulzio whom he found at dinner with his family, celebrating his transition from regent of Milano under Galeazzo Maria to favored supporter of Ludovico.

"GuidAntonio, my friend, join us for dinner!" Trivulzio waved a leg of lamb in the air.

"We must speak, Gian Giacomo," whispered Arcimboldi.

Trivulzio rose from the table and escorted him to a small study off the dining room. "Well, my friend, what is it?"

GuidAntonio looked him in the eye. "Simonetta's head was separated from its body earlier this week. The only one in attendance was the Englishman—the musician."

Trivulzio gave his friend a sad grin. "So Ludovico has slipped away from us for the moment. Too bad. He feels his debt to Sanseverino stronger than to ourselves." His expression turned hard and cold. "A temporary turn of fortune." He put a reassuring hand on Arcimboldi's shoulder. "Fear not. The names Trivulzio and Arcimboldi shall echo for five hundred years."

Arcimboldi relaxed. They returned to the feast, arm in arm.

Trivulzio confided his secret. "Secretary Stanga asked me what a fair price of a condotta would be at this moment in time—"

"Si, si." Arcimboldi, once the third regent under Bona of Savoy, savored the thought. "Yes, Capitano-Generale Sanseverino's contract comes up for renewal very soon."

The soldier made a fist. "You see how things work out?" He smacked Arcimboldi's arm with a light hit. "We will tell him that not less than five to six hundred ducati would compare favorably with other contracts given."

Arcimboldi thought for a moment then smiled. "Si, si. Six hundred ducati. A small price—for questionable loyalty." They laughed.

In the candlelit bedchamber of his wife, Trivulzio knelt down beside the sleeping form of Marguerite, who coughed frequently as she slumbered. He drank in the sight of her and touched her hair with affection. Taking out his dagger, he swiped at the candle nearest the bed, cutting it in two. As the candle fell to the floor, he muttered, "Sforza!"

With the sleeping Cecilia pressed against his hip, Ludovico reclined against a pillow and stared through the darkness out the window. The grounds and the woods below invited him.

Torches illuminating the castello glowed with great round halos. He could see a fine mist covered the brick edifice with a silky dew, giving everything a shimmer. The sky turned darker than a bottomless cave, as if a squall were brewing.

In the world-beyond-time stillness, Ludovico felt the betrayal of Ascanio to the depths of his soul. For many years, he and his brothers had acted with one mind, as though the spirit of their father had drawn them into a tight, resolute ball of intention. Nothing could dent, crack, or dissolve it, not even death. Galeazzo had never been one of them. As the heir to the throne, he had always been arrogant and self-serving beyond belief. Death had taken his arrogance away, stolen away Sforza Maria's boldness and zest for life, as well as Ottaviano's innocence in the prime of his life. Now, betrayal, the handmaiden of all the vices in the world, had taken away Ascanio, the dearest of all his brothers.

At a time when Ludovico and Ascanio could have been looking ahead to the profound effect they might have had on the future of the duchy, they faced the possibility of greatness, not as one indivisible chain linking themselves with their father and grandfather, but as two broken links, one broken by betrayal and the other by the deep injury inflicted by his closest friend, his most trusted and reliable brother.

In the darkness, a deep wave of sadness engulfed him, and tears welled up in his eyes. The faces of those whom he had lost to the Specter of Death came to him—his father, his mother, Tristano, Ottaviano, Sforza...and Galeazzo as well.

Suddenly he was startled by the sound of his own sobbing as pain and grief overcame him. Instantly he quieted his sobs as Cecilia stirred.

"What is it, *amore*? You are restless."

"*Niente, carissima,*" he whispered. *Lord God, let nothing happen to her.* He thought again of Ascanio. *Why? What would he have gained by being regent—that he could not have had as pope? Perhaps Simonetta's death had something to do with it?*

Cecilia drew him down to her and enfolded him in her arms. "Sleep, my dear. Sleep."

*How sad,* Ludovico thought, *how profoundly sad to have lost a friend and a brother all in the same evening.* With everything to live for, life seemed so pointless. Carrying on the family ambitions all by himself felt empty. *What is ambition? What is accomplishment? What is power—when those with whom one should enjoy such fruits reveal hearts full of envy, greed, and deceit?*

He doubled up in pain as if something inside him, down deep behind his navel, was trying to digest an object much too large for so ordinary an organ. He tossed and turned in fits.

At last, he nestled up to Cecilia, wrapping his arms around her, cupping his hands beneath her breasts—life-giving and seeming to glow like Carrara marble in the cold, bluish, predawn light. Their warmth and her faint heartbeat brought him back to earth, and he slept.

# 15

## *Moro's Vision*

*The Consiglio Segreto*
**CASTELLO DI PORTA GIOVIA**
MILANO, ITALIA
1480

The members of the Consiglio Segreto found their places and sat down on the benches of the chamber whose dark mahogany interior gave the room a warmth so unlike the mood of the counselors and ambassadors in it. Not present were a number of noble families which had set the body of men to wondering about their own fates.

All around the room, members of the Panigarola and Marliani families whispered among themselves, as did Ambassadors Stanga, Panigarola, Gallerani, Grimaldi, Tranchedino, Pallavicino, and Bishop Branda who sat in a special section of the chamber.

"Giovanni Borromeo told me he has been forbidden to attend the Consiglio," murmured Andreas Missaglia, a member of the notable family of armorers.

"I have heard of a plot to overthrow Ludovico," added Francesco Marliani. "Ascanio was behind it."

"What think you, cousin?" Francesco Visconti turned to Trivulzio. "Was it Ascanio?"

Trivulzio nodded. "With the death of Simonetta, the Borromeos became confident they could gain the throne for themselves—and Sanseverino thought so, as well."

The chamberlain announced Ludovico's arrival, and the

chamber quieted.

Seating himself, Ludovico gazed around the room.

"As you may have noticed, some members of the council are not here. They have been found guilty of conspiring against the state, the duchy of Milano, and have been expelled from the counsel. Henceforth, they will no longer hold positions of ambassador, secretary, or counselor. In time, their loyalty may win them again to our presence."

He spoke in a forceful but unemotional voice.

The members of the noble families whispered among themselves. "If Galeazzo Maria was still duke, Borromeo would have lost his head," observed Francesco Visconti, a handsome cousin of the Sforzas. "Perhaps others among us would have as well."

"It was the thing to do, otherwise he would have had to execute his brother, Ascanio," agreed Trivulzio.

"So far Dama Fortuna has looked with great favor upon his every enterprise," continued Visconti. "Let us hope it continues for a while." He spat on the floor, and Marliani laughed.

Trivulzio gave them all a contemptuous look. "Fools," he muttered to himself as he walked away.

Ludovico looked over at them from the regent's chair, giving each man a hard, imperious glance. Visconti recoiled in fear. Marliani stared at the floor, then looked up to see what appeared to be a twisted little smile on the regent's face, as if he had overheard all of their thoughts and fears —and was well ahead of them. Marliani shuddered.

Some distance away, Trivulzio watched the exchange of looks darting back and forth. *I belong in the field, not here! I am barely able to keep my head above water battered by the mercurial tides of this court.*

Ludovico glanced around the room and found Trivulzio by himself, eyeing Marliani, Visconti, and Pusterla. He gave the soldier an appraising look.

Trivulzio caught Ludovico's smile of approval.

That evening in the great hall of the castello, members at the court settled into their seats. To the right of the duke's empty chair, Duchess Bona of Savoy sat in the place of honor. Next to her were two empty chairs that Ludovico and Cecilia would soon occupy. On the right side of these very important personages sat First Secretary Calco, Bishop Branda, and his nephew William Castle.

On the other side of the duke's empty chair sat Captain-General of the Milanese forces, Roberto Sanseverino, with his son, Galeazzo, and several younger sons.

William noticed that Bona appeared annoyed and downcast, perhaps for want of love. Her lover, Tassino, had been found trying to loot the treasury and had been sent back to Ferrara in a hurry. She may also have been distressed at the thought that Ludovico now had a magnificent woman in his life, Cecilia Gallerani. The liaison between Ludovico and Cecilia could hardly be of comfort to Bona.

At that moment, a trumpet's fanfare sounded. Those seated rose and began stamping their feet.

"Moro! Moro! Moro, Bravo!" the members of the court hollered as he appeared, holding his hand out so that Cecilia might precede him into the room.

William watched the two of them, saddened but resigned to what was.

The entire room was abuzz at the sight of Cecilia Gallerani. Beautiful and elegant, bedecked with sparkling diamonds and a ruby in her hair, she had every inch the appearance of a queen.

"Moro has chosen well!"

"How beautiful she is!"

"They say her moans can be heard all night long!" the crowd murmured.

The crowd noise began again.

"Long live the duke! Bravo! Bravo!"

A moment later, Gian Galeazzo entered the room at a brisk pace, head high, looking very regal at age eleven. The hurrahs were much less vigorous for the duke than for his uncle, Regent Ludovico, who followed.

As the duke and the others sat down to their meal, Ludovico caught a few of the phrases bandied about, then turned to his beautiful consort.

"You have taken them by surprise, *cara mia*," he whispered. She smiled and said nothing. After a glass of wine, Ludovico leaned over and touched her hand.

"Mmm," Cecilia murmured, warmed by his skin.

The two lovers consumed their dinners with little awareness of the world outside themselves. Ludovico gazed down the length and breadth of the many tables filled with courtiers and damsels, then leaned toward her.

"You see, our Milano is an oasis in a desert. All around us evil and stupidity—animals of the night, wolves and pythons—wait for the sheep and the antelope to incline toward the cool waters."

"Mmm, yes."

First Secretary Calco, Bishop Branda, and William leaned in to hear what he was saying.

"But if we remain wary, outshining all others," he gazed into her eyes, "like Roma during the republic, no one will dare attack us. Like Athens eighteen hundred years ago, we will create a place where reason and justice prevail, laws will be fair, our people will prosper."

He fell silent, feeling her body warming to his ideas.

"Gone will be the foolish, violent, rapacity of men like Galeazzo, the very reason tyrants are so despised."

"Go on," she whispered.

"Piety shall be honored, but ignorance cloaked in the robes of piety shall be cast out. Man shall be the measure of all things, and the center of this universe of ours."

Her hands began to stroke his neck. "Tell me all, for if you dream, you will be gifted with vision. And no one has a greater opportunity than my sweet Moro."

"Our enemies…" Ludovico glanced out at those around him, his voice rising, "…have their own interests in mind, content to exploit what others have. We shall honor our borders, seeking only to influence the minds of men, as does Messere Lorenzo in Firenze. Our first line of defense is this." He touched his head. "I *will* understand the desires and intentions of all those who enter the stage with me."

His eyes shown with a hard, bright look.

"Our second line of defense will be our prosperity with which we dazzle the world as did the kings of old. And we will employ the best armies in Europe. Fairness, prosperity, and celebration will be our legs to stand upon."

"And the fourth leg?"

He laughed, nibbling at her neck and feeling the vibrations of her desires coming up to meet him. "Cementing the bonds that hold those who rule the state—will be the presence of those men and women of artistic and intellectual brilliance who will inspire those who rule to have a vision—and to act upon that vision." The laughter in his eyes teased her, undressed her.

Beneath the table, Cecilia nudged her slim legs against his. "Sweet reason may benefit the duchy in time, but now I want you to bring that sword of yours to me and slice away the hours of boredom that surround my passion," she murmured.

Ludovico whispered to the young duke, who nodded 'yes'. He then arose and helped Cecilia to her feet.

At the doorway, Galeazzo Sanseverino held the door open for them. "Messere Ludovico has chosen a perfect gem to complete the crown of Milano," he smiled. "A sapphire among beads of amber."

Ludovico bowed. "What a fine way you have with words, Galeazzo. Surely you did not learn that at your father's knee."

"*Certamente, no, Illustrissimo—Excellenza,*" replied the handsome young courtier. "I learned it from the brothers Sforza."

"Ah, we thank you, Galeazzo, for your wise and clever observations." Moro gave Galeazzo a pat on the arm then turned to Cecilia. He kissed her on the neck, whispering, "Come, my sweet. The feast is just beginning."

Calco, Branda, and William looked at one another. It had been an inspiring speech. Although not meant for their ears, it had given them food for thought.

"He means to create heaven on earth," Bishop Branda murmured. "And we are the instruments of his surgery."

Bartolomeo Calco, seldom given to pure reflection, began at last to get a picture of what the years to come would bring. He leaned past Bishop Branda and caught William's attention. "Musicians, painters, architects, scholars. That's what he wants here. The best we can find."

William realized he was one of those chosen, a person with the energy and artistry to bring such people to Milano. *Hmmm, the Golden Age begins and I am in the middle of it.* He smiled to himself with a sense of deep satisfaction— despite his loss of Cecilia, perhaps the great love of his life.

Would she have been the great love of his life? The answer to that question—*?* Well, he would probably never know the answer. He did his best to put the question out of his mind, preferring to concentrate on his future.

*Castello di Vezio*

# 16

## *Eyes on the Future*

*Castello di Vezio*
**VARENNA, ITALIA**
ON LAGO DI COMO
1480

The late afternoon sun had begun to sink toward the mountains in the west as William Castle and Ludovico Il Moro Sforza stared out at the golden rays of light reflecting off the waves of Lago di Como in the foreground and a bit to the south, the split between Lago di Como and Lago di Lecco in the background.

"How beautiful it is." Il Moro scanned the horizon from their vantage point on the castle's parapets, and dropped his gaze to the rocks below. "But also a long way down is it not?"

William said nothing for a moment. "Yes, a long way down." Then he added. "But then we are a long way up."

"Yes, yes." Ludovico laughed. "Precisely why I placed a chapel in the uppermost castle at Bellinzona, the Castello Grande. It is as close to heaven as I ever expect to get. And as close to my father as I can hope to be."

"One day I hope to visit there, with your permission."

Il Moro gave William's shoulder an affectionate squeeze. "You are a man of courage and loyalty, William."

"Thank you, Eccellenza."

The young prince shook his head and laughed. "Let me remind you, I am not the duke. I prefer you address me by one of those wonderful titles you English have invented...."

"You mean 'sire' and 'm'lord,' that sort of thing?"

"Oh, yes!" Ludovico exclaimed. "Look at the word "sire." What does it suggest? The lord of an estate whose purpose it is to make things grow, as a boar would sire piglets."

The two men chuckled at Moro's astute observation and love of language.

Behind them two beautiful women sat at a table loaded with delicious foods—mostly fish from the lake, salads and wine from William's vineyard.

"The soil here brings out the tart, tangy qualities of what grows around us, my friend." Moro observed.

"Yes, the wines from the vineyard are excellent," declared William.

"I was referring to our beautiful companions." Ludovico gestured toward the two women and gave an appreciative nod to Cecilia, who overheard the comment and gave him a little puckered kiss in the air. She turned back to the other beauty who herself grinned at the men.

"Your fair lady, Vanozza Landriano, would have been my second choice as a consort had I not become so entranced by my dearest Cecilia."

"I was fortunate," William surveyed Vanozza's profile. Long, dark brown hair, glowing amber complexion, green eyes, long, slender limbs, a magificent bosom. Ludovico was right. She was delicious to look at and to taste. And a wonderful lover. "Fortunate for me that you were busy pursuing your dreams."

"Her skin. *Molto deliziosa.*" Ludovico sniffed the air. "Like dark, polished wood. She is from Calabria, no?" He drank in her beauty. "The limbs of a woman of the North. Her eyes? Green as the sea. Irish, without question. The hair. Now, the hair fascinates me. It has a burnished quality, like dark mahogany I have seen with the women from Spain. They have hair of that kind—very beautiful. But hers is curled in a way that is more like Sephardim women—either Jews or Arabs."

William chuckled. "It is true. All of it. Her mother was half Sephardic Jew, half Norwegian. Her father is from Calabria, but with an Irish grandfather."

Ludovico's mind had already drifted on another matter. "You have brought some very excellent qualities to our court, William. Courage, bravery, loyalty, artistry—all very rare in this day and age."

"Thank you—sire." Boldly, William emphasized "sire." The two of them laughed.

Il Moro turned serious. "You inquired about how you could help the duchy...."

"Anything you ask, I will do. You have but to name it, Eccell—" said William leaning closer.

"Moro. Moro. Friends, William. Amici. One day when you have a child, perhaps by this lovely lady, we will become compari. Until then, I am Moro. You are Guglielmo, William. Remember that."

William gave Ludovico an amused bow.

Once again Il Moro turned serious. "Now then, there is much work to be done." Ludovico paused for a moment. "This castello, for example. Look over there, at Bellagio's fortress across *il lago*. Any of our enemies coming south down the lake must pass beneath the guns of these two fortresses." Ludovico glanced around the parapets of William's fortress. No cannon were visible. "You have no cannon. None at all. So I will arrange for you to be paid to obtain cannon, ammunition and some soldiers."

"Yes, m'lord," William replied.

"In Milano we must rebuild the court. Musicians, artists, astronomers, mathematicians, historians, all of them. The musicians

I leave to you. You must find first-rate musicians to occupy the choirs at both the cathedral and the chapel. I want to see no less than thirty singers on the roll books by the end of the year."

William smiled at the thought of the responsibility being handed to him—to build the finest court in all Europe. "I have heard that several fine singers are willing to return to us—Loyset Compere for one, Gaspare Weerbecke, for another. A man of great talent who works for the king of France— Josquin des Prez. Also a singer and composer named Gafurio, lately of the court in Napoli."

"Fine. Fine." Ludovico waved his hands as if the details did not matter at the moment. "Singers are fine. But you have shown us the future. What you have done with brass instruments. *Trombetti* and *tromboni.* The brass choir. It begins and ends with your work."

"Mine?" William frowned.

"Your preparations for the Christmas Mass the day my brother was assassinated added enormously to your reputation. When the members of the choir left for Christmas to be with their families, that's when it began. 'Ah, you should have heard what I heard today,' they said, about the rehearsals. Word spread all over the duchy."

In the late afternoon sunlight, a small grin crossed William's lips. "Martino and I lamented the events of that sad day. We thought our careers had ended."

The prince tapped his thumbs together. His mind had drifted ahead of the conversation. "First, set up a school for the players of brass instruments. Not for experts alone. Even young children must learn to play. The best of them will be hired to play for all the local events. Secondly, the universities of Lugano and Locarno will soon be places of learning. You will set up departments of instrumental and vocal music at each university."

William gave Ludovico an appreciative look. "No musician could ask for more."

Ludovico motioned to Pontremoli, who approached, carrying a small, plain-looking box.

"Opening schools of music will be only one of your tasks," Moro confided.

William stared at the box as Pontremoli opened it. Inside lay a mechanism of some kind.

A slow grin crossed Moro's narrow face. "These are the secret codes of the chancery. They are called *cifari*. Only our most trusted ambassadors have them."

The Englishman, realizing he had been holding his breath, let it go.

"From this day on you are to be one of those who know its secrets—in fact, you will be my roving ambassador. Officially you are looking to recruit musicians to the court and to give concerts in support of these efforts. Unofficially, you are my eyes and ears—wherever I send you—whenever I need to know something."

"I am to become your spy."

Il Moro threw his hands in the air. "Do not worry. It will entail little danger for you—for the most part. A few florins to a member of the city council in Siena, a ducati or two to a Florentine banker, that sort of thing."

The significance of his friendship with Il Moro began to dawn on William. In just a very few moments, he had become a different person—new responsibilities, new knowledge, new secrets. It was as if he had been an ill-fed foot soldier in an army who was suddenly promoted to the command of a regiment of cavalry.

"I shall do my best, sire."

"Of course you will, my friend."

Deep in thought, William turned to his mentor. "Now I have a request, if I may—"

"Go ahead."

William paused to collect his thoughts. "Sad to say, most of the members of the court at Burgundy believed I was responsible for the death of a young woman, the wife of the chamberlain. It is true, I am probably not blameless. But I should like to find the real murderer."

Moro gazed at the young man. He nodded his head up and down. "Yes, it would be helpful to all of us if you could clear your name of this sad event." The Reggente of Milano pursed his lips. "Many reports from my ambassadors to the court of the duke of Burgundy can be found in the chancery. The First Secretary will find them for you and make them available. Somewhere you will find something." He folded his hands together. "You loved this woman?"

"Yes, I did. Well, in a way, she was—hardly more than a plaything…" William admitted, "…or so I thought at the time. I realize now that I did not take her seriously enough. For certain, she was a delight. A confection. That is the name she gave to herself. 'Bonbon. Solice La Bonbon.' Now that she is dead, she haunts me—I did not stay to find her killer. I ran because I was afraid of the threat of death."

"You betrayed her?" Ludovico Il Moro wondered.

It was the second time that Il Moro had reminded him of his betrayals. His eyes drooped, then he raised them, meeting Ludovico's stare. "Yes, that is true. That is the right word. By running away, I…I diminished the quality of what went on between us. Often at night, before I fall asleep, I hear her voice. It is soft, not accusing, *Make it right,* it says. *Make it right.*"

Ludovico remained silent for some moments then spoke in a very soft voice. "After the death of Ottaviano," he said at last, "I heard my father's voice, speaking the same words. Once he even appeared before me. *Make it right,*' the voice said. *Make it right.* I have tried to do that." He turned to William. "With your help and the help of others like Galeazzo Sanseverino, and with some whom you will bring to the court, we *will* make it right."

The unspoken bond between the two men swirled around them, a net of enterprise and ambition.

For a moment, William wondered if he was being ensnared in something too vast for his limited imagination and abilities. Secret codes, whisperings of betrayal, money for cannon to guard passage—these were the stories he heard at court when he was young—more appropriate for a member of King Arthur's round table than to a simple maker of music.

William leaned out over the parapet of the castello, resting his weight on his forearms. "A man can accomplish a great deal with a little bit of help."

Ludovico also leaned out over the parapet. He gave William a rueful glance and chuckled. "And he pays a price for everything he accomplishes."

The Englishman looked out over the waters of Lago di Como, sparkling in the moonlight.

"You have suffered the loss of two brothers, whom you loved very much…."

"As well as the arrogance of a third and the betrayal of a fourth," Ludovico sighed. "What price could be steeper than that?"

"Despite the price you have paid, you have brought peace to Italia," William assured him. "For that, you are known and loved."

"Peace?" Ludovico's voice was soft and humble. His lips carried no smile of satisfaction. "No, not I."

"Si, si. To Italia. You have brought peace."

Ludovico rolled the concept over on his tongue. "*Pace in suo tempo.*" He savored the words. "A phrase often used in singing the praises of my father. But certainly not myself. Not yet. The pope and his nephews are forever at work, lining their pockets with gold.

They care nothing for *la tranquilita d'Italia*. I have heard rumors; more plots, more conspiracies—"

"Conspiracies, Eccellenza—sire?"

"Mmmmm. Yes. There is much going on that would keep most men awake if they knew what was happening." Ludovico stared out at the waters, so peaceful, so buoyant in the light of the moon. The silver orb hid, then danced out from behind the billowing clouds above, then hid once more. *"Tranquillo.* The waters of Il Lago. That is my goal for Milano. *Mantenere l'ordine pubblico* (To keep the peace.) Even more, to keep the peace among the states of Italia. Only in this way will we be able to use our wealth—"

"Our wealth, m'lord?"

Ludovico tapped the side of his head. "What the human mind can invent and create is limitless." He shook his head, marveling at the prospect as it unfolded in his mind. "Before long, the members of our court, together with the faculty at the University at Pavia, will stand among the most creative and inventive people who ever lived. What they will accomplish will stun the world for hundreds of years to come."

The look on William's face betrayed his uncertainty. He did not yet understand what Ludovico had in mind. He yearned to know.

"Yes, yes…I know. I know. It is all very—what?—unclear?—abstract? But wait and see. If we are to be remembered for all time, there are only two ways for that to happen—in the first instance, one builds a state, or develops a reputation for destroying someone else's state. In the second, one creates something out of nothing—images in stone, compositions in sound, geometric signs and symbols—and causes great things to be built or discovered."

William began to understand. He recollected the look on Simonetta's face when it became clear to Simonetta that he hoped he would be remembered. "I understand," he said simply.

"Money allows this to happen," Ludovico continued. "And peace. The former we have in abundance. The latter is more elusive. But it is a worthy goal." He chuckled. "*Il Magnifico* has his academy, but soon the court of Milano will be on everyone's lips." As he folded his arms across his chest, his gaze came to rest far beyond the moon.

"I am thankful to be here, at the beginning, Signore," William smiled.

"The beginning." Ludovico ran the fingers of one hand up and down his chin. "Yes, yes. The beginning—" He pointed toward the lake. "If we can keep the waters of the state *tranquillo, molto tranquillo.*" The expression on his faced relaxed, taking on a look of fascination and amusement. "Then it will be interesting, amico."

Warmed by the fire in the open pit, the two men joined the ladies. Together they laughed with merriment and joy.

Their laughter rang out through the castle, down through the trees and onto the lake. It cavorted with the fish in the depths of the lake, at once placid, then turbulent. The waters shimmered in the moonlight—calm, cool, yet ever changing, world without end.

The old man tending the fire glanced over at the happy foursome. His eyes were small, wary pellets. His ears were cocked, drinking in every word—every whisper of feeling that flowed from Ludovico Il Moro.

Gian Giacomo Tivulzio stood at the parapets of his castle at Mesocco, gazing southward down the valley of the Moesa River. The steep mountains surrounding him provided a serene atmosphere.

The only calm that Trivulzio knew and trusted was the quiet center of a raging battle. While his opponents probed and nibbled—looking for a fatal weakness—Capitano Trivulzio guided his forces to the hot points of battle with a flexibility and clarity only the finest commanders ever achieved. The feints, thrusts, and counterthrusts of battle suggested that to him warfare was but a game—a deadly game, but nonetheless a game.

So far, Trivulzio's enemies had found no such flaws in him, in his armies or in his strategies.

Two men stood beside the soldier. One was GuidAntonio Rebucco, Trivulzio's longtime friend and confidante. The other was the elderly servant who tended to the needs of William Castle at the musician's Castello di Vezio in Varenna. Trivulzio turned to the old man.

"Grazie, Vicenzo, mille grazie." Trivulzio patted the old man on the shoulder. "Well done." With a wave of the hand, he dismissed the old man. Vicenzo fell to one knee then backed out of sight.

"Already Ludovico dreams of leaving his mark," murmured Rebucco.

"He has been seeking power like this since he was quite small." Trivulzio's voice was soft like the wind. "Of course, he is not the only one to do so." He chuckled to himself.

"Moro is very confident," Rebucco replied. "Fortuna seems to favor him in all things."

"Mmm, perhaps so." Trivulzio picked up a rock and hurled it high into the air. The piece of granite fell for a long time and finally made a little *pip* as it hit the ground.

Trivulzio said nothing for a while then whispered at last. "Sometimes an action takes time before its consequences are seen or felt."

"You have in mind the restlessness of the pope, his desire to see his family members prosper?"

Trivulzio smiled. "The pope has no end of ambitions, dreams, stratagems. He is sure to test the mettle of young Moro. But then the doge in Venice has been unusually quiet. No doubt he has something in mind. The Venetians love nothing so much as to feed on the wounds of others. For certain, one or the other will soon aim his arrow high—with a rope attached to Moro's ankle, hoisting him up high in the air. He will dangle there, arms and legs flailing about, embarrassed and filled with fear."

"And if Moro fails to unknot himself—" Rebucco gave his friend a wicked smile.

Trivulzio chuckled. "—why, then, we shall be ready with a net of our own design?" Trivulzio leaned on the parapet and gazed down the valley of the Moesa River above Bellinzona and the Ticino River.

"I sense your destiny is fast approaching, my friend." Rebucco stared into the mists lying low in the valley. "The pope becomes our unwitting friend."

Trivulzio remained silent for several moments. "Pope Sixtus IV, Francesco della Rovere, is a fool," he answered at last. "A short-sighted fool."

Rebucco shrugged. "What can you expect of the family into which he was born? Ligurian, I am told."

The soldier glanced at his friend, shaking his head. "How is it that men of small minds come to have ambitions worthy of kings? Why they become merchants, like the Florentines. For such people, all life is merely exchanging capital and goods. They discover and nurture an artist, a talented paint- er whose work redounds to one's glory...and trade him, like a cow or a pig, to another house for a small favor? A piece of land? A wife?" Trivulzio sneered with disgust. "Francesco della Rovere—Pope Sixtus IV."

He spat on the ground. "The conspiracy of the pope's nephews together with the Pazzi family in Florence against

Lorenzo *Il Magnifico*—his war against Florence—his foolish designs mocked the stability created by Duke Francesco."

"Creating opportunities for ourselves," said Rebucco, brushing back his thinning, grayish hair. "We have always landed on our feet. Who is to say we will have greater difficulty in the future?"

Trivulzio contemplated his friend's words. "Yes, Moro is young and inexperienced. He has little knowledge of men—of the depth of their guile." Trivulzio's head rocked up and down. "But do not underestimate him, my friend. He is still wise and crafty beyond his years."

Rebucco gave his compare a twisted grin. "Nevertheless, Dama Fortuna has her eye on Il Gran Trivulzio."

Trivulzio's pugnacious jaw jutted out a little more than usual. "We shall see. We shall see."

He leaned forward—as if through will power alone, he could penetrate the mists of the alpine valley—the only thing obscuring a future so certain that he could almost touch it.

Rebucco smiled wryly. "Perhaps we shall pour upon the head of Ludovico the same maledictions with which he anointed our beloved Simonetta." He crossed himself. "God rest his soul."

Trivulzio warmed his hands, rubbing them together. "The young regent should learn to avoid playing games of chance in arenas reserved for the ambitions of men—like his father and his brother—"

A hint of a smile still hovered around Rebucco's mouth. He watched Trivulzio musing over the mists of the river valley and saw a mysterious smile slowly form on his lips, a smile of naked ambition. "—and the next *Duca di Milano*, Gian Giacomo Trivulzio," Rebucco whispered.

Trivulzio starred out into the mists of the valley of the Moesa River. "Mmm—" The wan smile had hardened into a thin slit of resolve like cooling lava that had burst over the lip of the man's almost inhuman intentions.

*Only one man shall rule Italy.* Trivulzio's eyes glittered in the moonlight. *That man's name is Gian Giacomo Trivulzio.*

Below the Castello di Vezio in Varenna, a hooded figure moved through the darkness of a grove of trees and stopped. Dappled rays of moonlight filtered through the branches, revealing the outline of an English longbow slowly elevating toward the castle's highest point, where William and Ludovico leaned out and gazed into the moonlight, planning Milano's future.

Two fingers curled around the end of the arrow, behind its three feathers, where the bowstring was fitted to the notched end of the arrow. The fingers drew the arrow backwards, stretching the bowstring taut. The muscles of the man's forearms bulged as the tension increased.

Sighting along the arrow upwards toward the two men, the archer raised the bow and aimed the arrow just above their heads. Moonlight glistening on its shaft, he released the arrow. The bowstring made a loud twang, shooting the arrow upwards. Reaching its apogee, the slim missle hovered for a moment, then spun downward, gathering speed as it plunged toward the two men who stood frozen in time and space, each the fragile target of an implacable foe.

---

## For the next installment of the Sforza/Castle series look for

## *PREDATORS*

# Glossary

**benefice**: It. a church holding which guarantees a certain income to the holder (originally an ecclesiastic). This income may be distributed (by contract with the Pope) by the duke, usually to artists, especially musicians in Milano who hold ecclesiastical titles. (see  Merkley)

**castello of Porta Giovia**: It. the original name for the Sforza castle in Milano locat-ed at the Porta Giovia entrance to the medieval/Renaissance walled city of Milano

**consiglio de guistizia**: It. council of justice--the court system

**consiglio segreto**: It. secret council (like the "congress" of the United States) with both the noblility, ambassadors, and trades people represented

**certo**: It. for certain

**compare**: It. a close family relationship of a powerful man to other families he desires to help and support. This relationship often opens the door to promotion within the court and the government.

**comprendo**: It. I understand

**capella**: It. chapel

**capella ducale**: It. ducal chapel

**Dama Fortuna**: It. lady luck

**fratello**: It. brother

**gentilezza**: It. a manly sense of ease and comfort

**ghigliottina**: It. guillotine

**grazie**: It. thank you

**gran/Il gran**: It. great (grand) The great

**pane**: It. bread

**puti**: It. a little cupid-like figures

**"per amor di Dio"**: for the love of God

**portcullis**: It. heavy metal grating that can be raised and lowered, found at entryways to castles.

**rocca**: It. fortress

**rochetta**: It. a smaller more secure fortress within a larger fortress

**sprezzatura**: ease and comfort in the most arduous of circumstances, cultivated during the Renaissance by diplomats, courtiers, and men of the world.

**Sforza castle**: Castle of Porta Giovia in Milano

**tenore**: It. tenor, upper-middle range of the voice (soprano, alto, tenor, baritone, bass)

*APPENDIX I*

# ADDITIONAL BIOGRAPHIES

*All are actual persons unless otherwise noted*

### *Milano*

## DUKE FRANCESCO "Il Gran Franceso" SFORZA (1402—1465)

Stately, wise and courageous. One of the greatest *condottieri* (commanders of an army for hire*)* of his age, he was merciful to his enemies, fearless as a leader, and patient as a ruler. One of the most admired men of his time, retaining his vigorous, soldierly appearance until well into his sixties. Had more than twenty children, most of them illegitimate. As head of the Milanese armies under Duke Filippo Visconti, he married into the ducal family. After Visconti's death, Milano formed a republic—the Ambrosian Republic. Francesco Sforza's army surrounded Milano until it capitulated and installed him as duke. Over the next ten years, his wise leadership brought peace and tranquility to Milano.

## GENERAL ROBERTO **SANSEVERINO (1440—1496)**

One of the more capable *condottieri* of his era. Rugged, ambitious, and self-assured. Was a trusted captain in the army of Duke Francesco, rose to the command of all the Milanese armies under Duke Galeazzo Sforza. Is a first cousin to Duke Galeazzo. Mistrusts both Trivulzio and Simonetta..

Sanseverino's hatred of Simonetta lay in his family's ties to the ancient nobility of Napoli. Simonetta and his clan, on the other hand, are upstarts from Calabria in the kingdom of Napoli. After the death of Duke Galeazzo, he maintains close ties to the Sforza brothers.

# SFORZA MARIA SFORZA (1450-1479)

Beefy, ambitious, impetuous older brother of Ludovico Ill Moro. Died of a heart attack before Il Moro came to power.

# ASCANIO SFORZA (1456-1505)

Brother of and wise adviser to Ludovico. Made cardinal in 1482, he became a wealthy patron of the arts in Roma. More powerbroker than religious figure.

# TRISTANO SFORZA (1422-1479)

Wise and trusted natural brother to Galeazzo, Sforza, Ludovico and Ascanio. One of more than twenty natural children sired by Francesco Sforza.

# PIER FRANCESCO PONTREMOLI

Assigned by Francesco Sforza to be the trusted companion, wise tutor, and friend to the Sforza brothers, from the birth of Galeazzo Maria onward.

# GIAN GALEAZZO SFORZA (1468—1494)

Gentle, mindless son of Galeazzo Maria and Bona of Savoy.

# BONA OF SAVOY (1450—1503)

Widow of the murdered Duke Galeazzo Maria Sforza. Became regent for her young son, Gian Galeazzo, along with Trivulzio and Simonetta.

## GASPARE WEERBECKE, MARTINO LACTORELLA, JOHANNES CORDIER, JOSQUIN DI PICARDIA

Prominent musicians at the court of Duke Galeazzo Maria Sforza. (See Merkley)

## GIOVANNI AMBROSIO (*Guglielmo Ebreo*) (1420—1480)

Master of dancing at princely courts throughout northern Italy, including the courts of Francesco and Galeazzo Sforza, from 1433 to 1480. Authored one of the most widely used manual on the art of dancing, *De practica seu arte tripudi (1463),* dedicated to Galeazzo. Converts to Christianity and takes the name of Giovanni Ambrosio.

### *Napoli*

## FERRANTE OF ARAGON (1424—1494)

King of Napoli. Arrogant, brutal, often irrational, though crafty.

## GIOVANNI PONTANO (1422—1503)

Wise and realistic First Secretary to Ferrante and Alfonso of Napoli. Humanist scholar, thinker and political writer.

### *Firenze*

## LORENZO "Il MAGNIFICO" DE MEDICI (1440-1493)

First Citizen and the most powerful person in Firenze from the 1470s to his death in 1493. A subtle, skillful negotiator, he helped keep the balance of power in Italy even though Firenze had less military power than any of the other states in Italy. The Medici Bank began to decline under Lorenzo. The Medici political influence declined as well.

*Francia*

# LOUIS XI (1423-1483)

King of Francia. Gathered the various factions in Francia under the banner of the Fleur de Lis. Defeated Charles *the Bold,* duke of Burgundy, at Nancy in 1478. His sister, Iolanda, married Amadeus IX, duke of Savoy.

*Burgundy*

# CHARLES "THE BOLD" (1431—1478)

Duke of Burgundy. Presided over the richest domain in Europe from his court in Bruges. His lands stretched from the English Channel (Hanault, Bruges) to Savoy on the Mediterranean Sea. Intended to extend his rule to Savoy. The finest musicians in Europe resided at his court in the years before his death. Relationship to England is quite strong; his wife is the daughter of Edward IV of England.

# ANTOINE, "LE BATARD (THE BASTARD)" OF BURGUNDY, COUNT OF RUPEFORT (1421-1504)

Half-brother to Charles the Bold, he is the ducal chamberlain and the second most powerful person in the duchy of Burgundy. A proud warrior and first rate tournament knight, he is the fiancé of Solice d'Anselm.

# SOLICE d'ANSELM, future COUNTESS OF RUPEFORT (1454—1476) *

The beautiful, talented, and mysterious fiancé of the ducal chamberlain, and the lover of young William Castle, this fictional character has more irons in the fire than William can ever know. She is privy to all the secrets of state, thanks to her relationship to Antoine, the duke of Burgundy's half brother.

## *Ferrara/Francia*

# FRA GIROLAMO SAVONAROLA (1452-1498)

Son of the court physician to the d'Este family, rulers of Ferrara, he becomes a significant voice for reform in the Catholic church, in the upper nobility, and in artists' guilds throughout northern and central Italy (Milano, Ferrara, Firenze) later in the 15th century. Mesmerizing speaker, he frightens many rulers into reviewing and repenting their morality, including Lorenzo di Medici and Sandro Botticelli, and perhaps Ludovico Sforza.

*Fictional

## *APPENDIX II*

# *Bringing History to Life*

This book, in fact virtually all history, starts with the characters who acted and reacted to the problems they faced, The following sources provide the reader with places to learned more about these characters.

**WILLIAM CASTLE**  Sources for musical, political, and ambassadorial activities of musicians like Castle can be found in Paul and Lora Merkely's *Musicians at the Sforza Court,* as well as an earlier work, Gregory Lubkin's *The Court of Galeazzo Maria Sforza. (The pisspot incident is taken almost directly from Merkley's book.)*

**BRANDA CASTIGLIONE**  Sources for his life and work as well as the many family members who profited by his position can be found in Lubkin's work, as well as by visiting his estate in Castiglione Olona near Varese.  He is the uncle of William Castle (fictional) and uncle to Baldassare Castiglione (actual), author of *The Book of the Courtier.*

**LUDOVICO MARIA SFORZA**  Sources for his life and ambitions are almost too numerous to name. I found Julia Cartwright's *Beatrice d'Este: Duchess of Milano* to be a good general place to begin to understand the dynamics of Ludovico's reign. Likewise, Colin Morissey's *Life of the Sforza* provided a good overall picture. Specific problems encountered by Il Moro were addressed with considerable insight in articles by Ady, Bueno de Mesqita, Hicks, and Ianziti.

For color photographs of the Sforza castles where the events described in the book took place, please see my book *The Hidden Treasures of Renaissance Milano,* as well as my web site.

**GALEAZZO MARIA SFORZA** For a thorough understanding of the structure of the court of Duke Galeazzo, see Gregory Lubkin's *The Court of Galeazzo Maria Sforza.* Excellent insights and narratives of his activities can also be found in the works of Vincent Ilardi, Julia Cartwright, and Colinson-Morley.

**GIAN GIACOMO TRIVULZIO**  The source that provides the most information for Trivulzio's life and ambitions is Carlo de Rosmini's *Dell'istoria intorno alla militari impresse e alla i viti di Gian Giacomo Trivulzio*. The relevant chapters were translated for me by Flavio Frontini, a graduate student at UCLA in the 1990's.

**KING FERRANTE and DUKE ALFONSO of NAPOLI**  By far the best book on the subject, well-written and insightful, is Jerry Bentley's *Politics and Culture in Renaissance Napoli*. It provides insights into Ferrante, his son Alfonso, and into the work of Pontano as well.

**LORENZO DE MEDICI**  Sources for Lorenzo di Medici's life and work are almost endless. Currently, excellent work on the Academy of Ficino is being done at UCLA by Michael Allen, with whom I have chatted on occasion. Much of Lorenzo's biography can be found in Cecilia Ady's *Lorenzo Dei Medici*.

# Geneologies:

## MILANO

(legend: 1) = married to 2) / or \ -- not married   3) ill. -- illegitimate   4) fictional)

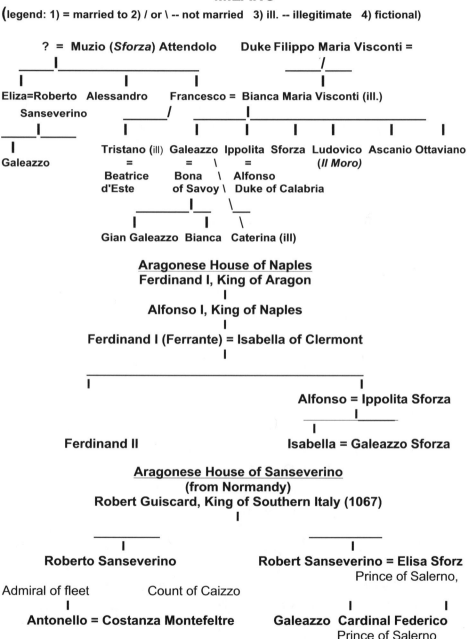

? = Muzio (*Sforza*) Attendolo        Duke Filippo Maria Visconti =

Eliza=Roberto   Alessandro        Francesco = Bianca Maria Visconti (ill.)
Sanseverino

Galeazzo        Tristano (ill)  Galeazzo  Ippolita Sforza  Ludovico  Ascanio Ottaviano
                =               =         \                (*Il Moro)*
                Beatrice        Bona      \  Alfonso
                d'Este          of Savoy  \  Duke of Calabria

                Gian Galeazzo  Bianca   Caterina (ill)

**Aragonese House of Naples**
**Ferdinand I, King of Aragon**
**Alfonso I, King of Naples**
**Ferdinand I (Ferrante) = Isabella of Clermont**

                                    Alfonso = Ippolita Sforza

**Ferdinand II**                    **Isabella = Galeazzo Sforza**

**Aragonese House of Sanseverino**
**(from Normandy)**
**Robert Guiscard, King of Southern Italy (1067)**

**Roberto Sanseverino**            **Robert Sanseverino = Elisa Sforz**
                                   Prince of Salerno,

Admiral of fleet      Count of Caizzo
**Antonello = Costanza Montefeltre**    **Galeazzo  Cardinal Federico**
                                        Prince of Salerno

# BIBLIOGRAPHY

## Books

### MILANO

Cartwright, Julia *Beatrice d'Este* Dutton N.Y. 1905

Ceroni, Lydia *La Diplomazia Sforesca nella Seconda Meta Quattro centoe i suoi cifrari segreti*
Fondi e Studdi VII Il Cento Di Ricerca E. 1970Collison-Mor ley, L. *Story of the Sforza* Routledge: London 1933

Ilardi, Vincent *Dispatches with Related Documents of the Milanese Ambassadors in Francia and Burgundy* Vol III 1450-1483 Northern Ill. U., Dekalb, Ill. 1981

Lubkin, Gregory *Court of Galeazzo Maria Sforza, U. of Mich.* 1982

Merkley, Paul and Lara *Music and Patronage in the Sforza Court* U. of Ottawa Press, 1999

Rosmini, Carlo de *Dell'istoria intorno alla militari impresse e alla i viti di Gian Giacomo Trivulzio (1803)*

Sparti, Barbara, *Guglielmo Ebreo's On the Art and Practice of Dancing* Oxford 1993

Welch, E. *Art and Authority in Ren. Milano* Yale: New Haven 1995

## Articles

Ady, Cecilia "Florence and Northen Italy," Cambridge Medieval Hist. VIII 206-31

Bueno de Mesqita, D. M. "The Conscience of a Prince," *Proceedings of the British Academy*, Nov. 1979. p. 416ff

———."Ludovico and His Vassals," *Italian Renaissance Studies,* ed. E. E. Jacobs, p. 184-216

———."The Place of Despotism in Italian Politics," *Europe in the Late Middle Ages*, ed. Hale, London 1965 p. 184-216

Hicks, D. "Education of a Prince: Ludovico Sforza and Pandolfo Petrucci," *Studies in the Renaisance VIII*

Ianziti, Gary "A Humanist Historian and his Documents: Giovanni

Simonetta, Secretary to the Sforzas," *Renaissance Quarterly,* XXXIV, Number Four, 491—

Ilardi, Vincent, "Fifteenth Century Diplomatic Documents in West ern European Archives 1450-1494,"*Studies in the Renaisance IX*

———. "Assassination of Galeazzo Maria Sforza and the Reaction of Italian Diplomacy", in *Violence and Civil Disorder in Italy, 1200-1600,* ed. Lauro Martines, Berkley and Los Angeles, 1972

Lockwood, Lewis, "Josquin at Ferrara: New Documents and Let-ters," *Proceedings of the Congresso Internationale Honoring M.L. Gatti Perer, 2* Volumes  Milano 1969 II

Lowinsky, Edwin "Ascanio Sforza's Life: A Key to Josquin's Biog-raphy and an Aid to the Chronology of his Works," *Con gresso Internationale sul Duomo di Milano*, ed. M.L. Gatti Perer 2 vols. Milano 1969  II 17-24

———. "Secret Chromatic Art in the Netherlands Motet," Music Quarterly, Oct. 1953, Note 73

———. "The Goddess Fortuna in Music—with a 'Special Study of Josquin's Fortuna d'un gran tempo," Music Quarterly, p. 45

## *NAPOLI*

Bentley, Jerry  *Politics and Culture in Renaissance Napoli*; Princeton U. 1987

## *FIRENZE*

Machiavelli, Niccolo  *The Prince*
de Roover, Raymond *Rise and Decline of the Medici Bank*
Ady, Cecilia  *Lorenzo Di Medici*

## *ROMA*

Pastor, Ludwig van *History of the Popes*  St. Louis  40 volumes 1913-1953

## VENEZIA

Finlay, *Robert Politics in Renaissance* Venice Rutgers: New
　　Brunswick 1980

## FRANCIA and BURGUNDY

Potter, David  *War and Gov. in Fr. Provinces*  Cambridge 1993

## GENERAL

Castiglione, Baldassare  *The Book of the Courtier* Garden City 1959
Ady, Cecilia  *The Bentivoglio of Bologna (1937)*
————.　　*Milan Under the Sforza  (1907)*
————.　　*Lorenzo dei Medici*  N.Y. 1972
Baron, Hans  *Crisis of the Early Italian Renaissance* 2nd. ed. Princeton,
1966
Breisach, Ernst  *Caterina Sforza* Chicago 1967
Bruchner, Gene *Story of the Renaissance Firenze* New York 1971
Castiglione, Baldassare  *The Book of the Courtier*  Garden City
Cartwright, Julia  (Mrs. Henry Ady) *Letters of Baldassare Castiglione*
————.  *Beatrice d' Este*  New York  1905
Chastel, Andre  *Myth of the Renaissance*  Geneva 1969
Cochrane, Eric,  *Historians and Hist. in the Italian Ren.* Chicago,
1981
Collison-Morley,  *Story of the Sforza* London 1933
Clark, Kenneth  *Art of Humanism* London 1970
————.  *Leonardo da Vinci*  Penguin: Baltimore 1938
Cassirer, Ernst  *Individual and Cosmos in Ren. Italy*  New York 1963
Chabod, Fred. *Machiavelli and the Renaissance*  New York 1965
Friedlander, Max *From Van Eyck to Bruegel*  London 1956
Gibbs-Smith, Charles  *Inventions of Leonardo da Vinci*  NY 1978
Guiccardini, Francesco  *History of Italy*  Princeton, N.J. 1969
Herrick, Marvin *Italian Comedy in the Renaissance* Urbana, 1966
Hale, J.H. *Renaissance War Studies*  London
————.  *Artists and Warfare in the Renaissance* New Haven 1990
————.  *Concise Encyclopaedia of the Italian Ren.* New York: 1981
Kristeller, Paul O.  *Renaissance Thought*  New York 1961

Lowe, Kate *Church and Politics in Renaissance Italy* Cambridge 1993

Lyle, G/Orgel, S. *Patronage in the Renaissance,* Princeton 1981

Martines, Lauro *Power and Imagination: City States in Italy* New York 1979.

Mattingly, Garret *Renaissance Diplomacy* Baltimore 1955

Melchoir-Bonnet, Sabine *Chateaux of the Loire* Paris 1987

Murray, P. *Architecture of the Italian Renaissance* New York 1963

Oman, C. *History of the Art of War in the 16th Ct.* London, 1937

Ridolfi, Rudolfo *The Life of Savonarola* Chicago 1963

Rosci, Marco *Hidden Leonardo* Rand McNally

Schevill, *Medieval and Renaissance Florence* New York 1961

Sypher, Wylie *Four Stages of Ren. Style* Garden City 1955

——————. *Art History: Anthology of Criticism* New York 1963

Trinkhaus, Charles *Studies in the Renaissance VI (1960)*

Young, Irwin *Practica Musicae of Franeschino Gafuri* Madison, 1969

Vasari *Lives of the Artists* London 1965

Vaspasiano, *Renaissance Princes, Popes, Prelates.* New York 1963

Von Martin *Sociology of the Renaissance* New York 1963

Welch, E. *Art and Authority in Ren Milano* New Haven 1995

Winternitz, E. *Leonardo da Vinci as Musician* New Haven 1982

## Books in Italian

Rosmini, Carlo de' *Dell'istoria intorno alle militari imprese e alla vita di Gian Giacomo Trivulzio* (1815)

Garlandini *I castelli della Lombardia* Milano 1991 Electa

Vincenti, A *castelli Viscontei e gli Sforzeschi* Milano 1981

Ghirardini, Lino *La Battaglia de Fornovo* Parma 1981